FIREFIGHTER PHOENIX

FIRE & RESCUE SHIFTERS 7

ZOE CHANT

❀ Created with Vellum

The Fire & Rescue Shifters series

Firefighter Dragon
Firefighter Pegasus
Firefighter Griffin
Firefighter Sea Dragon
The Master Shark's Mate
Firefighter Unicorn
Firefighter Phoenix

Fire & Rescue Shifters Collection 1
(contains Firefighter Dragon, Firefighter Pegasus, and Firefighter Griffin)

Series available in Kindle ebook, paperback, and audiobook.

All books in the Fire & Rescue Shifters series are standalone romances, each focusing on a new couple, with no cliff-hangers. They can be read in any order. However, characters from previous books reappear in later stories, so reading in series order is recommended for maximum enjoyment.

CHAPTER 1

If you want a happy ending, you have to make it yourself.

Rose Swanmay silently chanted the phrase in her mind like a mantra, focusing on the words to quell the butterflies in her stomach. She'd wasted enough time on regrets and might-have-beens. It was time to take matters into her own two hands.

Steeling her nerve, she rang the bell on the end of the bar.

"Time, gentlemen!" she announced in a loud, firm voice.

Mutters and groans rose from the men scattered throughout her pub, even though she'd given them the 'last orders' warning fifteen minutes ago. Most of the Sunday-night crowd had already finished up their drinks and left, but a couple of her regulars had clearly been hoping she hadn't really meant it when she'd announced that she was closing early.

"Aw, come on Rose," wheedled Wayne, one of Rose's most long-standing customers. He normally spent so long in the pub, he was practically a resident. "You can't kick us out. Where are we supposed to go?"

"There are literally hundreds of other pubs in this city." Rose folded her arms, giving him a stern look. "Not to mention bars, clubs, and drinking dens. I'm sure you'll find somewhere else that can serve you a beer."

"You know it ain't about the beer, Rose." Wayne attempted to give her puppy eyes. Given that he was a grizzled, grimy, half-drunk wolf shifter, this was not entirely successful. "There's no place like the Full Moon."

This was true. The Full Moon was the only pub in Brighton that catered exclusively to shifters. No ordinary humans were allowed in unless specifically invited. It was the one place in the city where all shifters, no matter what their animal, could relax and truly be themselves.

Even though shifters were secretly part of all levels of society throughout Great Britain, they still always had to be on their guard in public. No matter how powerful they were individually, they were still massively outnumbered by regular humans. The safety of all shifter-kind depended on ordinary people remaining happily oblivious to the hidden world running alongside their own.

"This ain't just our local," Wayne continued. "It's the only safe neutral territory in Brighton. You wouldn't kick an old lone wolf out into the cold, would you?"

Rose smiled, touched by the slightly slurred declaration. She'd worked hard to make her pub a welcoming haven for all shifters. It was nice to have it appreciated.

Nonetheless, she plucked his nearly-empty pint glass out of his hand. "Sorry, Wayne. You can have a free drink on me tomorrow. But I'm still closing early tonight."

"You got a hot date, Rose?" one of her other regulars called out teasingly from the other end of the bar.

Rose's heart skipped a beat, but she managed to keep her expression unruffled. "Just booked for a private engagement, you cheeky beggar. Now be off with the lot of you."

Wayne paused in the doorway, shooting her a curious look over her shoulder. Rose's empathic sense caught a surge of sudden interest from him, like a wolf pricking up its ears.

"Private party?" Wayne's gaze slid sideways, to a particular corner booth. "Is it Alpha Team? They're normally here by now."

"Nothing to do with Alpha Team," Rose said, which wasn't *entirely* true. "And mind you keep that long nose out of other people's business, Wayne, or I might forget about that free drink. Shoo."

It wasn't the first time she'd had to remind the old wolf to respect Alpha Team's privacy. And Wayne wasn't the only shifter she'd had to slap on the muzzle that way. More than a few people came to the Full Moon in the hopes of getting a glimpse of one of the famous firefighters of Alpha Fire Team.

It wasn't just that Alpha Team saved lives everyday, although that was impressive enough. It was what they were as much as what they did that attracted curious tourists from far and wide.

Dragon, griffin, pegasus, sea dragon, unicorn...even among shifters, they were rare and powerful.

And their leader was the rarest and most powerful of them all.

He was also, unfortunately, the most elusive. Which was exactly why Rose was closing her pub at the most profitable time of the week.

Shooing out the last few stragglers, Rose flipped the sign outside the pub to *CLOSED*. She waited, tapping her foot, until her innate empathic ability told her that there was no one lingering hopefully outside. Then she opened the door again, spun the sign back to *OPEN*, and dashed for the bar.

She barely made it in time. Even as she slid back into her usual position behind the taps, the door opened softly. For everyone else—even Rose—the old iron hinges always squealed, but somehow *he* never made a breath of noise when he entered.

And there he stood, on the precise stroke of eight o'clock, as always. Straight-backed, contained and controlled, formal in his day uniform of charcoal trousers and pale gray shirt. The warm light from the pub's scattered lamps caught the gold thread in the East Sussex Fire and Rescue badge embroidered on his sleeve.

Fire Commander Ash. The Phoenix Eternal. The most powerful shifter in Europe.

Rose's heart thudded against her ribs, so loud that she was certain he'd be able to hear it in the silent bar. As ever, Ash made the whole world tilt and refocus around him.

It wasn't his physical looks. Oh, he was well-built enough, especially for a man in his late forties, but still nowhere near as big or burly as many shifter males. There wasn't anything unusual about Ash's coloring, either. Slightly tanned, weathered skin, gray streaking his short sandy-brown hair—there was nothing out of the ordinary about him at all.

Except for the intense, leashed power burning behind those deep brown eyes.

He was the Phoenix. Not *a*, but *the.* Rose didn't know exactly how it worked, but there was only ever one Phoenix at a time, in all the world.

Even ordinary humans could sense the raging inferno hidden in the heart of that quiet, unassuming figure. To Rose's shifter senses, Ash blazed with alpha power. He was so bright, she could hardly bear to look at him, yet so compelling that she couldn't bear to look away. He was the most magnetic man she'd ever met.

Not our mate, whispered her inner swan.

"Ash!" Rose said brightly, drowning out her animal's unwelcome comment. "Come in, come in!"

He normally moved with utter assurance, but tonight he hesitated on her doorstep. His piercing gaze swept the deserted room, pausing briefly on the corner usually occupied by Alpha Team.

For some reason, Ash was the one person Rose's empathic sense didn't work on. But she didn't need psychic powers to be able to tell that Ash was baffled by his team's absence. Possibly no one else would have been able to read that from his still, remote face, but Rose had known him for a long time.

"I don't know where everyone is," Rose said, too quickly. "Maybe there's some sort of event going on. I've been bored stiff. Come keep me company, will you?"

Moving as gingerly as a cat on unfamiliar territory, Ash approached the bar. He clasped his hands behind his back, feet setting in parade rest. He had the air of a man who suspected a surprise party might be about to spring out at him.

"The usual?" Rose asked, already reaching for a glass.

Ash's chin dipped in a fractional nod. "Thank you."

Rose poured his drink. As always, Ash slid a twenty across the bar in return. Rose had given up arguing with him about this years ago. Although she'd at least managed to talk him down from paying *fifty* per glass of perfectly ordinary ice water. Even though he didn't drink, he didn't need to feel *that* guilty about occupying space in her pub.

Rose occupied herself cleaning an imaginary spill on the worn oak bar. "Busy day?"

"Evidently busier than yours," Ash murmured, staring around the empty pub again. His eyebrows drew down, his head tilting as though he was listening to something.

"Anything from the gang?" Rose asked, recognizing the look that Ash got when he was attempting to contact his fire crew telepathically.

"No," Ash said, his brow creasing further. "Their minds are closed at the moment. It is not like them to miss our customary social gathering."

"Oh, I wouldn't worry." Rose fought down a smile, forcing her tone to stay nonchalant. "No doubt they're all just enjoying some quality time at home tonight."

As a matter of fact, she knew for a certainty that they were. Thanks to a quiet word with their mates—and some assistance in arranging babysitters—she was confident that all the other firefighters of Alpha Team were currently having a *very* enjoyable evening. And would be far too preoccupied to answer their Commander's telepathic call for quite some time.

Ash let out a faint sigh. He settled onto a bar stool at last, though his posture stayed as straight as a soldier on duty.

"I suppose," he said, "that I should have expected this."

"Well, the whole team is mated now," Rose said, her voice softening in sympathy. "Not to mention most of them have children, or babies on the way. No how much they all might want to keep up the weekly pub meet tradition, they've got a lot of new demands on their time."

"That is true." Ash eyed her sidelong. "Though not what I was referring to."

Rose blinked at him. "Oh? What did you mean, then?"

The corner of Ash's mouth rose, ever so slightly. "That perhaps I might have saved you a great deal of evident effort and planning, had I simply agreed when you first asked me for a private meeting."

Rose laughed, shaking her head ruefully. "I can't get anything past you, can I?"

Ash's mouth quirked a little more, into what for him was the equivalent of a broad, beaming smile. "I have known you for a long time."

"Ten years." Rose flicked the corner of her dishrag at him in a playful swat. "Which should be long enough that it *shouldn't* be so hard to get you alone. Honestly, Ash, you could drive a woman to her own drink sometimes. Why do you have to be so evasive?"

Ash's gaze slid away. He didn't answer, toying with his water glass. His shirt cuff rode up a little with the motion, exposing the old, faded scar that twisted around his right wrist.

"I am here now," he said, in that deep, quiet voice. "What is on your mind, Rose?"

Rose licked her lips, her mouth suddenly dry. Even though she'd rehearsed this, it was one thing to practice the words in the silent solitude of her bedroom, and quite another to say them to Ash's closed, forbidding face.

She took a deep breath. "I know you aren't happy, Ash."

His head jerked back up, as though this wasn't at all what he'd been expecting her to say. "I assure you, I am content enough."

Rose shook her head firmly. "I may not be able to read your heart, Ash, but I've known you a long time, too. There's a difference between acceptance and contentment. And lately, you've been losing what little peace you ever had. Seeing the other members of the team happily mated...I know how hard it is for you."

Ash's expression shuttered down even further. "I appreciate your concern, but it is both unnecessary and unwanted. The only thing that I have ever asked is that you respect my privacy. Please continue to do so."

Rose had seen full-grown dragons cower in submission when the Phoenix used *that* tone. She gripped the edge of the bar, taking comfort from the familiar feel of the old, smooth wood.

"You're lonely, Ash." She steeled herself. "And so am I."

Ash—the Phoenix Eternal, the man who commanded the respect of even the most powerful shifters, the veteran firefighter who calmly walked into deadly danger as a matter of routine—*flinched.* His shoulders jerked as though her words had been a blow, driving all the air out of his lungs.

"I thought that *you* were content enough." He made a slight gesture around at the pub. "You do not lack for company."

"It's not enough." Rose blew out her breath in a long sigh. "I thought it was, but...Ash, I've stood here and served drink after drink to happy mated couples, and each time I do something inside me grows colder and darker. I'm not proud of it, but I'm jealous, and it's eating up my soul. I can't help it. I want what they have."

Ash stared down at his clasped hands, resting on the bar counter. His knuckles whitened.

"I would give anything," he said, very quietly, "to be able to bring your mate back to you."

"I know you would," Rose said, her own throat tightening with the old pain. "But no one can do that. Whoever he was, he's gone now."

She'd told Ash the story before, many years ago. Swans were renowned among shifter-kind for always being able to find their mates. Every swan just *knew,* when the time was right, where to go to find him or her.

Rose had felt that pull herself, when she'd been younger. She'd set off joyfully, certain of finding her happily-ever-after.

Only to wake up one cold, bleak morning to echoing silence in her soul. No mate calling to her. No instinct pulling her on.

Just silence, and her swan's deep, heartbroken grief.

The wound was still sharp and raw, even twenty years later. Rose swallowed hard, forcing the bitter memory back down.

"My mate died before I could meet him," she said. "But that doesn't mean I have to be alone forever."

Ash's eyes closed, as if in pain. "Rose," he said, his voice a barely-audible rasp.

It was now or never. Rose summoned up her courage, her heart beating fast as she reached across the bar. Ignoring her swan's muffled cry of protest, she rested her hand on top of his.

"It doesn't mean *you* have to be alone forever," she said softly.

She'd never touched Ash like this before, in all the years that they'd been friends. Oh, she'd tapped him on the shoulder or caught his sleeve often enough—even kicked him in the ankle on more than one occasion, when he was being particularly insufferable—but no more than that. He was so fiercely private, even the most casual gesture of affection was unthinkable.

Now, a strange tingle shot through her palm at the feel of his bare skin against hers. She caught her breath, a wave of longing crashing over her. The emotion was so intense, she couldn't tell whether it was Ash's or her own.

His skin burned against hers, as if she was holding her hand out to a roaring bonfire. But it was a welcome heat, warming her entire body. It was like she'd been frozen solid, never knowing how cold she truly was, until his fire thawed her.

Not our mate, her swan said again.

"Ash," she whispered.

His fingers stirred under hers. Gently but firmly, he pulled his hand away.

"No," he said.

Her hand felt cold, bereft of his heat. She yearned to reach out to him again, but he stood abruptly, turning his back on her. His spine was a straight, rigid line, every muscle tense.

"No," he said again, harsh and rough. "I am not your mate, Rose."

She wished that the bar wasn't still between them. She longed to touch his shoulder, to see if her empathic sense really *had* penetrated his armor, but she was pretty sure he'd bolt for the door if she moved.

"I know that," she said, trying not to let on how her heart was pounding just from that brief contact. "And if…if you met *your* true mate, I wouldn't keep you from her. I'm not asking for that sort of bond, Ash. I know that's impossible. But maybe…maybe we could both be a little less lonely. Together."

His fist clenched at his side, shaking. He stared at the door, but made no move toward it.

Was he hesitating? Hope rose in Rose's chest.

"We're more than our animals, Ash." She spoke quickly, as though she could throw words over him like a net. "We can still choose for ourselves. *I* want you, not my swan."

He let out a small, pained sound. "You shouldn't."

"Why not? I'm not your mate, not your perfect partner, but we've known each other for ten years. I know what a good man you are. Ever since we first met, my feelings for you have only grown. You've always been there for me, and I—"

She stopped. Ash's shoulders were shaking, very slightly.

But not with anger, or tears.

"Why on earth are you laughing?" she asked, bewildered and more than a bit hurt.

The near-silent, bitter sound cut off. Ash half-turned. The light caught the mirthless curve of his mouth, and the dark flames in his eyes.

"Because not a single word of that was true," he said.

CHAPTER 2

PAST

20 years ago...

The horizon was on fire.

Even with the windows wound up tight, the smoke still crept into Rose's small rental car. She could taste it, acrid and bitter, on the back of her tongue. For the past fifty miles, every single vehicle she'd passed had been barreling full-tilt in the opposite direction. All the local radio stations were broadcasting the same information over and over.

"Full evacuation orders are in effect countywide," repeated the flat voice of the emergency bulletin. "Do not attempt to stay in your homes. Do not try to rescue pets or livestock. Leave personal belongings behind. If you do not have transport, call 911 now. This is a mandatory evacuation order. All residents and visitors must leave the county immediately."

Rose switched off the radio, since it wasn't telling her anything she didn't already know. She took a firmer grip on the steering wheel, deliberately fixing her eyes on the road rather than on the ribbons of fire crowning the mountains ahead.

Faster, her swan urged her. Its wings flexed in agitation, longing to take flight. *He is calling us. Our mate needs us, now, now!*

Rose could feel that pull herself, deep in her soul. What had started as a faint, gossamer-slender tug was now like a fist around her heart, hauling her irresistibly onward.

Her aunts and cousins had warned her that the compulsion would become stronger the closer that she got to her mate. When she'd felt those first tiny stirrings, calling to her across the world, they'd urged her to wait, to ignore it for as long as she could. Twenty-three was young for a swan shifter to feel the mate-call, after all. There was plenty of time to mature, learn who she was as her own person, before she rushed into a permanent partnership.

But Rose *couldn't* wait. Even back home in England, the mate-call had felt like a fishhook set in her soul. She could no more have ignored it than ignore the need to breathe. Whoever her mate was, wherever he was, she knew at a bone-deep level that he was in mortal peril. She *had* to go to him.

Even if it meant driving into the heart of the worst wildfire in Northern California for a decade.

Flashing lights cut through the smog up ahead. A police car barricaded the road. Rose put her foot on the brake, slowing to a halt, even though her swan hissed in protest at the delay.

She tried on her most winning smile as she rolled down her window. "I'm so sorry, officer. I just need to pop back for—"

"Ma'am, I don't care what you've left behind, whether it's Fido or your family photos," the police officer interrupted her, in the weary tones of someone who'd already had this conversation too many times today. "I just heard on the radio, even the firefighters are pulling back. You gotta turn around and get out of here right now."

"But, but—my granddad!" Rose widened her eyes, the smoke helping her to fake tears. "I have to go and get him from, um..."

She wished she'd paid more attention to the map. She had only the haziest idea of where she actually was, other than that it had been a long, *long* drive north from San Francisco.

"His cabin," she finished, somewhat unconvincingly. "Up that mountain there."

The policeman gave her a suspicious look, but pulled his radio out of his belt. "Tell me where it is. I'll get one of the crews to swing by and pick him up."

"Oh, no, it's really hard to find," Rose said hastily. "He's a real backwoods hermit. Paranoid. He'll shoot anyone he doesn't recognize. But if you just let me through, I promise I can get there and back quick as a lick."

From the exasperated glare the police officer was giving her, he wasn't buying her story. "Girlie, I don't know what you're trying to pull, but I'm not letting you pass. Now scram, unless you'd rather I hauled you out of here in handcuffs."

Rose attempted to looks suitably chastised. "That won't be necessary, officer," she said meekly. "I'll just be on my way."

The officer's hand drifted down to rest on his holstered gun as she reversed. Very carefully, Rose turned her car around. The policeman stared after her, narrow-eyed, as she drove off.

No! Her swan beat its wings furiously, making her ears ring. *He needs us! Turn around!*

"Keep your feathers on," Rose muttered, looking in her rear-view mirror to check that the policeman was out of sight. "I have a plan."

Pulling over to the side of the road, Rose parked. She would have liked to conceal the car, but there was no hope of driving it deeper into the thick forest. She'd just have to hope that the police officer wouldn't waste time looking for her when he spotted it. He was only doing his job, and she didn't want him to get caught in the wildfire.

She also hoped that he wouldn't be along for a few minutes. Bad enough that he'd find an abandoned vehicle. If he found her taking all of her clothes off next to it, he probably *would* haul her off in handcuffs to the nearest mental institution.

Kicking off her shoes, she shimmied awkwardly out of her shirt and shorts. Not for the first time, she wished that she was a mythic shifter, like a dragon or a pegasus. It must be nice, never having to worry about being caught buck naked. Unfortunately swans shifters couldn't just magic their clothes away and back again.

At least she was big enough when shifted to be able to carry a few essentials with her. She grabbed her emergency pouch from the back seat, looping it around her neck. Then, stretching out her arms, she gave herself up to her swan.

As ever, the shift raced over her skin like a lover's caress. She thrilled at the sensation of stretching into her other shape, becoming sleeker and stronger.

Anyone who thought a swan was just some lumbering, overgrown duck had never been one.

Her shining black wings stretched over eight feet from tip-to-tip. Her powerful webbed feet and scaled legs could propel her equally well across land or water. She'd taught more than one arrogant would-be alpha not to underestimate her just because she didn't have claws and fangs.

Of course, the disadvantage of her size was that she needed a heck of a run-up to take off. Spreading her wings, she ran full-tilt along the road, flapping with all her strength. It was harder to get airborne from dry land rather than water, but she managed it, although it wasn't the most graceful process.

Once she was in the air, it was much easier. Heat rising from the burning forest caught her outstretched wings, lifting her higher like a child tossing a ball. Safely above the treetops, she circled, arrowing back the way she'd come.

The police officer was back in his car, talking on his radio. He never even glanced up as she soared overhead. No longer bound to follow the road, Rose turned her beak straight in the direction of her mate. The pull was even more urgent now, pulsing through her veins as strongly as her own heartbeat. It pulled her on irresistibly.

Straight toward the wall of fire burning on the horizon.

As she flew closer, she could see that it *was* literally a wall. The wilderness firefighters had cleared a wide strip through the forest. The deadly blaze roared hungrily right at the edge of the firebreak.

Burning leaves and sparks fell harmlessly onto the barren earth, unable to cross.

A group of firefighters were falling back, exhaustion clear in their stumbling steps. They must have been working all night to finish the firebreak.

Her mate was so *close*. Could he be one of the firefighters? A little thrill went through her. Call it a cliché, but she'd always had a thing for a man in uniform.

Not, she had to admit, that they were a terribly appealing sight at the moment. Once-yellow safety gear was now mottled with ash and mud. The men were as filthy as their uniforms. Most of them were hastily throwing chainsaws and cutting tools into the back of an off-road vehicle, clearly eager to be gone, but a couple seemed to be having an argument.

Rose swooped as low as she dared, passing so close to the firefighters that a few of them ducked. She scanned every upturned face, hoping for that lighting-bolt of recognition… but she saw nothing but surprise and fatigue in their eyes. None of them were her mate.

"…still in there!"

She caught the snatch of words as she swept past a pair of men at the back of the group. On impulse, Rose landed. They were so caught up in their argument that they didn't notice her sidling over to hear better.

"I'm telling you, I *saw* him." One of the firefighters pointed into the forest, looking agitated. "Just let me go back and check!"

"Anyone still in there is dead!" The other, who she guessed was the leader from the grimy insignia on his helmet, shoved him back. "Now clear out! That's an order!"

The other firefighter obeyed, though his reluctance was clear. With a last backward glance over his shoulder—and a double-take at Rose—he joined the others in the vehicle.

Rose's heart lurched as the truck roared off down the road.

They'd left someone behind.

And her mate was still calling to her.

The heat of the fire beat against her skin even through her feathers. Gouts of flame leaped up from burning pines. It would be difficult enough to try to fly over the wildfire. To fly *through* it, searching for someone collapsed on the ground...

Terror gripped her so hard that she could barely open her wings. She spread them anyway. Steeling herself, she faced the inferno head-on...and saw him.

For a second, she thought she was imagining things. But there *was* a dark, wavering figure, blurred by smoke and heat haze.

Sheer surprise made her shift back into human form. Rose stumbled, catching herself on her hands. Sharp-edged rocks cut into her knees, but she barely noticed the pain.

The roar of the inferno, the punch of heat against her fragile human skin...it all faded into irrelevance.

He came walking out of the blazing forest, as calmly as if the furnace-hot wind whipping his clothes was just a pleasant springtime breeze. The white-yellow glow backlit his lean, tall form, so that she couldn't make out his face.

But she could see how the flames bowed before him. They drew aside to let him pass, then leaped up again in his wake, roaring twice as high. Sparks and embers swirled around his head like a crown.

As she watched, dumbstruck, he reached the edge of the firebreak. For a moment he paused. Through the billowing smoke, she saw his head tip down a little, as though considering the barren ground.

He strode out onto the churned earth.

And the fire followed him.

Flames flared up where he stepped, the very rocks burning. Behind him, in the forest, the inferno mounted like a cresting wave, gathering, rising. Waiting to surge forward, down the narrow path that he was making for it across the firebreak.

She could see his face now. He was smiling.

"Stop!" she shouted, surging to her feet. She ran at him, waving her arms. "You can't—there are people—*stop!*"

He checked his stride, surprise flashing across his face. He was only two steps away from the edge of the firebreak. Narrow tongues of flame crowded behind him, muttering.

She planted herself square in his path, spreading her arms wide to bar his way. Smoke burned her throat as she fought for breath.

For the first time, she met his eyes.

Fire, nothing but fire. The dark inferno embraced her, burning away everything but him. The mate-call roared in her blood louder than the burning forest. She was dry tinder, and he was her match. One step, one touch, and she would be consumed utterly.

Every part of her yearned to take that step. Let the world burn around them. Nothing mattered, as long as they were together.

She clenched her fists, shaking with the effort of not falling into his arms.

"Stop," she said again. "I don't know why you're doing this, but it's wrong. The fire will hurt people if it goes any farther. You have to stop."

He blinked. The fire behind him died down, flames falling back into smoldering embers. The black fire in his eyes faded too, revealing a more human color. They were darkest brown, deep and clear. Even with his fires leashed, the power in them stole Rose's breath away. She'd been in the presence of alpha shifters before, but never one like *this*.

His eyebrows drew together a little. For all the burning force in his gaze, he had a very human look of puzzlement.

He lifted his right hand, almost but not quite touching her cheek. Intricate tattoos twined around his wrist, running up his bare forearm. They looked like runes, characters in some script she didn't recognize.

"I know you," he said.

His deep voice made her toes curl into the dirt. Her cheek burned where he almost touched her. The rest of her felt cold in comparison, cold down to the bone. She yearned to lean into his palm, but something about his raw, uncertain eyes made her hold still. There was a sense of wildness about him; an unpredictable, unstable power.

"I know you," he said again. "Who—?"

He gasped, suddenly stumbling back as though jerked away by an invisible leash. His left hand shot to his right wrist, gripping tight.

Rose stared, unable to make sense of what she was seeing. A moment ago the tattoo had just been black ink. But now color was blossoming up his arm. Each tiny, precise rune was outlined in crimson.

Then the thin red lines started to drip and run.

Blood. Blood welling up, as though the tattoo was tightening, cutting into his skin.

Her swan hissed in distress at the sight of their mate's pain. Rose started to reach out to him, but had to jerk back. The air around him was *hot*. She might as well have tried to put her hand into a furnace.

Behind him, the forest fire surged up with renewed force. The inferno was back in his eyes, black and all-consuming. He strained toward her, every line of his body yearning, but it was like a glass wall had slammed between them.

With a snarl of frustration, he turned away. He tipped his head back, throwing his arms open.

"Wait!" Rose was forced to scrunch her eyes shut as his human form dissolved into incandescent light. "Don't go!"

"No choice." The words hissed and crackled, formed by fire. "He's calling. I have to obey."

"Who?" His blinding form seared her sight even through her closed eyelids. "Who's calling? Who are you?"

"I am the Phoenix." Burning wings spread wide. "My name is Blaze."

CHAPTER 3

You're a fully grown, mature woman, Rose told herself firmly as she pulled pints. *You've got no call to be pining after a man like some melodramatic heartbroken teenager. Let it go.*

She'd offered; Ash had refused; that was the end of it. There was no need to feel awkward about it.

Nonetheless, she couldn't quite bring herself to look Ash in the eye. And it might have been her imagination, but he too seemed to be giving her rather more space than normal. He'd gone directly to his shadowed corner with barely a nod of greeting rather than coming up to the bar to chat—or rather, to listen in silence as she chatted at him—as he usually did.

Still, at least her rash declaration hadn't scared him off entirely. She'd been worrying all week that she'd embarrassed him so badly that he wouldn't want to set foot through her door ever again. And as far as she knew, Alpha Team's weekly after-work gathering was the entirety of Ash's social life. She'd fretted over the thought of him sitting abandoned and alone in the fire station, working on reports while everyone else went out for drinks.

But there he was, as usual. A still, quiet shape amidst the banter and laughter, sitting in his customary place at the edge of the group.

And if he was even more reserved and silent than usual...well, it would take someone who knew him well to spot that.

Unfortunately, she wasn't the only one who knew him well.

"So, Rose," Griff murmured in his rich Scottish accent as he waited to collect the drinks. The firefighter's gaze flickered from his commander to Rose. "Just how badly did that conversation go?"

Rose scowled at him over the bar taps. "And what conversation would that be, Griff?"

"I told him that you were angling to get Ash alone last week," Griff's curvy mate Hayley confessed. "Sorry, Rose. It's hard to keep a secret from your mate, especially when he's a griffin."

"Not that you need eagle eyes to see that something's up," added Chase. The pegasus shifter had ostensibly come up to the bar to help carry the drinks, but his black eyes were bright with curiosity as he too looked between Rose and Ash. "Our glorious leader is never exactly over-brimming with exuberance, but at the moment he's so rigid I could use him as a tire iron. I just told him the filthiest joke I know and he didn't even make the tiniest sigh of irritation."

"Stop staring," Rose hissed. "He'll think we're talking about him."

"We *are* talking about him," Hayley pointed out. "Come on, Rose! We all know that you've had a crush on Ash for years. Did you finally tell him? What did he say?"

"Judging from the way he looks like he's had his entire body Botoxed, I think we can guess," Chase said. He flashed a warm, sympathetic smile at Rose. "But do not despair, lovely Rose! No doubt he was simply paralyzed by astonishment. Give him a month or five, and he might be able to wrap his head around the idea to the point of being able to articulate a response."

Rose focused on getting the foaming head of beer perfectly to the top of the pint glass. "Oh, he made his position very clear."

Griff's brow furrowed. "That's odd. Ash is hard to read even for me, but I could have sworn he had a bit of a thing for you."

"Evidently not." Rose set the glass down on a tray rather too hard, beer slopping over onto her fingers. "And apparently he doesn't think that I truly have feelings for him either."

That still rankled, despite her best efforts to rise above it. It was one thing for Ash to say that he wasn't interested in her romantically. It was quite another for him to tell her that *she* couldn't really be interested in *him*. As if she couldn't be trusted to know her own mind.

It was almost insulting. No, it *was* insulting. Ten years they'd been friends, and he was suddenly insisting she didn't know him at all?

Griff was studying her expression. He winced. "Oh dear. Ash did not express himself well."

"For a man of few words, he does occasionally have an uncanny ability to open his mouth wide enough to insert his entire foot," Chase agreed. "But I'm sure he didn't really mean whatever he said, Rose. Perhaps he finds it hard to believe that a gorgeous, vivacious woman such as yourself could truly be interested in a graying and boringly responsible man like himself."

"I think he's scared," Hayley said.

"Scared?" It was so nonsensical that Rose let out a snort of laughter. "*Ash*? The man could incinerate this entire city with a snap of his fingers."

"And I think he works very hard to make sure that he *doesn't*," Hayley said. "He's so controlled and formal, it's like he doesn't dare to let himself feel any emotion at all. I mean, I've known him for a while now, and I don't think I've ever heard him laugh."

"You know, neither have I," Chase said, tilting his head to one side in consideration. "Despite my best efforts."

"That's not actually surprising," Griff said. "Your best efforts generally motivate people to punch you in the face."

"Which Ash has never done either, despite extreme provocation," Chase said cheerfully. "So your mate has a point. The question is, what are we going to do about it?"

Rose raised her eyebrows at him. "About Ash not punching you in the face?"

"No, about you and Ash!" Chase grinned at her, waving his hand to indicate not only Griff but the entirety of Alpha Team, oblivious in their corner behind him. "We're all *both* your friends, so we're doubly invested in helping you to find happiness together. Think of us as your improbably muscular and handsome team of fairy godmothers. You shall win your Prince Charming, Cinderella! Or at least Prince Uptight and Stuffy."

"Oh no." Rose shook her head firmly as she pushed the tray of drinks across the bar. "No matchmaking, thank you. Ash isn't interested. He said so himself. That's the end of it."

"No it isn't." Hayley wound her arm around Griff's waist. Their mate bond glowed in Rose's empathic sense, bright and clear as summer sunshine. "This big idiot tried to push *me* away at least three times, by my count."

"And the only reason I'm standing here today is because she didn't let me," Griff said, smiling down at his mate. "Hayley's right, lass. Ash has kept himself in such a narrow cage for so long, he's forgotten how to spread his wings. It'll take more than just opening the door for a moment to encourage him to fly out."

"So!" Chase clapped his hands together. "How are we going to get the world's most pig-headed and hidebound man to open his heart to the jaw-droppingly beautiful and delightful woman standing here before us?"

"I really don't—" Rose started, but no one was listening to her.

"We need to get his attention," Griff said thoughtfully. "Make him realize what he and Rose could have together."

"That's not going to be easy," Hayley said, frowning. "You know Ash, he's not exactly observant when it comes to things that aren't on fire."

Chase brightened.

"*No,*" Griff and Hayley said together.

"Come on, it's perfect. Can't you just picture the scene?" Chase held up his hands like a film director framing a camera shot. "A mysterious arson attack...the beautiful maiden trapped by the encroaching flames...the daring Fire Commander charging to the rescue and sweeping her up in his arms—"

"And the pegasus-sized pile of ashes when he realizes you set him up," Griff finished.

"Oh, Ash wouldn't burn Chase," Rose said, glaring at Chase. "There wouldn't be enough left after *I* got through with him. Do not even *think* of setting fire to my pub."

"Of course not," Chase said, looking mortally wounded. "How can you even think that I would do such a thing? This is a special place to all of us. Now, a very flammable disused warehouse that no one will miss, on the other hand..."

"Connie!" Hayley called across the room. "Come and tell your mate not to set fire to anything!"

"Don't set fire to anything, Chase," Connie called back, pushing herself up from Alpha Team's table. She was only in early pregnancy, but her bump showed prominently on her short, curvy body, thanks to the fact that she was carrying triplets. She joined her mate at the bar, radiating a mix of exasperation and curiosity to Rose's empathic sense. "Why do you want to set fire to something, anyway?"

"So that Ash will realize his deep and undying love for our very own Rose," Chase declaimed, far too loudly.

At the other end of the bar, Wayne lifted his head from his pint. The wolf shifter blinked, his bleary eyes struggling to focus. "Whazzat? Ash ish what?"

"Nothing," Rose said, her face hot with mortification. She grabbed a beer from the tray and slid it down the bar. "Have another on me, Wayne. And ignore Chase, he's just being ridiculous."

"Yes, you are," Connie told Chase, poking him in the side. "Even more so than usual."

"*Thank* you," Rose said.

"We can't possibly trap Rose in a fire just so Ash can rescue her," Connie continued. "How about a charity auction?"

They all stared at her.

"You know, like 'a win a date with a hot firefighter' sort of thing?" Connie said, looking round at their blank faces. "And then we pool together our funds to make sure that Rose wins the bidding on Ash."

"What?" Rose said.

She seemed to be the only person still confused. Everyone else now had a thoughtful look, as though what Connie had just said made perfect sense.

"You know, it *has* got potential," Hayley said. "But I've no idea how we'd get him to agree to it."

"Much as I'm delighted by the thought of our rugged leader forced to oil up and sell off his virtue, I concur," Chase said. "How about—"

"No," Griff, Hayley, and Connie said together.

Chase looked wounded. "I was only going to suggest that we arrange for them to get trapped together in Rose's beer cellar."

Rose looked down at the still untouched drinks on the bar. "Are my prices too high? Did you all get drunk on cheap spirits before coming here?"

"Ash can burn his way out of anything like that," Hayley said, as though Rose hadn't even spoken. "I know! We set Rose up with a fake boyfriend, so that Ash will be driven mad with jealousy!"

"Sounds dangerous for the fake boyfriend," Griff said, one eyebrow quirking. "Not sure we'll persuade anyone to risk their life like that. But what if Ash *is* the fake boyfriend? Say we invent a crazy stalker—"

"And persuade Ash that the only way to keep Rose safe is for him to pretend to date her so that the stalker will be scared off," Hayley finished eagerly. "And then of course the fake relationship will turn real!"

"Right, you are *all* being completely ridiculous," Rose announced.

Gathering up the tray of drinks, she swept past the whole silly lot of them. With her head held high, she marched across the room.

"About time," Hugh said, as she reached Alpha Team's corner booth. The white-haired paramedic passed a beer to his mate Ivy and took a whiskey for himself. "I was starting to wonder if you were having to distill the alcohol from scratch, Rose."

"You can blame your colleagues for the delay," Rose said, scowling over her shoulder at the group still whispering together back at the bar. "I don't know what's gotten into them, spouting such nonsense."

Red dragon shifter Dai cocked an auburn eyebrow at her as she passed him a beer. "Surely you should be used to gibberish from Chase by now."

"But not from Griff," his mate Virginia said, taking a white wine. "What was that about setting fire to something?"

"Just a joke," Rose said quickly, her face heating. "Here, John, Neridia. I brought non-alcoholic for you both."

Neridia smiled as she accepted the mixed juice cocktail. Her huge belly barely fit behind the table. "Thank you, Rose. Though John's not the one who's pregnant, you know."

"But I am on duty guarding the most precious treasures in the Pearl Empire," John said in his melodious sea-dragon accent. He saluted Rose with his own mocktail. "Honor demands that I maintain a clear head."

That left only one.

Rose cleared her throat, forcing her hand and voice to stay level as she set down a glass of water. "Ash."

"Rose," he said, in precisely the same neutral tone.

That had gone well.

Holding the tray like a shield, Rose swung round to flee back to safety—and ran smack into Chase's muscular chest.

"Gentlemen!" the pegasus shifter declared, draping an arm around Rose's shoulders before she could escape. "And beautiful ladies, of course. We were just having a very interesting discussion at the bar."

A desperate smile frozen on her face, Rose stomped hard on his foot.

Chase didn't bat an eyelid. "On a topic that I'm sure will be of great interest to all of you. I refer, of course, to romance."

Dai's forehead wrinkled. "But we're all already mated."

Virginia nudged him in the ribs, her eyes cutting across to Ash.

"Oh. Right." The tips of Dai's ears flushed faintly pink. "Sorry. No offense intended."

"None taken," Ash murmured.

"One word, Chase," Rose hissed as quietly as she could. If she'd been a mythic shifter, and able to communicate telepathically with the pegasus, she would have been screaming in his mind right now. "*One word*, and you will never drink in this pub again."

Chase adopted an expression of exaggerated innocence. "I only wanted to ask them what *they* thought made the perfect woman."

Rose stared at him. So did everyone else.

"Indulge him," Griff said, coming up behind Chase and—suspiciously—boxing Rose in so that there was no chance of escape. "Obviously we all have our own mates—with the exception of Ash—but pretend for a moment that you don't. What would you look for in an ideal partner?"

Dai exchanged a glance with Virginia, who raised her eyebrows at him in a *let's just roll with it* sort of way.

"All right," the dragon shifter said, shrugging. "Well, clearly the answer is a stunning, brilliant, Anglo-Saxon archaeologist."

"I think that's a little specific," Virginia murmured.

Dai grinned across at his mate, his bright green eyes crinkling. "True, though. But if we're talking general traits…I'd say intelligence is important."

"Courage," John Doe rumbled, taking Neridia's hand.

"Tenacity," Hugh said, his voice losing all trace of its usual sarcasm. Ivy met his eyes, her own going bright and soft.

Griff smiled down at Hayley, who was still tucked under his arm. "Compassion."

"You're all wrong," Chase announced. "Because clearly the correct answer is great pragmatism, even greater patience, and the ability to fly a plane upside-down at three hundred miles per hour."

Connie, who'd just come up to his other side, elbowed him.

"Also, extremely sharp elbows," Chase added. "To keep you on track."

"Chase, you are so far off track, I'm not even sure you ever had a destination," Hugh said. "Is there a point to this?"

"Patience, Hughnicorn," Chase said, ignoring the death glare that the unicorn shifter shot at him. "Not all of us are as pointy as you. And we haven't heard from everyone yet."

Rose's stomach lurched. She had a sudden horrible certainty as to where Chase was steering this conversation.

"Ash," Chase swung round to face his Commander, forcing Rose to turn as well. "What do you think is the most desirable quality in a woman?"

She was going to *skin* the pegasus shifter.

"There is only one." Ash looked directly at her. "That she is your mate."

The bottom dropped out of her stomach. For a moment, she couldn't breathe, hurt beyond words.

"But if, for argument's sake, you were an ordinary human—," Chase began.

"I am not," Ash said, in a tone that killed the conversation stone-dead.

A rather awkward silence fell. Rose's face burned with humiliation.

"Well, I don't agree," Hayley said. She turned to Rose, jaw setting. "Don't listen to him. Regular people fall in love every day, and it's no less real just because they aren't shifters."

"What's brought all this on?" Dai said curiously.

"Some jerk rejected Rose last week," Connie told him. She was very obviously *not* looking at Ash.

"What an idiot," Dai said, without any hint of guile. "Well, in that case, I fully agree with Hayley, Rose. Even though your mate's gone, there's no reason why you can't find happiness elsewhere."

"Hear, hear," Hugh said, lifting his glass in her direction. "You just need to find someone who appreciates everything you have to offer. Which, if we consider the checklist we've just heard, is considerable. Don't let one stupid bastard get you down."

From the genuine sympathy radiating from them, Rose was certain that Chase and Griff hadn't tipped them off telepathically as to precisely *who* had rejected her. Nonetheless, her face flamed. She didn't dare glance at Ash.

"There's no need to be making all this fuss," she said. She turned away, busying herself tidying up empty glasses from the next table. "I'm fine. Really."

"She's not fine," she heard Hayley whisper behind her back. "That sort of rejection is a slap in the face. Especially when it's the first time in years that you've dared to put yourself out there."

John let out a low, deep growl. "Who is the cur who has insulted our Rose? I will seek him out and demand that he face me in the duel for such disrespect."

Now she *knew* that Chase and Griff hadn't told their colleagues that it had been Ash. Thank heaven for small mercies. But her heart sank at the loyalty and outrage she could sense emanating from John, and from the other firefighters too.

They were trained to rescue people in distress. Now, apparently, they were determined to rescue her, whether she wanted them to or not.

And when they all found out that it was Ash who'd rejected her... the poor man would never hear the end of it.

She couldn't be responsible for him losing the tiny bit of peace he had left. She just *couldn't.* But how on earth could she persuade the stubborn firefighters of Alpha Team to drop the subject?

"I *am* fine," she said firmly, as inspiration struck. She half-turned, glancing at them over her shoulder. "In fact, I'm getting straight back on the horse."

"Good for you!" Hayley said, exchanging a triumphant glance with Connie. "So you'll ask him again?"

"No." Rose pulled her phone out of her pocket, brandishing it at them. "I'm going to set up an online dating profile."

The Ash-shaped silence behind her was deafening.

"That's a wonderful idea," Dai said warmly.

"No it isn't!" yelped Chase. "I mean, are you sure, Rose? Lots of strange men on those sorts of sites."

"I am literally an empath," Rose said. She was already busy typing —partly to prove to them that she was serious, and partly out of fear that she'd lose her nerve if she didn't do it straight away. "I think you can trust me to be a good judge of character."

"True," Hugh said, though he sounded a little dubious. "But still... online dating? What's wrong with meeting someone the old-fashioned way?"

"You mean on top of an acid-drenched elevator?" Ivy said dryly. "Or amidst the smoldering wreckage of a burning building? There's nothing wrong with meeting your mate in less dramatic circumstances, you know."

"I'm not looking for a mate," Rose said, focused on her phone. "Just a man."

She wasn't just saying it to get them off her back, she realized. She *did* want a man. She'd thought that spark had long since died, but Ash's touch had awakened a fire in her body again. She couldn't deny that she wanted more.

And if it couldn't be with Ash...well, maybe she could still find solace with someone else. Better to cup her hands around a candle than pine for the sun.

"Ash," Chase appealed. "You don't think this is a good idea, do you?"

Despite herself, she snuck a peek at him. Hoping for...she didn't know what. Some kind of reaction. Maybe even a flicker of jealousy.

His face was utterly expressionless.

"It is not my place to have an opinion one way or another," he said. His eyes met hers, very briefly. "But I wish you every happiness, Rose."

Wayne was good at three things.

The first was appearing to be a lot drunker than he actually was.

The second was noticing things.

And the third was noticing *what* to notice.

It was a surprisingly lucrative set of talents. And right now, his mouth was watering at the juicy scent of a big, fat payout coming his way. One that might keep a roof over his head for *months*.

He slumped over his beer, letting his eyelids droop as if he was utterly sozzled. In truth, he was watching carefully. Noticing.

Right now, he was noticing the Phoenix's hand.

It was no good staring at the man's face. Wayne had long since learned that no secrets ever slipped out from behind that blank, frozen wall. But his hands...those were another story. You could learn a lot, watching the Phoenix's hands.

Ash's fingers gripped his glass of water. He held it, and held it, and didn't once raise it to his mouth. Not even when all his friends finished their own drinks, excusing themselves with awkward, stumbling goodbyes. He held onto it for a good five minutes after they'd all left, sitting alone at the table, staring at nothing.

Finally, he released it, one finger at a time. Usually, he came up to the bar, to say goodnight to Rose. This time, however, he left without a backward glance.

Wayne slid off his own barstool. Affecting a stumbling, weaving gait, he staggered over to Alpha Team's corner booth. He pretended to stumble, catching himself on the edge of the table. His hand brushed against the Phoenix's abandoned drink.

Rose was wiping down a nearby table, her movements rather jerkier and more forceful than usual. She looked up at his yelp. "You all right, Wayne?"

"Yep," he mumbled, around his stinging fingers. "G'night."

The water in the glass was still boiling.

Fighting down a grin, Wayne made his way outside. He ducked down an alleyway, pulling out his phone. The *special* phone, that he only used for one number. The one that *he'd* given him.

Wayne blew on his reddened fingers, trying to cool them, before opening up a new text.

Got a good one for you, he typed. *I think the Phoenix is in love.*

He started to put the phone back in his pocket. To his surprise, it buzzed in his hand.

Tell me everything, said the reply.

CHAPTER 4

PAST

20 years ago...

Blaze arced across the sky like a comet, trailing fury. His rational mind was stretched paper-thin, barely containing the raging inferno underneath. Only the binding biting into his soul kept his humanity from being consumed utterly.

Unchecked, his beast would have scorched a firestorm of devastation across the state. Its burning rage grew with every unwilling wingbeat. The binding forced him on, but there was a new pull resisting it. An equally demanding call, tugging him back.

Back to *her*.

He was used to the constricting agony of one leash. But now he was caught between two, and the opposing forces threatened to rip his mind in half.

Blaze, I am Blaze. He held onto his name like a lifeline, a point of certainty amidst the howling wildfires sweeping through his soul. *Not just the Phoenix. Not just a beast. I am Blaze. I am in control.*

Though he barely had control. He could stop his beast from starting new fires, but he couldn't help its rage from reaching out to the parts of the forest that were already alight. Whenever he passed over smoldering patches of wilderness, the inferno roared up anew.

He swooped low through the flames, seeking solace. But for once, not even their heat could cool him.

For the first time in his life, it was not the fire's embrace that he craved.

Anger burned in his soul—and not just from his animal. It was as much his own fury as the Phoenix's that set fire to the sky as he arrowed toward home.

Mundane people were blind to him in this form. But the compound he called home was guarded by more than mere humans.

The alarms were already wailing at full volume as he shot over the outer perimeter fence. The complex boiled like a kicked anthill, people streaming out of the scattered dormitories and labs. Armed soldiers barked orders at panicked acolytes and staff, trying to maintain order as they herded everyone into the emergency underground bunkers.

Part of him—the tiny part that was still vaguely human—was darkly amused by the sight. Like mere blast doors and concrete walls would do anything to protect them if the Phoenix was ever *truly* unleashed.

His binding tightened in warning. It bit into his wing like barbed wire, making him lurch in the air. Hissing, he tumbled ungracefully into the landing courtyard, scorching the already-blackened stones with a fresh layer of soot.

Pulling the Phoenix back into his skin was like swallowing a sun. Even in human form, it burned beneath his chest.

His binding burned, too. The tattooed runes cut deep into his right arm, deeper than they ever had before. Blood dripped from his fingers, scarlet drops vivid against the scorched flagstones.

The pain was irrelevant. So were the four guns trained on him, and the four shaking soldiers who held them. There was only one person he wanted to see.

"Corbin!" he shouted, heedless of the way the soldiers' fingers tightened on their triggers. "Damn you, Corbin! Let me go back! I have to go back! *Corbin!*"

"I am here," said the familiar, calm voice. "And we will speak once you can do so like a man rather than a beast, Blaze."

A fresh throb of pain shot through Blaze's binding. He clenched his fist as a tall, austere figure stepped out from the shadowed doorway.

As always, Corbin wore the black, full-length robe and gold-lined hood that marked his rank. A casual observer might have mistaken the outfit for traditional academic dress. With his graying hair and lined, thoughtful face, Corbin did look the part of an absent-minded college professor.

In truth, he was something far more dangerous.

Corbin folded his hands into his wide sleeves, regarding Blaze with cool appraisal. "You are not in control of yourself. You know what that means, Blaze."

The Phoenix rose in his soul, alight with hatred. With gritted teeth, Blaze forced his beast back down. He didn't like this process any more than his animal did, but fighting only made it worse.

Blaze's binding burned. His vision went dark, a wave of dizziness sweeping over him. His beast shrieked in outrage and fear—and fell into strangled silence, as Corbin fully opened the link between them.

Blaze swayed, power running out of him like blood from an open vein. Across the courtyard, Corbin drew in a soft, sharp breath, his chest rising as he siphoned off the Phoenix's fire.

The warlock kept the connection open for a long, agonizing minute. By the time Corbin finally released him, Blaze was on his knees, hands braced on the flagstones.

"There," Corbin said, calmly. "Better?"

For a moment, all he could do was breathe. His ears rang with the sudden silence in his mind. There was a sick, sour taste in his mouth.

But the warlock *had* drawn off the rage that had threatened to consume him. The Phoenix fire burned low and fitful in his soul, leaving him space to think.

Painfully, he got back to his feet. "Thank you, High Magus."

The warlock tipped his head in acknowledgement. "And now that you are not half-feral, you can explain yourself. I summoned you back the instant I sensed you start to lose control, but even so, I was nearly too late. What happened, Blaze?"

"I don't know." He swallowed hard, still feeling dizzy and nauseous. "I went to the fire. It was helping to calm my beast, just like it always does. But then—there was—"

He stopped, words failing him. His memories were a confused jumble, as they always were after he walked in a wildfire. It was like awakening from a dream, and trying to pierce together sense from jagged, too-bright fragments.

A voice like a song, calling to him. Skin as soft and dark as soot, every rich curve gloriously, maddeningly bare. And her eyes, her *eyes*...

"There was a woman," he said, haltingly.

Corbin went very still. "A woman?"

"Yes. The most beautiful woman...and I knew her." Just the thought of those heart-stopping eyes made fire rise again in his soul, even though Corbin had only just drained him. "But I've never seen her before. High Magus, how is that possible?"

A muscle ticked in Corbin's jaw. "I do not know."

The warlock had raised Blaze from childhood. Corbin had been parent and mentor and prison warden for as long as Blaze could remember. Their very souls were bound together. He knew Corbin better than anyone.

And he knew when Corbin was lying.

"You do know something! Or you suspect it, at least." Unable to contain himself, Blaze took a step forward. "Tell me! Now!"

The soldiers in the corners of the courtyard tensed. Corbin lifted a hand slightly, motioning them back down.

Corbin's gray eyes never left his. Blaze was used to being studied by the warlock for any sign of instability, but this much unwavering scrutiny was unnerving.

If he didn't know better, he would have said that the High Magus was...*afraid*.

"Tell me," Blaze repeated. Though he felt like he was burning from the inside out, he forced his voice to match Corbin's calm, measured tones. "Please. I need to know. Who was she?"

For a long moment, he thought the High Magus wasn't going to answer. Then Corbin let out his breath in a resigned sigh.

"Someone very dangerous," Corbin said, a hint of grimness shadowing his usually level voice. "Especially to you."

A disbelieving laugh escaped him. If he hadn't known that the warlock possessed absolutely no sense of humor, he would have thought it was a joke. "One naked, unarmed woman is a danger to the Phoenix Eternal?"

"Yes," Corbin said, his jaw tightening again. "And if you use your head rather than letting your beast continue to rule you, you will understand. Think, Blaze. When you looked into her eyes, how did you feel?"

Heat rose in him at the mere memory. "Like she was the only person who mattered in the entire world."

The warlock looked at him, silently, and waited.

"The only person who mattered." Blaze repeated his own words more slowly, ice replacing the fire in his veins as he realized what he'd said. "One word from her, and I would have gladly burned anything she asked."

"You see now," Corbin said.

He did. He scrubbed his hands over his face, sickened at the thought of how close he'd come to endangering the population of the entire country. Of the *world.*

"But who was she?" he asked, dropping his hands again. "To have such power over my beast...*what* was she? Some kind of witch? A rival of yours, even more powerful?"

Corbin's severe expression turned even more icy. "Of course not. I am the High Magus. No other warlock could come close to breaking my binding of you. No. She was something else."

The High Magus turned away, heading back into the building. Blaze didn't need the slight tug on his binding to know his cue to follow. He fell into his accustomed place, half a step behind Corbin.

The plain gray corridors of the menagerie building were deserted. He could sense the knotted, feral fires of some of the other shifters behind the heavily-reinforced doors they passed, but none of the dimmer, steadier energies of human souls.

On a normal day there would have been plenty of people around; cleaning staff mopping out the cages, soldiers bringing in freshly-captured feral shifters, brown-robed acolytes hurrying on minor errands for their mentors. But all the residents of the complex usually made themselves scarce whenever Blaze was out of his cell.

They were afraid of him. And he knew that there were whispers about the way Corbin handled him. Mutterings that he had too much freedom, that Corbin treated him too much as if he was a person.

Other warlocks at the facility never let their familiars range out of sight. When their shifters grew too agitated, they let them vent their bestial urges hunting within the extensive grounds of the secluded, private base.

But the Phoenix was not a mere wolf or bear, to be pacified by ripping up a deer. Only wildfire soothed the creature that lived in Blaze's soul. Corbin could hardly accompany him into the heart of the inferno, but it made the other warlocks nervous whenever the High Magus allowed him off-site.

Blaze could have told them not to worry, if they would have listened to a mere shifter. The runes around his arm bound him equally tightly regardless of whether Corbin stood two feet away or the other side of the planet. No matter how far he might fly, Corbin could always pull him back.

Or at least, he always *had* been able to. Blaze glanced down at his right arm, uneasily. The cuts edging the inked runes stung. Even shifter-fast healing struggled with the wounds inflicted by the binding whenever he fought it.

He hadn't fought it for a long, long time. As far as he was aware, he wasn't deliberately fighting it now.

And yet still the binding cut into his arm, seeping blood in slow drips.

Perhaps the other warlocks were right after all.

He looked back at Corbin, trying to judge his mood from the straight line of his back and the set of his head. With most people, Blaze could get an idea of their general thoughts from the patterns of their soul-energy...but not Corbin. Despite the bond between them, the warlock was—and always had been—utterly impenetrable to him. Nonetheless, Blaze had the impression that his mentor's mind was working furiously.

That was comforting. Corbin was the most powerful warlock in generations. He was the High Magus, the only one ever to bind a shifter as powerful as the Phoenix. He had not only studied all the ancient lore on shifters, he had substantially added to it through his own research. If anyone would be able to work out what was going on —and more importantly, how to stop it—it was him.

"You said she was naked." Corbin spoke without looking round, his stride measured and unhurried. "Did she also appear to recognize you?"

He nodded, knowing that the warlock would sense his assent down their bond. "She seemed drawn to me. As much as I was to her."

The sweet, searing heat of her skin against his palm, close, so close...

Corbin shot him a sharp glance over his shoulder, and Blaze tamped down his rising fire as much as he could. He had no desire to have his power drained twice in a single day.

The warlock's eyes narrowed slightly, but to Blaze's relief he made no move to re-open the link. Corbin continued on, without even a scathing comment about Blaze's lack of discipline.

That unnerved him. It wasn't like Corbin to pass up what he called a 'teaching opportunity'. The High Magus *was* preoccupied.

"Given what you say, I believe that she is a shifter as well," Corbin said, sounding thoughtful. "A lesser kind of animal, if she was unable to shift with her clothes."

"A shifter?" Blaze said, startled. "But she had no binding. And she spoke to me. She shouted at me to stop the fire. How could she maintain her human mind, with no warlock to help her?"

"Some feral shifters, particularly those with weak beasts, can do surprisingly well at maintaining the pretense of humanity." Corbin's shrouded shoulders were set in a tense, straight line. "But do not be misled. Underneath the veneer of civilized behavior she is driven by base animal desires. No better than a bitch in heat. And that was what drew your own beast."

Blaze stared at the back of the warlock's head. "My animal is in some kind of…mating frenzy?"

"It is a sickness that can strike some shifters. An urge to rut, which drives out all other thought. When it occurs, madness is the inevitable result." Corbin sighed. "We have sometimes had problems with it here, with other familiars. But I never thought it would affect you, given your singular nature."

She certainly couldn't be the same species as him. There was only one Phoenix, thankfully. Blaze would not have wished his own inner monster on anyone else. Yet he couldn't deny that his body had responded powerfully to the mysterious woman.

Not *just* his body, though.

She'd run toward the wildfire. Toward *him*. He'd been nearly lost to the inferno, more elemental force than man, and yet she'd faced him without flinching. In the defense of innocent lives, she'd defied the fire, standing bare and unafraid. Her courage and compassion had arrested him as much as her feminine curves.

"You truly think that it was only my beast?" he asked, uncertain. "She was very…striking. Not to mention very naked. Surely any man would have responded to her as I did."

Corbin made a slight, impatient sound. "Becoming instantly infatuated? To the point of throwing away all training, all discipline, all ethics and morals? *Think*, Blaze. How long were you in her presence? How many words did you exchange? And you have the idiocy to think that this sudden passion you feel can possibly be real?"

Blaze dropped his gaze to the hem of the warlock's robe, stung by his scorn. Corbin was right, of course. Even as isolated as he was, he knew enough of regular humans to understand that love—*true* love, the kind that lasted—didn't work that way. You didn't lock eyes with a woman and instantly know that she was the one and only for you, always and forever.

But it had felt so real.

It still felt so real.

"You said this drove shifters mad," he said, quietly.

Corbin stopped, turning. His mouth was set in a thin line, eyes as hard as steel.

"I will not allow that to happen," the warlock said. "But you must fight this as well, Blaze. No matter how much your beast rages, you *must* keep control. The Phoenix must be contained. You cannot let it rise."

His binding throbbed, an ever-present ache ebbing and falling in time with his own pulse. He was used to constant pain.

But there was a new hurt in his heart now. And ache of the binding was as nothing compared to it.

He took a deep breath, closing his eyes. As a child, he'd adjusted to the cage of pain that contained the ravenous force consuming his soul. He was a man now, stronger, more disciplined. He could adjust to this new torment.

He would have to.

"Will you do one thing for me?" he asked, opening his eyes again to meet Corbin's impassive ones. "Can you find her? To explain things to her. And to help her. If she has been struck with this sickness as well, if she feels this pain, she will need your aid as much as I do."

"Oh, I shall find her," the warlock said, his jaw tightening. "But I cannot bring her here, Blaze. You know why."

"Yes." Blaze bowed his head. He forced himself to say the words out loud, no matter how the inferno within him raged and howled. "I must never see her again."

CHAPTER 5

Ash knew that he shouldn't be here.

He sat in the high-backed restaurant booth, pretending to study a menu. In reality, most of his concentration was focused on very lightly singeing the minds of the people around him.

It was an art he'd perfected decades ago, during the darkest years. Just the barest brush of his flame, carefully sending a single thread of short-term memory up in smoke, and people's eyes skipped straight over him. He wasn't invisible; they still saw him. They just instantly forgot that they had.

There was only one person's mind he didn't touch. He'd sworn that he never would.

Not ever again.

Nonetheless, Rose was oblivious to his presence. He could only see the back of her head, over the wall of the booth ahead. If he'd been anyone else, she would have sensed him watching her—but he knew her empathic abilities didn't work on him.

That was his fault too.

She stirred, and he tensed, ready to duck behind his menu—but she only tipped her head back, laughing at something her companion had just said. Her spiraling curls bounced with the motion, floating in a black halo around her head. He hadn't seen her wear her hair in anything other than a plain, practical bun for years.

She'd quite literally let her hair down.

Ash stared at his menu, and concentrated very hard on not incinerating it.

Out of the corner of his eye, he saw the man opposite Rose laugh too, white teeth gleaming in an charming, roguish grin. Even Ash had to admit that he was dismayingly handsome. Although he must have been in his mid-forties, his artfully-tousled hair was thick and dark, without a hint of gray. He sat with the spread-legged, relaxed confidence of a man who knew he looked good, and wanted women to notice too.

Rose was certainly noticing. Ash didn't need to be able to see her face; he could read her body language. Her tilted head, the way she kept toying with her hair…she was attracted to the man.

Ash clenched his hand around a fork, so hard that his fingernails bit into his own palm. He was not Rose's mate. Why shouldn't she smile and flirt? She deserved to find someone who could make her happy.

If he was truly her friend, he would leave her to enjoy her date in peace.

He stayed.

"You did *not*," Rose was saying. No—giggling. When was the last time he'd heard her voice ripple with girlish laughter like that?

"I most certainly did." Her date leaned forward, resting his arms on the table. His shirt sleeves were rolled up, exposing sculpted muscles emphasized by black tribal tattoos. "Looked him in the eye, laid down my cards, and picked up the keys to his Lexus. I thought the old man was going to have a stroke on the spot."

"But you didn't really keep the car, did you?" Rose sounded half-appalled, half-tickled. "I mean, he clearly shouldn't have gambled it."

"It's in the car park out front now." The man's voice dropped to a low, intimate purr. He ran one finger over the back of Rose's hand. "Beautiful things belong with guys who'll treat them properly."

"Sir? Um, sir?"

In his distraction, he'd slipped up and allowed a waitress to become aware of him. She'd frozen next to his booth, her gaze riveted on his hand.

Ash glanced down. His fork had melted into a white-hot puddle of steel, gleaming against his weathered skin.

"I am not quite ready to order." He flicked away the molten metal, hiding it under his menu. "Would you be so kind as to bring me another fork? This one appears to have…malfunctioned."

"Right away, sir," the waitress said faintly.

He was going to leave her a very large tip.

Rose's date was still leaning forward, his hand covering hers. "Tell you what. How about we quit this joint and go have some real fun? I'll take you for a drive."

"Oh." To Ash's relief, Rose drew her hand back. "But we're having a lovely evening here. And we've both been drinking. This wine's nearly gone."

"Nah, I'm still fine. I've hardly had any."

This was true. The man had barely touched his drink. It also hadn't escaped Ash's notice that he had been quietly topping up Rose's glass at every opportunity.

"Come on, you know you want to." The man winked at her. "You may have described yourself as 'mature' in your profile, but I think there's a secret part of you that's still wild and carefree."

"Oh, no." Rose toyed with her wineglass, her head lowering. "Maybe in my youth, but that was a long time ago. I'm afraid that if that's what you're looking for, you won't find it in me."

"Maybe I can see you better than you see yourself," her date murmured. He reached out, this time drawing a finger seductively down her bare arm. "Forget being grown-up and responsible for one evening, Rose. Live a little."

Ash concentrated on his breathing. He lifted his hands away from the table, before the linen could burst into flame.

"I…have to pop to the ladies' room." Rose stood up abruptly. "Excuse me for a moment. I'll be right back."

Ash froze, caught between hiding under the table and leaping to his own feet. He was sitting barely six feet from her. If she turned her head, she'd see him, right there in plain sight. She'd be utterly furious.

But at least she'd know that he was there.

Turn your head, part of him willed, despite his better judgment. *Look at me. See me.*

But she was deaf to his mental plea. She never looked around as she headed for the bathroom.

Left behind, her date slouched back against the back of his seat. He scratched his crotch absently, then took out his phone. His eyes scanned the room—skipping straight over Ash—as he dialed.

"Hey," the man said into his phone. His voice was pitched low, but to Ash's shifter-sharp hearing he might as well have been yelling into a megaphone. "It's me. Listen, I have to push back delivery."

A pause, then, "Nah, no problems." An unpleasant smirk spread across the man's face. "Just picked up a hot piece of ass."

Ash clenched his jaw.

"Pussy so wet she's practically on my dick already," the man said, unaware of how close he'd come to making headlines as a mysterious and tragic case of spontaneous human combustion. He lowered his voice even further, eying the nearest waitress cautiously. "Promise, the stuff is all safe. It's in my car now. I'll just be an hour or two later than planned, okay?"

Ash's instincts pricked up at the man's furtive air. He hesitated, wrestling with his conscience…but only briefly.

Closing his eyes, he opened himself to the man's soul.

His most feared power was the ability to burn thoughts and memories. What few people ever realized was that meant he could *see* them as well. He couldn't skip at will through someone's head like surfing TV channels, but he could examine their mind and weigh their very nature. See the way experience knitted together to form patterns of personality. And then, if he chose, he could alter them with flame.

He only did *that* in direst need. It was one thing to quietly remove his own image from people's surface thoughts, and quite another to transfigure someone's entire personality. He generally tried to avoid even looking into other souls. He valued his own privacy too highly to casually breach that of others.

He didn't do it casually now. Even so, part of him whispered that he was just allowing his own feelings to override his ethics. But if there was the slightest chance that Rose's date might not be all he seemed...

Ash reached out, sinking into the man's mind.

And what he found there...

Opening his eyes again, Ash exhaled, slowly. When he could trust himself, he slid out from the booth.

Pausing only to leave a twenty for the waitress, he left.

~

In the safety of the bathroom, Rose stared down at her phone. She bit her lip, wondering if she was being over-dramatic. Mack had been coming on a little strong, but perhaps that was her fault.

She *had* been laughing at his outrageous stories. Too loudly, too enthusiastically, to cover her awkwardness. And he must have caught her staring at his sculpted forearms with their swirling black tattoos, and the breadth of his shoulders under his well-tailored shirt. No doubt he thought she was checking him out.

She had been checking him out. Looking at his undeniably attractive physique, the sort of body any straight woman should desire... and wondering why he left her utterly cold.

A handsome, charming man was flirting with her, and she didn't feel even the slightest flicker of interest.

She knew that he was interested in *her*. The hungry anticipation and sharp-edged lust she kept sensing from him was unmistakable.

The intensity of it made her uneasy. She couldn't shake the feeling that his dark-tinged, predatory anticipation could easily turn to anger. Especially when she told him no...

She was probably being silly. She hadn't dated anyone since...well, ever. She wasn't used to being looked at with desire. Perhaps Mack's emotions were perfectly normal.

Not our mate, hissed her swan again.

It had said the same thing about Ash, of course. But not in the same way. Her swan's rejection of him had always been tinged with strange, wistful regret. He'd never made her inner animal *nervous.*

Not like Mack did.

Rose found her thumb hovering over Ash's name in her contact list.

"Now I *am* being ridiculous," she muttered to her reflection in the mirror. She could hardly ask the Phoenix Eternal to call her so that she'd have an excuse to get away from an uncomfortable date. He was probably on duty at the fire station, anyway.

Shaking her head, she dropped her phone back into her bag. She was a grown woman. She faced down drunk alpha shifters on a regular basis. She could handle one ordinary man, no matter how much of a dangerous vibe he gave off.

She'd finish her meal and wine, politely thank Mack for a lovely evening, and head home.

At least, that was the plan until she heard the scream.

Dashing out of the bathroom, she was confronted by a scene of confusion. Mack was on his feet, fists clenched. Shock and anger boiled off him, so strong Rose could almost see it clouding the air around him. A waiter barred his path, holding up his hands in a pacifying manner.

"Sir, you really can't go out there," the waiter was saying. He was doing a good job at maintaining a professionally calm expression, but Rose could sense the panic bubbling behind his face. "It's not safe—"

"Out of my way!" Mack shoved the smaller man aside.

"What's going on?" Rose asked, but Mack was already bolting for the door. Ignoring the waiter's garbled protest, she followed on his heels.

The instant she stepped outside, the breeze blew a cloud of smoke into her face.

"My car!" Mack howled in agony.

Coughing, Rose blinked to clear her streaming eyes. She was no expert on cars, but she guessed that the bright red convertible parked in front of the restaurant was Mack's treasured Lexus.

She also guessed that it wasn't usually on fire.

Thick black smoke poured from the windows with the stench of burning leather. The car alarm gave a last valiant, strangled shriek, and died.

Mack charged for the car, as though he thought he could beat out the flames with his bare hands. Rose pelted after him, barely managing to catch his arm before he hurled himself into the blaze. She dug in her heels, hauling him back with all her shifter strength.

"Don't go near it!" she shouted over the roar of the fire. With her free hand, she dug in her purse. "It could explode any minute! I'll call the fire department—"

The wail of a siren cut her off.

"Goodness," Rose said as a fire truck screamed around the corner. "That was fast."

The appliance pulled up in front of the restaurant. Even before it had fully come to a stop, the doors were swinging open. Two firefighters in full turnout gear piled out.

With a start, Rose recognized Dai and Griff. They didn't seem to notice her in return, completely focused on the job at hand.

She'd never seen Alpha Team at work before. Moving in perfect synchronization, the two shifters threw open a side compartment on the truck, hauling out lengths of hose. Dai hefted the nozzle, while Griff took up the slack behind him. The two firefighters ran toward the burning car...and stopped.

"Don't just stand there!" Mack yelled at them. "Save my car!"

Griff and Dai's heads turned, but not in Mack's direction. They both looked around as if searching for something.

"The fire is right there, you morons! Get it under control!"

"Oh, that fire's already under control," said Chase's distinctive Irish brogue.

The firefighter had dismounted from the driver's seat and come up to them. Like his colleagues, he was dressed in heavy fire-resistant gear, reflective bands on his sleeves luminous in the swirling lights of the fire engine. For once, there wasn't even a trace of a grin on his face. It was strange to see the pegasus shifter so focused and serious.

"Is there something wrong?" Rose asked him in concern. "Should we run?"

"No, everyone's perfectly safe," Chase said absently, still studying the burning car with narrowed eyes. "It's just an unusual situation. We're not sure if we *should* put it out."

"What kind of cowards are you?" Mack spluttered. With a jerk, he broke free of Rose's grasp. "My taxes pay your damn salaries! I don't care if you burn to death, get in there and do your job!"

Before Rose could stop him, he took a swing at the firefighter. Without even looking, Chase caught Mack's fist in his hand. Mack yelped as Chase's fingers tightened.

"Please calm down. I'd hate to have to break your arm. The paperwork would be a nightmare." Still holding onto Mack's fist, he glanced at Rose, and waved his free hand in casual greeting. "Evening, Rose. We knew you had a hot date tonight, but we didn't think it would be *this* hot."

"Neither did I." Rose anxiously kept an eye on the burning vehicle. Despite the thick smoke, the fire actually didn't seem to be that bad. "Mack, calm down. I think it looks worse than it is. Maybe someone threw a cigarette through the window out of jealousy or something. See, it's just the passenger seat that's actually on fire."

She'd thought that the observation would reassure him. Instead, he went stark white.

"Th-the passenger seat?" he stuttered.

"Good news!" Chase announced brightly, as a police car pulled into view round the corner. "We just got the go-ahead to proceed. Don't worry, we'll have it doused in no time."

"No!" Mack yelped. "Let it burn!"

Rose blinked at him. "What?"

Griff had already crowbarred open the door of the car, allowing Dai to spray the seat with some kind of white foam. The crackling flames died away quickly, revealing scorched, crumbling leather.

"Make them stop!" Mack tried to pull himself out of Chase's grip as Dai prodded cautiously at the wreckage of the seat. "That's my property, he can't just poke around in there!"

"We have to check for hotspots," Chase said. Rose sensed a distinct, wicked sense of glee behind his too-innocent expression. "Very thoroughly. Our Commander's orders."

"Ash is here?" Rose said in surprise.

Looking past Chase, Rose's heart give an odd little skip. Ash *was* there, though she hadn't noticed him getting out of the fire truck. He was in profile to her, back to the still-smoking vehicle, talking to a couple of police officers. Unlike the other firefighters, he wasn't wearing protective gear—just his usual gray duty uniform.

Mack let out a strangled moan as he too noticed the watching cops. "Oh fu—"

"Officers?" Dai called, pulling something out of the smoldering seat. It looked like a plastic-wrapped white brick. "I think you might want to take a look at this..."

The wave of guilt and terror from Mack made Rose physically take a step away from him. "That's not mine," he babbled, desperately trying to jerk away from Chase. "I have no idea what it is. Someone else must have put it there."

"Then you won't mind telling the nice police officers all about it," Chase said, his eyes glittering dangerously. "Come on. I believe there are some people who would like to have a chat with you..."

"What?" Rose said, but Chase was already frog-marching Mack off in the direction of the police car. From the expressions on the faces of the waiting officers, Rose didn't think she'd get any answers from *that* direction.

Giving the smoking, foam-encrusted wreckage of Mack's car a wide berth, she hurried over to Ash. He stood a little to one side, watching calmly, his hands clasped behind his back.

"Ash, what's going on?" Rose demanded.

Ash turned his head to look at her. Rose's breath caught.

Even though he was facing away from the burning car, flames reflected in the dark depths of his eyes.

Just for a moment. Ash blinked, and when his eyes reopened they were as cool and remote as always.

"There was an incident," he said.

"I can see that. Why have the police arrested Mack? What was that thing they found in his car? And how did it burst into flames in the first place?"

Ash shifted his feet fractionally, his gaze sliding away from her. She was certain he was rapidly trying out and discarding various responses in his head.

"Ash." She narrowed her eyes at him. "How did you get here so fast, anyway?"

He didn't respond for a moment. Then his shoulders fell in a long sigh.

"I owe you an explanation," he said.

~

"Mack's a drug dealer?" Rose said incredulously.

"I am afraid so."

His blood burned at the mere recollection of the darkness he'd seen in the man's mind. He kept his hands folded under his arms, forcing his face to stillness.

Rose sighed, staring down into her mug of tea. He'd put sugar and milk in it, the way she liked. Steam curled up between her cupped hands.

She looked unusually small and fragile, curled in his desk chair with her feet tucked up. He'd brought her back to the fire station, to his own office. He'd told her that it was mere pragmatism. The station was closer to the restaurant than Rose's pub, and she'd needed treatment for shock straight away.

In truth, he'd wanted—*needed*—to bring her back to his own nest. Even if it was just an office and the tiny adjourning room where he slept, it was his territory. The one place where he could be certain she was safe.

She'd washed her hands and face in the station's shower room, but she was still flushed and disheveled. Her beautiful red silk top was marred where soot from the burning vehicle had blown onto her.

The black marks were yet another guilty stain on his soul. He clenched his fist, still angry with himself for putting her in such danger. If he'd known how closely she would approach the blaze, he would never have started it.

Of course, he should have known.

She'd always run toward the fire.

"You must think I'm such an idiot," Rose said.

It was so at odds with his actual internal monologue of self-castigation that he could only stare at her for a moment, nonplussed. "Of course not. Why would you say that?"

"I'm an empath. I knew there was something off about Mack. But I was so happy to have someone interested in me that I ignored all the red flags slapping me in the face." She rubbed the bridge of her nose, pulling a face. "I have terrible taste in men."

He couldn't disagree with *that.*

"Oh." Rose dropped her hand, looking mortified. "Oh, Ash, I didn't —not you, of course. That is, not that I'm still—well, you know. No offense meant, anyway."

"None taken." He hesitated, but couldn't resist asking. "Though I am very curious as to what you could possibly have seen in that...individual."

Rose looked, if possible, even more embarrassed. "If I tell you that, you *are* going to think I'm an idiot."

"I will never think that. Tell me, Rose. Please."

Rose dropped her eyes to her coffee again. She tugged his blanket a little closer around her shoulders as if trying to hide within its gray folds.

"Tattoos," she muttered, blushing.

"I beg your pardon?"

"I agreed to the date because I saw his tattoos in his profile picture." She shrugged. "I don't know why, but I always do like a man with tattooed forearms."

The scar around his own right wrist burned, as though the binding was still there. Ash found he was rubbing at it, and made himself stop.

Fortunately, Rose hadn't seen. She still had her head bowed, her hair shadowing her face.

"And, well, then I met him in person, and he had that hint of danger too, and..." Rose broke off, taking a sip of her tea. "I guess I have a type."

"Dangerous men with tattoos," he said softly.

"I didn't say it was a good type." She pushed her hair back, glancing up at him. "Just as well you were there. But why were you there?"

He looked at the papers on his desk. The city map on the wall. Anywhere but her face.

"Ash." Her voice was soft, but brooked no evasion. She leaned forward a little, capturing his gaze. "Why?"

The truth leaped into his mouth. He swallowed it back again.

"I am your friend," he said instead, which was at least a different truth.

"And the car just happened to burst into flames," she said, her mouth twisting wryly. "Well, to save further property damage—not to mention your career—I'll try to pick my date more wisely next time."

Cold stabbed his heart. "There will be a next time?"

She held his gaze steadily. Her deep brown eyes were clear and unguarded, offering him the depths of her soul. "That's up to you, Ash."

He was the one to look away first.

"No more dangerous men with tattoos," he said, rather more harshly than he'd intended. "Promise me that, at least."

"No more dangerous men with tattoos," she agreed, with a faint sigh. "I promise."

CHAPTER 6

PAST

20 years ago...

This is a terrible idea, the sensible part of Rose's mind screamed as she circled over the compound. *Turn around and go home!*

She ignored her fears, stretching her wings to stay as high as possible. The thin air burned in her lungs. If any of the soldiers patrolling the high barbed-wire fences happened to look up, she'd be nothing more than a dot in the sky. Just another bird.

The mate-call tugged at her, trying to pull her down to a grim, plain concrete building at the heart of the complex. She swept around it in wide, steady circles, waiting her moment.

She'd spent three days covertly studying the strange base. It was hidden deep within an otherwise untouched stretch of forest, with no other buildings for miles around. Only a single dirt path led to it. In all the time she'd been watching, she'd only seen a handful of vehicles approach or leave. They'd all been plain black, with smoked glass windows hiding their occupants.

What kind of place is *this?*

She still couldn't decide if it was a military compound or some kind of peculiar academic retreat. The barbed wire and watchtowers—not to mention the uniformed soldiers with their semi-automatic rifles—definitely suggested the former.

But she'd seen other people too, in strange flowing robes, looking for all the world like students heading to a graduation ceremony. And though the compound was lined with low, utilitarian barracks, there were older, grander structures as well.

A mansion, built in the elegant old style with sweeping porticos. Smaller houses lining quads and formal gardens. A big, stately stone hall that wouldn't have looked out of place in Oxford or Cambridge University, set behind a manicured lawn.

It was like someone had taken a very private, very exclusive college, and fortified it.

She had no idea what it all meant. All she knew was that her mate was down there.

And he needed her.

So she circled, and waited.

Her pulse picked up as she heard the sound of honking. The flock of wild geese was returning, as they had every evening at sunset, calling back and forth to each other. Their voices sharpened in disgruntled affront as she slid into their midst.

Don't mind me, she silently willed, as beady eyes stared at her in suspicion. *I just need to fly with you for a moment. Don't make a fuss.*

Beaks clacked at her, but the flock still swung down to their usual pond. Rose landed too, stretching out her webbed feet to splash into the cool water. As quickly as she could, she paddled away from the irritated geese. She hid herself in the reeds lining the water, surreptitiously craning her neck to peer out.

So far so good.

No one seemed to have noticed the geese's noisier-than-usual arrival. The pond was off to the eastern side of the campus, surrounded by manicured lawns and formal flowerbeds. Over the past few days, she'd seen the robed people strolling through the garden or relaxing on the scattered benches, but never any of the soldiers. She had the impression that this part of the complex was reserved for the students, if that's what they were.

Now for the tricky part.

Rose scrambled out of the pond. A large, jet-black swan was hardly inconspicuous, but still less likely to attract attention than a naked woman. Sticking as close as she could to the shadow of bushes, she set off toward one of the low buildings.

She'd seen people go in and out enough times to know that it was where they stored cleaning supplies. Even more importantly, it didn't seem to be locked or guarded. Who would break into a secret base in order to steal mops and buckets?

Someone who really, really needs to borrow a janitor's uniform.

She was halfway there when a crunch of gravel warned her that someone was approaching. Two people, from the sound of footsteps. Rose looked around frantically, but she was stuck in the middle of an open lawn, away from any cover. All she could do was duck her head, pretending to poke around in the grass for food.

"Damn assignments," a male voice complained loudly. "I just got back from Brazil, and now they want to send me to some armpit place in the Middle East. Who do those bloody military stuffed shirts think they are?"

"Our employers," said a second voice, dryly. "Funnily enough, the U.S. government expects a certain level of return for its investment."

"They can kiss my cat's ass. I deserve a vacation after that last mission."

Just a swan. She nibbled at the grass, silently willing whoever it was to pass her by. *Nothing to see here.*

Two men came into view around some shrubbery. They were both dressed in those strange, long robes, with the unselfconscious ease of people who wore such garments every day. One of the men stalked along as though the gravel path had personally insulted his mother. The other was eating a sandwich.

Neither of those things was what made Rose jerk her head up in shock.

An ocelot slunk behind the angry man. Its spotted coat was dull and matted, the fur thin and patchy on its right foreleg. It stumbled along as though jerked by an invisible lead. Its lips were drawn back from its fangs in a continuous, maddened snarl of hatred.

But its eyes, its *eyes*...

They were human. Not in shape or color. But in intelligence, and awareness. Rose met that unblinking, tormented gaze, and knew that a human mind was trapped inside that animal body.

The other shifter froze on the path, staring at her. It had recognized her in return.

"Hey, what's wrong with your animal?" the second man asked, casually waving his sandwich at the ocelot.

Please don't give me away, Rose mentally begged the ocelot shifter.

It was futile—usually only shifters of the same type could communicate telepathically with each other. And even if she *had* been a cat, she had a horrible certainty that the other shifter was too far gone in the depths of its own personal hell to understand human words any more.

"Oh, for the love of—I'm not going to let you eat that swan," the first man said irritably to the ocelot. "*Heel,* you idiot beast."

He made a slight, sharp gesture, and the ocelot's body jerked as though he'd yanked on a choke chain around its neck. Nonetheless, its eyes stayed fixed on Rose.

The ocelot's jaw worked oddly for a moment. Then it slunk on its belly to the angry man's side. He made the gesture again, as if in punishment. The ocelot let out a moan, a horribly human sound from that animal throat. Frozen in horror, Rose could only watch as it cringed at the man's feet.

"You shouldn't do that," the second man said to his companion in a tone of mild rebuke. "Your cat's on its last legs as it is. You keep drawing power from it, you're going to finish it off early."

"Then the damn bastard General can't order me to the ass-end of nowhere to assassinate whatever stupid target he has in mind this time," the first man said, smirking. "Not until the High Magus finds me another shifter, anyway."

The second man shook his head, a touch of jealousy shading his voice. "Don't get cocky. You'll be lucky if the High Magus *lets* you have another one, the rate that you burn through them."

"He gives them to me because I know how to use them." The first man pulled a cigarette from an inner pocket, placing it in his mouth. He snapped his fingers, and the tip spontaneously lit.

Rose blinked.

"Anyway," the man said around his cigarette, "rumor has it that the hunters have tracked down an entire wolf pack. Once the High Magus rounds them up, it'll be like Christmas come early."

"*Finally*. I'm sick of theoretical research. In that case, let's hustle. Never hurts to earn some brownie points from the seniors when there's shifters coming up for grabs." The second man idly tossed the crust of his sandwich in Rose's direction. "Hey, you got enough juice to jump us straight there?"

The first man pushed back his left sleeve. An intricate tattoo twined around his wrist. It was identical to the one she'd seen on her mate's skin, except in two respects. It was on his left arm rather than his right...and it wasn't dripping blood.

The man muttered something that didn't sound like English, holding up his left hand. Rose's beak dropped open as his tattoo lit up with an eerie golden glow. Sparks crackled over his fingers in flaring arcs.

With quick, practiced motions, the man sketched a rectangular shape, like a doorway. Light trailed in the wake of his fingertips, the glowing lines hanging impossibly in mid-air. Between them, the view of the garden rippled and warped, like a reflection in a wind-blown lake.

Rose caught a glimpse of a white-tiled room lined with laboratory equipment before the two men blocked her view. As casually as stepping through a doorway, they disappeared into the shimmering portal.

The ocelot glanced at Rose one last time as it followed them. Its mouth worked again, making the same exaggerated motion that it had before.

She'd been wrong. The other shifter *wasn't* entirely lost to madness.

Run, it was saying, with lips that were never meant for human speech. *Run.*

Even in a secret base, a black woman carrying a mop was effectively invisible. The patrolling soldiers didn't give her so much as a second glance.

Rose kept her head down and her stride brisk, as though on an urgent errand. She prayed that the trailing hems of the too-big janitor's uniform would hide her bare feet. There hadn't been any shoes in the supply cupboard.

The mate-call guided her unerringly across the compound, toward the large, ominous building at the very center. Its matte gray walls were sheer and featureless, completely without windows.

She hadn't been able to guess what it was from the air. Now, after her encounter with the poor ocelot, she was horribly certain that she knew its purpose.

A prison.

And her mate was inside.

Two uniformed soldiers stood guard on either side of a narrow doorway, guns held low. The weapons were smaller and lighter than the ones she'd seen the perimeter guards carrying. As she drew nearer, she realized that they were tranquillizer guns. Each man had a pouch of darts at his hip, the feathered ends sticking up for easy access.

Both guards shot her disinterested glances as she stopped in front of them. Rose's palms were slick with sweat. She licked her lips, trying to moisten her dry throat.

She hadn't been able to come up with any plan for this part. She'd hope that sheer necessity would spark inspiration. Unfortunately, her mind had gone completely blank.

"What, you want us to hold the door open for you?" one of the soldiers said as she stood there in mute terror. He jerked his head, rolling his eyes in exasperation. "Hurry up and do something about that mess in cell six. I can smell it from here."

"Yes, sir," Rose squeaked.

She quickly sidled through the doors, keeping her eyes downcast. The soldiers didn't even turn to watch her.

Maybe all the guards and guns weren't to keep intruders out...but to keep the occupants *in.*

She hurried deeper into the building, her eyes struggling to adjust to the gloom. The wide, plain gray corridor was lit only by fluorescent tubes running along the ceiling. A steady, irritating throb of extractor fans hummed overhead, but the air still hung thick and lifeless. She wrinkled her nose at the pervasive, animal reek.

It was the smell of misery. Of creatures who had been penned up in the dark until they'd lost all pride, all hope, all sense of self.

It smelled like the ocelot had looked.

Despite the mate-call urging her on, Rose hesitated. The corridor was lined with thick, reinforced metal doors. From behind the nearest one came a steady *click-click-click* of claws on concrete. A large animal, a wolf or a bear, pacing in endless, mindless circles.

Rose tugged at the door, but it was locked. She couldn't find a keyhole, or even any indication as to how it opened. Maybe it *didn't* open. People who could make magic portals in mid-air probably didn't need anything as mundane as a door handle.

She spread her hand futilely against the metal, hoping that the shifter inside could sense her. "I'm sorry," she whispered, as loudly as she dared. "I'll come back, I promise. I'll get help. Just hold on a little longer."

The constant *click-click-click* never altered.

She lost count of the doors she passed as she headed deeper into the building. The rough concrete floor chilled her bare feet, but it was nothing compared to the chill in her heart.

So many shifters imprisoned and tormented. And if she'd understood the two robed men earlier, this was all sanctioned by the U.S. military. By the *government.* How could they do this to their own people?

She took a deep breath, pushing down her sickened anger. She'd free her mate. Once they were free of this terrible place, they could expose it for what it was. There were secret shifter governments and countries all around the world. Surely someone would be able to put an end to this atrocity.

The mate-call pulled her through a door and down a staircase. There was another set of doors at the bottom. A double set, one after the other, like an airlock.

Ribbons of plastic sheeting hung down behind the final door. Pushing through them, Rose had a powerful memory of visiting the tropical house at the zoo as a child—ducking through heavy plastic curtains just like these, the surprise of leaving the cold outside and entering a warm, humid wonderland.

It was the opposite way round with *these* doors. Rose gasped as cold struck her in the face. Her breath steamed in the suddenly freezing air.

This room was tiled all in white, stark and sterile. Three other doors circled it, one per side. Each one was even more heavily reinforced than the doors she'd passed earlier. Thick steel bars ran across them, chained to rings set deep in the walls.

Rose's heart leapt into her mouth as a deafening *crash* echoed through the small room, coming from behind the door to her left. It sounded for all the world like a bull had charged full-tilt into it.

The thudding impact came again, with a ringing clash of horns hitting metal. Hooves clattered against concrete as the hidden creature gathered itself for another strike.

"Shh, shhh!" Rose hurried over to the door, terrified that the poor shifter would either injure itself or make enough noise that someone would come to investigate. "It's all right, I'm here to help. I'm going to—ow!"

She snatched her hand back from the door, sucking at her fingertips. The metal was *cold,* cold enough to burn. As she watched, ice crystals spread over the surface, sharp and bristling.

"Hungry." The whisper sounded more like wind over a frozen glacier than any human voice. "*Hungry.*"

"I'll get you out," Rose repeated, though she was no longer sure that was at all a good idea. "Just wait."

The wind-swept voice chuckled and moaned, like the sounds of a distant blizzard. Claws scratched against metal. The cold followed her as she backed away.

The next door was open. The cell beyond was as blank and featureless as an empty meat locker. Rose didn't think it had been occupied for some time, if it ever had been.

The final door wasn't a door. Just a solid lump of blackened metal, fused into the wall. The surface was frozen in lumpy ripples, thicker at the bottom, as though at some point the door had been subjected to such intense heat that the metal had started to melt and run.

The mate-call beat through her blood.

A wide observation window was set into the wall next to the not-door. Ice crystals frosted its surface, hiding the room beyond.

She put her hand to the glass. Cold numbed her palm as she wiped frost away.

Another cell. A narrow bunk, made up with a thin gray blanket. A small desk, bare, with a hard, straight-backed chair. In the corner, a toilet and washbasin sat in full view, unscreened from either the rest of the room or the window.

That was it. Nothing else.

Except him.

He was shirtless, doing push-ups on his knuckles with mechanical, rhythmic precision. His bare back gleamed with sweat despite the freezing air. The tattoo twining around his right arm stood out stark against his pale skin, black ink flexing with every motion.

Her numb, blue fingers pressed against the glass. "My mate," she whispered.

His steady rhythm faltered. He glanced up sharply. His eyes searched across the window, not focusing on her.

One-way glass. He couldn't see out. Yet his whole cell lay bare to any onlooker. Not a scrap of privacy.

In one smooth motion, he surged to his feet. He took a single step toward the window, then seemed to check himself. His fists clenched at his sides.

"Corbin." His voice crackled from a speaker grill set under the window. "You shouldn't have brought her here."

Who's Corbin? Rose wondered. One of his captors, or a secret ally? Irrelevant for now—she was painfully aware that she was on borrowed time.

"No one brought me," she said, hoping that he'd be able to hear her in return. "I'm alone. I've come to rescue you."

His head jerked up, eyes widening in alarm. "No!"

"Listen, we don't have much time," Rose said urgently as he backed away from the window. "How can I get you out?"

He'd retreated to the far side of the small cell, as far away as he could get. His upper body was still canted toward her, though, betraying secret yearning.

"You can't," he said. "You *mustn't*. I'm the Phoenix. This is where I belong."

The bleak certainty in his voice made her throat constrict with pain. What had they done to him, what lies had they fed him, that he could think that this was how he had to live?

"That's not true," she said fiercely. "No matter what your animal, you're still a person. There's no justification for treating anyone like this."

He shook his head. "Shifters have to be contained. Controlled. For the safety of humanity."

"Is that what they've told you? The men in robes, the...wizards?"

"Warlocks," he corrected, as though it was a perfectly normal, everyday concept. "They find feral shifters, bind them. Harness their power for the good of all."

"It's not good for the shifters!"

"It's better for them than the alternative," he said, though he looked a little sickened, as though he didn't really believe what he was saying. "At least here, when they go mad, they don't hurt anyone."

"The warlocks are the ones *driving* them mad. Can't you see that?"

His throat worked. He took a step forward, and another, hesitantly approaching the window. He put his hand flat on the glass, precisely over her own.

"I've never spoken with another shifter before," he whispered.

He couldn't see her, yet their fingers perfectly aligned. She could feel his heat even through the thick double glass.

"Well, now you have," she said. "I'm a shifter. I'm your *mate*. And I'm not mad, or dangerous, or a wild beast to be locked up in a cage. Everything they've taught you here is a lie, Blaze."

He closed his eyes, leaning his forehead against the glass. Across the width of the window, frost curled into steam.

"I don't even know your name," he said.

She pressed her hand harder against the glass, willing it to melt away like the frost. "Rose. Rose Swanmay."

"Rose," he repeated softly. Longing shot through her at the way his mouth caressed her name. "You have to go. Now. This isn't safe."

"I'm not leaving you here. Please, just trust me—"

"It's you who cannot trust me." His hand fisted. Some of the red, angry-looking scabs edging the black tattoo on his forearm broke open, fresh droplets of blood welling up. "You may claim that other shifters are not mad, but *I* am mad. From the moment we met, my human will has been burning up. I am more dangerous now than I have ever been."

"You won't ever hurt me. We're mates."

"Mates," he repeated, as though it meant nothing to him. "Why do you keep saying that word?"

She stared at him through the glass. "You really don't know anything about mates?"

His eyebrows drew together. "Do you mean the sickness? Corbin told me about that. A breeding madness that afflicted some shifters, allowing animal instincts to overcome human reason."

Rose was beginning to think that whoever this 'Corbin' was, he'd better pray that she never caught up with him.

"It's not a *sickness*." She opened her soul wide to him as she spoke, hoping that he would be able to sense the truth in her words. "That's another lie, Blaze. What you feel is right, and natural. A mate is—"

A siren drowned out her words. She leaped back from the glass as a flashing red light turned the white room the color of blood.

"They know I'm here!" she shouted over the alarm.

"No," Blaze gritted out through clenched teeth. His left hand gripped his right forearm, as though his tattoo was burning him. "Temperature alarm. Too hot. Out of control—*go!*"

Rose rushed instead to the cell door, her hands searching for some gap or crack in the fused metal. "Not without you! How does this open?"

"It doesn't, Corbin portals in!" Blaze's fist slammed against the window, leaving a bloody smear on the glass. "Rose, they're coming, *hide!*"

Booted feet clattered down the stairs. Too late, Rose bolted for the empty cell.

"Freeze!"

Rose whirled, and found herself staring down the business end of a gun. Not one of the harmless, nonlethal tranquillizers carried by the entrance guards, but a semi-automatic assault rifle.

"Hands on your head," barked the soldier training the weapon on her. "No sudden movements."

"Rose!" Blaze hurled himself at the window.

Across the room, the unseen creature in the other cell was howling and snarling as well, throwing itself against its door. One side of Rose's face was numb with cold; the other, as hot and flushed as if she stood next to a raging bonfire. In her soul, her swan beat its wings frantically, trying to claw its way out of her skin.

Slowly, shaking from head to foot, she raised her hands.

Never taking his eyes off her, the soldier tilted his head to speak into a small radio clipped to his collar. "Intruder in the cold room. Specimens highly agitated. Orders?"

A tinny voice crackled from the speaker. "Eliminate the threat."

The soldier's finger tightened on the trigger.

"No!"

The world went white.

For a split second, Rose was convinced that she'd died and gone straight to hell. Incandescent fire swirled around her. She dropped to the floor, burying her head in her arms, but the furious light still scorched through her closed eyelids. Heat seared through her body, her mind, her very soul.

"Rose. *Rose.* You have to go."

The light faded a little, to merely eye-searing. Rose blinked, tears streaming down her face.

Blaze knelt in front of her, his right arm crimson from elbow to wrist. A stench of molten metal hung in the air. His cell door was a wreckage of red-hot, twisted steel.

There was no sign of the guard.

"You have to go," Blaze said again.

She clutched at his arm, gripping tight. "Not without you."

Black flames filled his eyes, the only darkness in the blazing inferno raging around them. "I can't! The binding—"

He stopped dead, staring down at his blood-slicked arm.

"The binding," he whispered. "It's gone. I'm free."

He pulled away from her, standing up. Tipping back his head, he flung his arms wide.

"*Free!*" he cried, in a voice that was no longer human.

Rose flung up a hand to shield her eyes as he went up in flame. His body vanished, utterly consumed in seconds.

From the fire, the Phoenix rose.

He filled the room with fire and fury. Every feather burned, white-hot at the base, flickering yellow at the tip. Concrete and debris exploded outward as he spread enormous wings, shrugging off the ceiling as easily as cracking an egg.

Rose reached inward for her swan. Her animal surged up eagerly, wrapping her in ebony feathers. Shakily, she got to her webbed feet, stretching out her own wings.

The Phoenix's crested head bent to hers. For a moment, the great golden beak caressed her own.

Then, together, they flew.

CHAPTER 7

This is nice, Rose told herself firmly.

The man sitting opposite her was certainly nice. Jim—or was it Tim?—had nice eyes, a nice body, nice…everything. Even his voice was nice, a pleasant, gentle tenor. He liked cats and gardening and long walks on the beach.

Rose had never been so completely, utterly, mind-numbingly bored.

She became aware that Tim—or possibly Jim—had paused, looking at her expectantly. She jerked herself back to the present, trying to remember what he'd been talking about. Something about hiking in the Lake District?

"That sounds…nice?" she ventured.

His nice mouth curved in a nice smile, showing nice teeth. She could sense the shy hope kindling in his heart. "It's so good to finally meet a woman who shares the same interests. I wasn't sure about coming to this event tonight, but now I'm glad that I did."

Rose's polite smile was so fixed, she feared she might never change expression again. She desperately wanted to look at her watch.

To her intense relief, the shrill blast of a whistle broke the awkward pause. "Time's up!" announced the organizer in a bright, cheery voice. "Gentlemen, please find your final lady!"

Tim-maybe-Jim gave her another of those shy, sweet smiles as he rose. "I'll definitely be marking your name down on my form, Rose. I hope you'll mark mine?"

Rose forced out a strained laugh. "Oh, you know it's against the rules to talk about that now. And you still have one date left. You might like her even more than you like me, Tim."

His face fell a little. "Jim."

She winced. "Yes, sorry. Too much chatter in here." She fiddled with her pen, pretending to write on her form. "Anyway, it was nice to meet you."

She gusted out a long sigh, slumping in her chair as Jim-not-Tim headed for his next date. Morosely, she followed his retreating back. It was a perfectly nice back. He was a perfectly nice man.

Not our mate, said her swan.

"Oh, be quiet," she muttered under her breath. "We're not looking for a mate, remember? Just a nice, normal man."

She stared down at her list of names. All of them had been nice, normal men. Mostly a little nervous and awkward—as was to be expected at a speed dating event for the over forties—but perfectly pleasant. None of them had had tattoos, or even the slightest hint of danger.

None of them had had dark eyes filled with leashed fire.

With a grimace, she banished Ash's still, intent face from her mind. If she was going to insist that her swan stop pining after their long-lost mate, she could hardly cling onto a silly crush of her own.

Squaring her shoulders, she forced herself to think positively. She still had one more date to go this evening. There was still a chance she might feel a spark of attraction.

The chair opposite her scraped against the floor. Fixing a welcoming smile on her face, Rose looked up at the man who'd just sat down.

"Wayne?" she said incredulously.

The graying wolf shifter flashed his teeth in what she assumed was meant to be a smile, but looked more like a rictus snarl of pain. "Hello, Rose," he mumbled, not meeting her eyes.

She blinked at him, completely taken aback. She'd deliberately picked this speed dating event because it was human-run. Shifters tended to organize their own versions of such things, with much larger numbers. When you could recognize your true mate on sight, there was no need for five minutes of getting-to-know-you chit-chat.

"I wasn't expecting to see any other shifters tonight," she said, lowering her voice. "What are you doing here?"

Wayne shifted uncomfortably in his chair. "He told me to come."

"He?"

Wayne jerked his head in a strange, convulsive motion. A sharp, bitten-off whine escaped through his teeth. "Can't. Can't talk about that."

Is he drunk? Rose wondered. Her sense of him was oddly foggy. He was such a dense, swirling soup of contradictory emotion, she couldn't get a fix on him.

"Wayne, are you all right?" she asked in concern.

"No." He twitched again, and she sensed a jagged lightning-bolt of pain shoot through the roiling turmoil of his aura. "Yes. *Yes*. I said yes!"

"You're hurt," she said, noticing a bandage wrapped around his right wrist. Fresh red spots were spreading across the dirty gauze.

"New tattoo," Wayne said, his aura darkening with a peculiar sharp, stabbing splatter of black humor. His left hand closed over the bandage, hiding it from view. "Still getting used to it. Don't ask me questions."

Rose knew the old wolf well enough not to pry any further. At least, not right now. He was a proud, stubborn man, and a hard life had taught him to lash out rather than admit weakness. Whatever trouble he was in now, she'd only be able to help him if she was patient enough to let him come to her in his own time.

"Got a question I have to ask you, though," Wayne continued. "What are *you* doing here, Rose?"

"Looking for a date, obviously." Rose raised her eyebrows at him.

"And please don't be offended, Wayne, but I'm not interested in getting involved with a shifter."

"Specially not me, huh?" Wayne let out a growling laugh. "It's all right. You're not my type either." He eyed her sidelong. "Thought there was one shifter you *were* interested in, though."

"I'm sure I don't know what you mean," Rose said, in the chilling voice she normally reserved for aggressive drunks.

Wayne should have known better than to mess with her in *that* mood. Nonetheless, to her surprise, he persisted. "Thought you were sweet on the Phoenix."

Rose narrowed her eyes at him. "I've told you before to mind your own business, Wayne. Keep your nose out of other people's private matters."

If Wayne had been in wolf form, she was sure that his ears would have been flat against his skull and his tail plastered between his legs. "Can't. Have to ask." Wayne's bloodshot eyes fixed on hers, oddly pleading. "Rose. Is there anything between you and Fire Commander Ash?"

"No," Rose bit off, curtly. "And if you ever want to drink in my pub again, Wayne, you'll drop this *at once.*"

Some of the tension drained out of his lean shoulders. "Good. Good. That's good. Don't..." He twitched, his hand tightening on his wrist. "Don't—just *don't*. I'm sorry."

"Sorry for what?" Rose said, utterly baffled. "Wayne, what's going —Wayne?"

She was talking to his retreating back. Rose started to get up to follow him, but the speed-dating organizer was already chasing Wayne herself, waving her clipboard.

"Sir? Sir! Time isn't up yet, and you need to hand in your—"

The old wolf rounded on the blonde human, snarling something. Rose couldn't see his face, but the organizer recoiled, clutching her clipboard like a shield. Without a backward glance, Wayne stalked out, slamming the bar door behind him.

White-faced, the organizer fumbled for her whistle, raising it to her lips. The shrill noise was rather shakier than it had been previously.

"Th-that's the end of the evening, ladies and gentlemen!" The organizer cleared her throat, rallying herself. "I hope you've all enjoyed your dates. Now it's time to make your final decisions. Gentlemen, if you could come to the bar to hand me your forms. Ladies, please remain at your tables. I'll come to each of you in turn after I've collected the men's data. I'm sure you're all eager to discover who you've matched with!"

Rose sank back into her chair. She was still half-minded to go after Wayne, but she'd have to push her way through the crowd of men congregating at the bar in order to reach the door. She didn't want to reject Jim-not-Tim or any of the other perfectly nice men *that* obviously.

I'll find out what's wrong with Wayne tomorrow night, she decided. No matter what was troubling him, she was sure he'd still come to the Full Moon as usual. Chasing madly after someone usually only made them run away faster, after all.

Ash was certainly proof of that.

She was thinking about him *again.*

Rose stared determinedly down at her form. Her pen hovered over the empty checkbox next to Jim-not-Tim's name. He *had* been very nice. Exactly the sort of man she should want. Undemanding. Uncomplicated.

Uninteresting.

"Are you all done with that, Ms. Swanmay, or do you want me to come back in a few minutes?" The organizer had come over to her table, smiling brightly. "There are so many wonderful men here tonight, I know it's difficult to choose!"

Rose guiltily twitched her sheet up, so that the woman couldn't see the blank, empty column where she was supposed to mark the men she'd like to see again. She opened her mouth to ask for more time—and paused.

The organiser's smile was just a shade too fixed. She held her clipboard close to her chest, as though she too had something to hide.

Rose focused her empathic sense on the woman, and had a distinct impression of pity.

Rose abruptly knew, without a shadow of a doubt, that none of the men had written *her* name down.

She thrust her unmarked sheet at the organizer. The woman glanced down the empty column, and her tight expression relaxed.

"Oh, what a pity. There'll be a lot of disappointed gentlemen," the organizer lied, relief practically steaming off her. "Well, it's only your first time. I'm sure if you come back—"

"Thank you," Rose interrupted, desperate to be out of there. "But I don't think I will. Excuse me."

Brushing aside the organizer's half-hearted attempt to stop her, she fled. The men were still hanging around the bar. Head down, mumbling apologies, Rose pushed through them. She tried not to catch anyone's eye, but was still painfully aware of Jim-not-Tim glancing in her direction. His gaze passed straight through her, without a flicker of acknowledgment.

Guess he was just being polite too. They were all *just being polite.*

It shouldn't have mattered. She hadn't wanted any of them, after all.

But…it did matter, it did. So many men, and none of them had chosen her. She'd been so *sure* that at least some of them had been interested.

Then again, she'd been sure of Ash too.

She burst out into the cool evening air, face hot with humiliation. She started walking, fast, her feet automatically turning in the direction of her home. She needed to be back in the Full Moon. Back in her place, behind the bar, where she belonged.

She'd been stupid to ever leave. Stupid to reach for anything more. Stupid to dream.

She scrubbed angrily at her eyes, brushing away the stupid, *stupid* tears. She didn't have anything to cry about. She was the person people turned to when *they* needed to cry. That was her role. That was what she was good at. She provided comfort and support, a welcoming space and a listening ear.

There wasn't anywhere to go when *she* needed those things.

As she turned down an alleyway, Rose became aware that there was a slight echo to her footsteps, a soft tread falling not quite in time with her own. She halted, and the sound stopped too. Silence enfolded her like vast, gentle wings.

She squeezed her eyes tight shut. "Ash," she said, without looking round.

"Rose," he said quietly, from right behind her.

"This is becoming a habit." She fought to keep her tone light, betraying nothing of the tears streaking her cheeks. "At least you didn't have to set fire to anything this time."

He made a wordless, noncommittal noise as he came up to her side. Rose turned her head away, hoping that the darkness would hide her face.

A jolt went through her as his fingers brushed her elbow, very lightly. "Let me walk you home."

"Just a minute." Keeping her head ducked down, Rose rummaged in her handbag for a tissue. "Sorry, I-I've got a cold."

Moonlight silvered the side of his face, casting a shadow over his eyes. He said nothing.

Rose made a show of blowing her nose, surreptitiously wiping her tears as she did so. "There," she said, shoving the tissue in her pocket. She tried to smile up at him. "I appreciate you watching out for me, Ash, but there's no need to put yourself to all this trouble. I can find my own way home."

His hand was still on her arm. It was the barest touch, but she felt it through her whole body. His fingers tightened fractionally, in unspoken command. Without conscious thought, Rose found herself falling into step with him.

"You are upset." He stared straight ahead as he spoke, not looking at her. "What is wrong?"

"Oh, nothing. I'm fine."

"Rose," he said, and nothing more.

She let out her breath. "If I tell you, do you promise not to set fire to anyone's car?"

His eyes cut sideways. "No."

That startled a snort of laughter out of her. "Honest as ever."

She could feel his heat against her side, warm and comforting. After the forced small talk and glaring auras of the speed dating event, his quiet presence was restful. She could sink into his silence like a featherbed.

She sighed again, surrendering. "It's stupid. I went to this speed-dating event...well, I guess you knew that." She hesitated, glancing up at him. "*Were* you there?"

His chin dipped in a fractional nod. He still didn't look down at her.

Friends, she told herself, commanding her silly heart to slow. *Just friends. Of course a friend would be worried, after what happened on my last date.* I'd *be shadowing me too. It doesn't mean anything.*

"Thank you," she said, meaning it. "For looking out for me, I mean. Lord knows I don't have a good track record in men. Though it turns out you needn't have bothered." Despite her best efforts, her voice wavered a little, her bottom lip trembling. "It was a complete wash. No one was interested in me."

He didn't say anything for a moment. "That is not true."

If he'd been lurking just out of sight, perhaps he'd seen her so-called dates flirting with her. He had no way of knowing that they'd just been pretending. *She'd* been fooled, and she'd been sitting at the same table, after all.

"It is. They were all just taking pity on me, being polite." Oh, for heaven's sake, she was going to start crying *again.* She fumbled for her tissue, her voice thickening. "If they'd actually been interested, they would have put my name down at the end."

"They would have done." Ash's voice sounded strange, rasping, as though each word was fighting free of his throat against his will. "If they'd remembered you."

Rose stared at him, caught off-guard with her tissue halfway to her face. "What?"

Ash turned his head away. "They did not remember meeting you. Because I burned their memory of doing so."

"*What?*" Rose stopped dead. Grabbing his upper arm, she hauled him round to face her. "Ash! Why on earth—?"

All the breath slammed out of her, her back hitting the rough brick wall. For a second, the world spun, her mind struggling to catch up with the sudden motion.

Ash's hands bracketed her head, his muscled forearms tense. The dark flames of his eyes filled her vision.

"I burned away their desire to stop them from choosing you." He was so close that his breath brushed her lips. "Because I could not bear the thought that you might choose one of them in return."

His intense heat enclosed her. He held himself the barest inch away, his body not quite making contact with her own. The bitter scent of scorched rock rose from where his hands pressed against the wall.

Not our mate! cried her swan.

She brought her hands up to his chest—but not to push him away. His rigid muscles trembled under her palms. She felt the wild hammering of his heart, echoing her own.

"I only want you, Ash." she whispered. "I will only ever want you."

Fisting her hands in his shirt, she pulled him closer, banishing that last inch of space. Her swan's protest was lost in flame. Heat rushed through her, setting every part of her body on fire. If he hadn't been pressing her so hard against the wall, she would have fallen, utterly consumed.

"Rose." He said her name like it was the air he needed to breathe, like rain after drought, like his very life. He bent his head, his mouth seeking hers. "*Rose.*"

Blindly, she turned her face to his, opening to him like a flower to the sun. She was on fire with need, wanting his lips against hers, his body in hers.

He pulled back just before their lips met. She made a desperate, inarticulate sound, winding her hands round his neck, stretching up to him, but he held firm, not letting her close that last tiny gap.

"Rose," he said again. He leaned his forehead against hers, closing his eyes. "There's something I have to tell you."

CHAPTER 8

PAST

20 years ago...

"This isn't safe. I shouldn't have left." Blaze paced back and forth across the small motel room, hands tucked under his arms as though he was scared to touch anything. Even from several feet away, Rose could feel the searing heat radiating from him. "I should go back."

"The only reason you should ever go back is to burn that terrible place to the ground," she said, busy rummaging through her first aid kit. "Now let me see that arm."

He shook his head with a tight, sharp motion, his shoulders hunching even further. "No. You mustn't touch me. I'm burning up, I'm not in control—"

"Blaze," she said, cutting across his rising voice. Going over to him, she held out her hands. "You're my mate. You can't hurt me."

He stared at her outstretched hands for a moment, the rapid rise and fall of his chest betraying his agitation. He was still shirtless, dressed only in plain army-issue pants. There hadn't exactly been time to stop off at a mall to pick him up some clothes.

After their escape, Rose had led him straight back to the motel where she'd been staying, a couple of hours' flight away from the secret base. It was just as well Blaze seemed to be able to do the mythic shifter trick of taking his clothes with him when he shifted, otherwise he would have been stuck naked. None of *her* clothes were going to fit him, given that his shoulders were about twice as wide as hers.

Right now those impressive muscles were rock-solid, wound tight with near-panic. Rose longed to touch him, to soothe away his tension, but she made herself keep still. Holding his gaze steadily, she waited.

Gradually, his breathing slowed. His tongue flicked over his lips, moistening them. With a final deep, shuddering sigh, he took her hands.

She closed her fingers around his, not too tight, savoring the hot roughness of his callused skin. He caught his breath as she raised his hands to her lips. She softly kissed his knuckles, and felt the shiver that ran through him.

"There," she said gently. "See? Now come here."

He didn't resist as she tugged him down to sit on the bed. Fighting the desire to push him flat down onto his back and straddle him, Rose knelt down instead, reaching for a packet of antiseptic wipes.

She tried to be as gentle as she could, but his breath still hissed between his teeth as she cleaned the dried blood from his right arm. She bit her lip as the extent of the wound was revealed.

His tattoo—or binding, as he'd called it—was completely gone. Raw, livid flesh marked where it had been, spiraling up his arm from wrist to elbow. The burn-mark seemed clean, but she couldn't see any sign of shifter-fast healing starting to knit the skin together.

"Maybe we should get you to a hospital," she said, worried.

He flexed his fingers experimentally. His jaw clenched, but he shook his head. "It looks worse than it is. Just bind it up."

"Are you sure? It's going to leave a nasty scar if we don't get it treated properly."

"Better a scar than getting caught. Corbin has connections with more than just the military. I imagine there's already a nation-wide alert going out."

"Let them search," Rose said stoutly, though her stomach clenched in apprehension. "They won't find us."

His free hand cupped her cheek. For a moment, the Phoenix looked out at her from his dark eyes. "If they do, they'll regret it."

"Why didn't you free yourself before?" she asked as she started to wind a bandage around his arm.

"I couldn't. The binding stopped me from using my powers, unless Corbin allowed me to." He fell silent for a moment, staring down at his arm as though it belonged to someone else. "I used to try to break it. When I was too little to know better. Sometimes Corbin would drain my power, stop my rages, prevent me from hurting myself. And sometimes he...didn't. Eventually I learned that I couldn't break it, and stopped trying."

"You broke it now, though."

"They threatened you," he said, very softly.

She glanced up at him. He was watching her intently, with utter focus. A thrill ran through her at the memory of how glorious he'd been, rising like the sun from the wreckage of the prison. Even now, she could feel the sheer, raw power beating through his veins.

"Why aren't you afraid of me?" he asked. He appeared genuinely baffled. "I'm the Phoenix."

"You keep saying that as though it's a curse," Rose said, tucking in the edges of the bandage. "Whatever your animal, you're a shifter. Just like me."

"I'm not, though." He hesitated for a moment. "You were born with your swan."

It wasn't quite a question. She nodded anyway.

"I'm different. The Phoenix is different." His free hand came up to touch the center of his chest absently, as though he wasn't really aware of the motion. "There's only one. Eternal, forever reborn. When one host dies, the Phoenix flies to another. To someone that's...suitable fuel. A soul that can burn bright enough to sustain the undying flame."

She stared at him. "Do you remember them? Your other lives?"

He shook his head. "It's not like that. The Phoenix is eternal, not me. I'm just the latest in a long line of hosts. The Phoenix came to me when I was very small. Five or six, I think. I don't really remember. Fortunately, Corbin found me not long after."

"Fortunately?"

His arm muscles went rigid under her hands. "Fortunately for everyone else. The Phoenix isn't a mere beast, Rose. It's a force of nature, ravenous, the wildfire to end all wildfires. If it had its way, it would burn down the world. All it wants is to destroy."

"Does it?" Rose leaned forward a little, forcing him to meet her gaze. "The warlocks were driving those poor shifters mad, Blaze. Is your animal really that angry, that dangerous, or was it just goaded past the point of endurance?"

He was silent.

"I believed Corbin when he said it needed to be bound," he said at last.

"Well, everything he ever told you was a lie." Rose covered his hand with her own, gripping it tight. "You aren't dangerous, and neither is your animal. There's no evil in you."

There was no fire in his eyes now. They were pure human, dark and vulnerable, showing her the tormented depths of his soul.

"How can you be so sure?" His voice was the barest whisper.

"I'm your mate," she said, surprised that he could even ask. Then she groaned out loud, smacking herself in the forehead. "And I *still* haven't told you what that means, have I?"

The faintest shadow of a smile crossed his haunted face. "I'm beginning to suspect it's fairly important."

She sat back on her heels, opening her mouth to explain—and found herself stuck. No one had ever told *her* about mates. It was just…a thing that all shifters knew, bone deep, in the marrow of their souls.

How could she explain mates to him, when he'd never known even a scrap of human kindness? All his life had been a lie, a prison built as much around his mind as his body. How could she make him understand with mere words what he was to her?

Don't use words, then, her swan said, pragmatically.

"You're smiling," Blaze said, looking a little uncertain.

"My swan made a good suggestion," she said, her smile widening. Bracing her hands on his taut thighs, she pushed herself to her feet. "Sometimes our animals are much wiser than we are."

He drew in a soft breath as she stepped close to him, between his braced legs. She was taller than him in this position. He had to tip his head back to search her face. His eyes were pools of black, just the barest ring of deep brown showing around his dilated pupils. Fire kindled in their depths as she leaned in close.

"Rose," he whispered, his breath warm on her lips. "What—?"

She stopped him with a finger across his mouth, her other hand curving around the back of his neck. "I'm listening to my animal. Listen to yours, Blaze."

He held very still. He wasn't even breathing as she drew her finger across his lips, slowly, tracing the line of his mouth. With her fingertips, she explored the planes of his cheek and jaw.

In years to come, she knew, she would know the shape of his body better than her own. They would match each other so well that they would move as one, two parts of the same whole. There would be a joy in that deep, earned familiarity.

But oh, there was a profound sweetness in unfamiliarity too. In discovering him for the first time—the slight roughness of his jaw against her palm, the way his mouth parted with a shuddering gasp as she trailed her fingers behind his ear and down the strong, sensitive column of his neck.

His hands fisted in the bed covers. She smelled smoke, rising from where he gripped the sheets. She felt his pulse beating wildly against her fingertips, in the hollow of his throat.

"Rose," he said hoarsely. "I want—I can't—I don't want to burn you."

"I'm already burning," she whispered, against his mouth. "I always will be."

His hands came up at last. His fingers wound into her hair, his whole body arcing up as he pulled her down to him. And if she'd been on fire before, it was nothing compared to the explosion at that first touch of his lips on hers.

There was nothing restrained or tentative about his touch now. He devoured her like wildfire, hot and hungry, claiming her mouth with fierce need. Every kiss and bite fanned her own desire. She pressed against him desperately, her fingernails digging into the thick muscle of his shoulders. She needed more of him, all of him, but she couldn't bring herself to pull away for even an instant.

He solved that problem by hooking two fingers into the neck of her sundress. With a sharp, impatient motion, he ripped the thin cloth apart, never relinquishing her lips. Her bra and panties went the same way, falling in tatters to the floor.

Now, *now* she could glory in the heat of his bare skin against hers. She bit his lip to stifle her cry as his hard chest pressed against her sensitive nipples.

A deep, feral growl rumbled through his throat. He broke their kiss at last, pulling back just enough to be able to slide his hands up over the soft curve of her belly. Everywhere he touched, her skin burned with need.

He spread his fingers wide, cupping her breasts as if they were priceless treasures. She squirmed against him, pushing herself into his hot hands, shameless and urgent. His thumbs teased her hard peaks, making liquid fire pulse between her legs.

"This is right?" His voice was a harsh rasp, shaking, edged with the crackle of an inferno. "This is what it means to be mates?"

"Yes." She tipped her head back, abandoning herself to ecstasy. "Yes, Blaze!"

With a groan, he pressed his open mouth to the base of her throat, tasting her skin. She could barely stay standing as he trailed lower, across her collarbone, down the swell of her breast. When his lips closed over her nipple, her vision went white, sparks exploding through her.

"Blaze!" she cried out, lost to everything except the heat of his mouth and her own aching need to be filled. "Please, more, now!"

His hands slid down to her waist, her thighs, though his tongue never stopped its exquisite, tormenting circles. He stood, scooping her up effortlessly, lifting her so that he could continue to feast. She wrapped her legs around him, back arching, his supporting fingers tantalizingly close and yet unbearably far from her slick, yearning core.

Shifting his grip, he held her up with one hand, his other diving between them to fumble with the button of his pants. Through the waves of pleasure, she felt him snarl in frustration against her breast. Releasing her nipple, he lifted her even higher for a moment. She gasped, startled, as a wash of intense heat licked against her thighs.

"What—" she started to say—and then lost all coherent thought, because he was lowering her again. Only now he was bare as well, his hardness pressing into her folds. Just the barest contact, his straining tip stretching her entrance. She writhed, trying to take more of him, but his arms were like iron.

"Rose," he gasped, holding them right on the edge of fulfillment. "I feel—I know—this is forever?"

Her wetness slicked his shaft, her body completely ready and open. The mate bond was a broad, brilliant path between them, leading straight into her innermost heart. She had a sense of gathering power at the other end, a raging inferno held back by the thinnest of firebreaks. Ready to sweep over her, through her, consuming and transforming.

She wasn't afraid.

"Yes." She opened her body and mind and soul to the fire. To him. "Forever."

His power lanced through her, a white-hot ecstasy as great as the surge of his body into hers. He drove in deep, into her mind, into her soul.

Our mate! her swan sang, black wings stretching wide, welcoming him home. *Our mate!*

CHAPTER 9

It was wrong, he knew. But he was so thoroughly damned already, what was one more small sin?

Her fingers intertwined through his. The soft sweetness of her pulse echoed through his own veins. He couldn't let go.

Not again.

So Ash held Rose's hand, and let her lead him through the darkening night.

The streetlamp was lit outside the Full Moon, bathing the old, homely building in a warm yellow glow. Rose tugged him up to the front door, casting a shy, hesitant smile up at him. Even in the flickering artificial light, he could see that there was something new in her expression. A tentative unfurling, like the first flower of spring turning to the sun.

He looked away, unable to bear that faint, shining hope in her eyes. But he still didn't let go of her hand.

After decades apart, every second in contact with her was a gift. A grace. He was not strong enough to refuse it.

Especially not now.

Rose unlocked the door. The main room of the pub was dark, chairs upturned onto tables for the night. By sheer force of habit, he turned in the direction of Alpha Team's usual corner, but Rose tugged on his hand.

"Not down here," she said, guiding him past the bar and through the door at the back. "Come on."

The corridor was even darker than the front room, but he didn't need light to know the way. The worn stairs were familiar under his boots. He'd climbed them many times over the years, usually due to some crisis. Whenever one of the team needed help, whenever something threatened their mates…it was always to the small private room at the Full Moon that they came.

Dai, Chase, Griff, John, Hugh…he'd witnessed all their struggles and their triumphs here. Helped them, inasmuch as he could. Watched them gather together, friends, colleagues, family. Sometimes at odds with each other, like any group of brothers, but always, ultimately, united.

Tonight the meeting room was locked and silent. He went past it without a pause.

There was a door at the end of the corridor. This one he had never been through. He'd dreamed of opening it so often that it seemed unreal to step through it now.

"Well," Rose said, peeking up at him sidelong. "Here we are."

She opened her fingers. After a moment, he made himself open his, releasing her hand. She left his side, moving around to turn on a couple of lamps. Darkness gave way to a soft, welcoming light.

His first impression was vibrant color and warmth. Her room above the pub was not much larger than his own living space, but whereas his territory was plain and utilitarian, hers was filled with homely details.

A thick rug with a geometric orange pattern that reminded him of flames softened the worn oak floorboards. A single armchair, deep and comfortable, with a tangle of half-finished knitting draped over one arm. From the rich indigo color and wave-like texture, he guessed it was a baby blanket for John and Neridia's yet-unborn child. Half the shifter infants in Brighton slept swaddled in the loving work of her hands.

She only had a small kitchenette up here—just a hot plate and a microwave. Of course, she would do her cooking downstairs in the pub, much as he prepared his own meals in the fire station's kitchen. A single plate and cup were upside-down on the draining board next to the sink. She ate alone, as he did, above the place that was her life's work.

A half-open door on the other side of the room showed him a glimpse of her bed. He jerked his gaze quickly away, and found himself staring at a wall of framed photos. He recognized some of them—Brighton Pier, the shingle beach, the sweeping view over the city from the top of the enclosing hills. An open day at the fire station, a long time ago, Dai and Chase with their arms draped over each other's shoulders. Young, so young.

Others were clearly family photos. Aunts, cousins, nephews, nieces. Some of them dark-skinned, some pale, but all with Rose's elegant, swan-like poise. A succession of pictures tracked half a dozen children growing from chubby-cheeked infants to smiling or scowling adolescents.

There were photos that an ordinary human would have assumed were digital paintings, but he knew better. Hayley leaning against the side of a great golden griffin, his beak preening her hair. Two sea dragons sporting in the waves. A unicorn glimmering through a winter-bare wood.

And one that looked like a misprint, an error. Just a yellow-white blur streaking over a faded blue, overexposed, all the colors blown out.

Rose came to his elbow, following the direction of his gaze. "You remember that day?"

He touched the glass over the photo, carefully. It had been her fortieth birthday. A picnic in the countryside, sunlight caught in her hair. Dozens of shifters, a little drunk, a little silly, safely out of sight of human eyes. He'd asked her what she wanted as a present.

"I warned you it wouldn't come out," he said, looking at the bolt of fire across the sky.

"It's my favorite anyway." She didn't say anything for a moment, gazing at the photo of the Phoenix. "How long, Ash?"

He knew what she was asking. "Always. Since the day we met."

Her breath sighed out of her. "Ten years...and you never said anything."

"Neither did you."

She slanted her eyes at him, a flash of the fire that he knew so well. "I did eventually."

"Yes." He couldn't delay any longer. "Which is why we need to talk."

She sighed again. "Wait a moment."

He stood back, a misplaced, foreign presence in her cozy home, as she dragged her single dining chair over so that it was opposite the armchair. She gestured him to sit down, but didn't take her own place. Instead, she went to a low cabinet, crouching to rummage around inside.

"This sounds," she said, emerging with a tawny bottle and a pair of tumblers, "like a conversation that might require a stiff drink." She hesitated. "Or do you still want the usual?"

He'd tried to numb himself with alcohol, a long time ago, when he'd been younger and the self-inflicted wound still fresh. It hadn't worked. He'd avoided it ever since, the taste forever associated with bitter grief and hatred.

He took the glass from her anyway. "This is not a usual situation."

She poured a generous measure for both of them. He knew the bottle—Scotch, from Griff's family distillery up in the Highlands. Made for shifters, by shifters, with a punch that could fell a full-grown bear.

He knocked it back in a single swallow. Smooth smoky sweetness. Ashes and rage and emptiness.

When he lowered the glass, Rose was watching him, her expression troubled. She put her own drink down on the coffee table between them, untouched.

"You're starting to scare me, Ash," she said.

"Good." His voice came out hoarse, his chest still burning with the unaccustomed whiskey. "You should be scared of me."

She gave him an exasperated look. "Not *of* you, ridiculous man. *For* you." She leaned her elbows on her knees, her whole body intently focused on him. "Whatever this secret is, you've been keeping it for a long time. And I think it's been eating you alive."

Now that the time had come to speak, his throat had closed up. He said nothing.

A little hesitantly, she reached out. He couldn't bring himself to pull away as she folded her fingers around his. For once, she was the warmer one. Her touch burned like a brand against his cold skin.

"Tell me, Ash," she whispered.

His time had run out, decades ago. He had been living on stolen grace ever since.

But he couldn't lie to her any longer.

He forced himself to meet her eyes. Her beautiful, trusting eyes, even now looking at him with nothing but love and openness.

"I need to tell you about your mate," he said.

CHAPTER 10

PAST

20 years ago...

My mate. Rose would never, ever get tired of those words, whether spoken out loud, sent down the telepathic bond, or just in the privacy of her own thoughts. **What's your waistband size?**

A bemused feeling spread from that warm, eternal glow in her soul. **In truth, I haven't the faintest idea. Clothes just always...happened.**

Rose flicked through a rack of men's jeans, pursing her lips in thought. She held up her hands in mid-air, curving them around an imaginary waist. After last night, her body knew the shape of his in intimate detail. The sharp angles of his hips, the hard planes of his flanks, his way his muscles surged in smooth motion as he filled her...

Need I remind you, I am currently sitting in the car wearing nothing but a sheet, he growled down the mate bond, sounding rather pained. She sensed him shift position uncomfortably. **And if you keep up* that *line of thought, I'm going to get arrested for public indecency.**

She giggled. **Serves you right for burning your only pair of pants.**

She gasped as heat ran over her skin, caressing her curves like a phantom hand. **You appeared to have no complaints last night.**

"Stop that," she hissed out loud, winning a slightly strange look from another shopper. "*I'm* in a public place."

A distinctly smug, masculine chuckle echoed in her mind. With a last tweak that made her legs buckle, the sense of warmth withdrew.

Our mate, her swan murmured in contentment.

Grinning like an idiot, Rose selected a pair of jeans. She pushed her shopping cart onward, scanning the shelves. A couple of soft cotton T-shirts, in a deep red that would complement his coloring. She hesitated over sweatshirts, trying to find one that wasn't covered in crass slogans or over-patriotic stars and stripes, before giving up. He was the Phoenix, after all. He wasn't going to get cold.

Boxers or briefs? she asked him.

He didn't answer for a moment. She felt a strange stillness from him, as though it was a question of huge import.

I've never had to pick anything for myself before, he said softly. **I don't really know how to do it.**

She wrapped wordless comfort around him, and waited.

Boxers, he said at last.

Is that what* they *gave you? she asked as she grabbed a couple of packs. **At the warlock base?**

No.

She brushed her mind against his, light as the tip of a feather, so that he could feel her silent understanding.

She paid for the shopping, counting out bills from her dwindling supply. She had more in her savings account, but she didn't want to risk going to a bank if she could possibly avoid it. Neither she nor Blaze thought that the warlocks had any way of identifying her, but better safe than sorry.

Exiting the store, she made her way to the back of the parking lot, where she'd left the car. Blaze opened the door as she approached, still carefully clutching his sheet. His relief shone down the mate bond.

"See?" She gave him a long, lingering kiss before handing him the shopping bag. "Perfectly safe. You could have stayed at the motel after all."

"You'd have come back to find a smoking hole in the ground," he said wryly, ripping tags off clothes as he spoke. "It was bad enough having to wait outside. I couldn't stand to be any farther apart from you."

She kissed him again, curling her hands over his smooth, bare shoulders. "You'll never have to."

Once Blaze was decent once more, they set off down the freeway. Rose would have liked to head straight north, but the wildfires were still blocking off the most direct route to the border. She switched on the radio, scanning frequencies for news updates as she drove.

Blaze rode shotgun in silence, his bandaged forearm resting along the open window, the wind ruffling his short brown hair. His dark eyes drank in the sky, the horizon, the ugly strip malls and billboards, all with equal wonder.

"Where are we going?" he asked at last.

"Since you don't have any sort of identification, our options are a bit limited." Rose flashed him a sideways glance, something occurring to her. "Do you even have a last name?"

He shook his head, an ironic smile lifting the corner of his mouth. "Officially, I don't exist. I suppose I must have a birth certificate on file somewhere, but I wouldn't know where to begin searching for it. I don't even remember the country where I was born."

"You have an English accent," she said, the strangeness of that only just striking her.

His jaw tightened. "Corbin," he said, and nothing more.

His warlock. The only person who'd talked to him. Of course he'd grow up copying his captor's speech patterns. And if this Corbin was English, no wonder that he'd fled here to the far side of America. Great Britain was a shifter-ruled country. Rose didn't know if the Parliament of Shifters was aware of warlocks, but they certainly came down very, very hard on anything that threatened either the secrecy or the wellbeing of shifter citizens.

"Well. We can't get you a passport, and that means a plane ticket is out," she said. "I think our best bet is to get as far north as we can, then shift to cross the border. Canada's a Commonwealth realm—our Queen is still their ceremonial head of state. It's a shifter-friendly country. We just need to find a British embassy, and we'll be safe."

"Safe," he echoed, as if it was a foreign word. "You really think that your country will grant me asylum? I am—"

"You're not dangerous," she said firmly, cutting him off. She hesitated, but she had to be honest with him. "They might have...conditions, though. I've only heard of a few shifters with your sort of elemental power. The sea dragon Pearl Emperor, for water, and the Queen herself, for earth."

His hand tightened on his knee. "I will not be used for harm. Not ever again."

She put her hand over his, rubbing her thumb in gentle circles over his hot skin. "I won't let that happen. If the British government tries to harness your abilities, we'll go somewhere else. It doesn't matter where we live, as long as we're together."

He was quiet for the next hour or so, lost in his own thoughts. Rose left him in peace, the mate bond reassuring her that nothing was wrong. He just needed some time to breathe, and be.

They stopped at a tiny roadside diner for lunch. Blaze stared down at the single-page menu in frank alarm, clearly paralyzed by options, so Rose ordered for both of them. Nothing fancy—fried chicken, mashed potatoes, green beans—but Blaze treated the food like a revelation. She enjoyed his astonishment, and ordered four types of dessert.

"What did they feed you in there?" she asked, as he gazed at a forkful of apple pie as if it was a work of art.

"Military rations." He turned the fork, feeding her the flaky morsel. "Nothing like this."

She licked her lips, tasting cream and cinnamon as if for the first time. The light of the mate bond glowing in her soul made everything fresh and new, reborn.

Even the sun-faded diner, the scratched plastic tabletops, the worn linoleum floor—they were all perfect, beautiful. Young lovers had carved that heart into the table. The scuffs on the floor were from weary feet, finding a place to sit down and rest. The old diner's imperfections were like laughter lines or stretch marks. They were scars of love.

"I'd like to have a place like this," she said wistfully.

Blaze's eyebrows shot up. "A restaurant?"

She snorted. "Believe me, no one would want to pay for my cooking. No, not a restaurant. But a place where people could come to be together. A safe haven, somewhere to relax, just for shifters. A pub, maybe."

From his quizzical look, this was evidently one aspect of English culture he hadn't picked up from Corbin.

She patted his hand. "Another thing that will be easier to show you than explain."

A heated gleam lit his eyes. His leg slid against hers under the table. "Will I enjoy it as much as the last thing you showed me?"

She laughed, feeding him another bite of pie. "Maybe not quite *that* much."

His wicked expression faded as he chewed and swallowed. She thought at first that he was just lost in flavor again, but he put down his fork rather than scooping up another mouthful. She sensed a slight darkening down the mate bond, something shadowing his thoughts.

"What is it?" she asked.

"You have a dream." He looked down at his plate. "I don't know how I fit in with it."

"You're my mate. You *are* my dream."

"Yes, but..." He let out his breath, running a hand through his hair. "You have a life, a place you come from, family. I don't know...any of those things. All I know is fire and destruction. What can I do, in your world?"

Reflexive reassurances sprang to her lips, but she held them back. He needed more than empty platitudes. He looked so lost, so out of place, this creature out of legend dropped into mundane life. What *would* he do?

"Firefighter," she said firmly.

His gaze jerked up, startled, as though he hadn't actually expected her to come up with an answer. "What?"

"You know fire. Better than anyone. You can use your powers to control it." A slow smile spread over her face as she realized how perfect it was. "To save lives, rather than destroy them."

"Firefighter," he said softly. "Yes. I would like that."

She leaned over the table to kiss him. "You'll be the best firefighter ever."

She never knew what had warned him. Mythic shifter senses, perhaps, even keener than her own. Or just greater wariness, from his lifetime of captivity.

One moment she was snuggling up against his side as they walked back to the car—and the next she was down on the tarmac, his body covering hers. A crackling lightning-bolt of green energy sizzled through the space where her head had been.

"Warlocks!" Blaze shouted, a ring of fire roaring up to shield them.

Another bolt shot overhead, passing clean through the flames, but at least their attackers couldn't get line of sight on them through the roaring inferno. Blaze pulled her to her feet, shoving her in the direction of the car.

"Go," he said, his voice crackling with power. Flames haloed him, spreading from his back like wings. "I'll deal with them."

She knew better than to try to argue. Rose ran for the car, her heart hammering, fumbling in her pocket for the keys. Behind her, she heard the *crack* of another lightning bolt, and a piercing scream—but it wasn't Blaze's voice. Heat washed over her back.

She screamed herself as the air in front of her split in two, parting like a curtain. She had a glimpse of foam-flecked fangs and maddened eyes lunging at her out of the portal.

Instinct took over. She flung herself flat, rolling. A stinking, furry body passed over her, jaws snapping shut on thin air. She scrabbled to hands and knees as the wolverine turned, snarling—

And went up in flame. Between one breath and the next, it was simply gone, no more than embers on the wind. The portal blinked out, cutting off a human howl of agony. Somewhere, a warlock had just lost his shifter, and his power.

"Not the shifters!" she cried out, covering her head as another jagged blast of energy shot past. "Blaze, don't hurt the shifters!"

"I have to!" He turned, and she saw the agony in his eyes, behind the black flames. "They're linked—"

He broke off, spinning round. A wolf bounded across the car park, leaping for him. Blaze dodged it, instead throwing fire at the warlock who'd just stepped out of thin air. The unfortunate man didn't even have time to scream before he turned to ashes.

And the wolf—just stopped. It collapsing in mid-stride, like a puppet with cut strings.

"They die together," Blaze finished, stepping over the fallen shifter. His hand closed around her arm, pulling her up. He shielded her with his own body as he turned, ready to fend off any further attack.

Rose stared into the wolf's glazing yellow eyes. Maybe it was just her imagination, but she thought it looked relieved.

A sound of frantic chanting came from behind a nearby fence, but no lightning bolt followed. Blaze bared his teeth, thrusting out one hand as if throwing a ball. The wooden fence vaporized, revealing a crouching warlock desperately sketching the shape of a portal in mid-air.

"Oh no you don't," Blaze growled.

The warlock screeched, doubling over. The half-formed portal flickered out, glowing lines fading into nothing.

"Try that again and you lose both hands at the wrist." Releasing her, Blaze stalked toward the man.

Cradling his burnt fingers, the warlock turned to flee. A wall of fire blazed up, stopping him in his tracks. His eyes flicked desperately left and right, searching for escape. Rose recognized his face…and the ocelot cringing at his feet.

"Not him!" She ran after Blaze. "She helped me, don't kill him!"

"I won't." Not entirely suiting actions to words, Blaze seized the warlock by the throat. The man made a strangled scream as Blaze lifted him off his feet with no apparent effort. "But I can hurt him a great deal without harming his shifter."

"Please," the man choked out, scrabbling at Blaze's fingers. "I'll tell you—anything!"

Blaze opened his hand, allowing the man to fall to the ground. "How did you know where we were?"

"Corbin," the warlock wheezed. Livid red burns ringed his throat. "Spent years—studying—the Phoenix. Knows how to—track it."

Blaze went very still. "He can find me?"

"Always." The warlock spat on the ground, a hint of sadistic satisfaction breaking through his terror. "How do you think he ever found you in the first place, as a child? Your beast burns so bright, he could see you on the other side of the world. Run all you want. You can't hide from him. You *or* your bitch."

"*No,* Blaze!" Rose grabbed his arm, digging her fingernails into his rock-hard muscles. "His shifter, remember?"

Blaze's hand unclenched, the fire around it fading. He stared down at the cowering ocelot for a second, then turned to her, his face bleak. "I can't let him live, Rose."

"But she helped me," Rose said again, throat closing up. "She's innocent."

She knelt, holding out her hands. The warlock glared, but didn't stop the little cat from creeping forward. Rose stroked it, her tears dappling the soft, spotted fur. The ocelot's shivering body relaxed a little.

"Can't we make him release her?" she asked Blaze.

The warlock spat again. "I'm dead anyway. If I'm going down, might as well take the mangy beast with me." He bared his teeth at her, eyes glittering with malice. "Since it hurts you."

Sirens sounded in the distance, getting closer. Fire engines, or police, responding to the disturbance. Rose knew they didn't have much time.

"There must be something we can do," Rose said, hopelessly.

Blaze stared down at the ocelot in her hands. It looked back at him, and something passed between them. Not telepathy. Just understanding, between two souls who'd shared the same torment.

"Are you sure?" he asked it, very quietly.

The ocelot's thin flanks rose and fell in a long sigh. It turned its head, exposing its throat in submission.

Blaze leaned down and touched its head.

Fire flared.

"No," Rose sobbed—and then realized that she could feel bare human skin.

The woman sat up, her long, tangled hair her only cover. She turned her hands over in front of her own face, looking at them in wonder.

"No!" howled the warlock—and was gone, in a flash of heat.

"Thank you," whispered the woman. She seized Blaze's hand, pressing it to her forehead. "*Thank you.*"

Blaze nodded. His own face had gone stark white. He swallowed, hard, before he spoke. "We have to go. Will you be all right?"

"Yes." The woman turned toward the direction of the approaching sirens. "Hurry. I won't tell them you were here."

Rose cast a last backward glance over her shoulder at the woman as they hastened away. She didn't seem hurt...and yet Rose couldn't shake the feeling that she *was*.

She is, her swan whispered. It hadn't been frightened during the fight, but now it was cowering in her heart, frozen as a mouse in the shadow of a hawk.

"What did you do?" Rose asked Blaze in a low voice. "How did you free her?"

He stared straight ahead, his mouth set in a sick, flat line. "I burned away her animal."

CHAPTER 11

"My mate?" It was so far from anything she'd expected Ash to say that for a moment Rose wasn't sure she'd heard him correctly. "What about him?"

"Your mate is the reason I never said anything about...my feelings." Ash's head made the tiniest jerk, as though he'd started to look down but then forced himself to keep holding her gaze. "And he is the reason why I cannot be with you."

"Ash, we've already been over this. I refuse to let my life be dictated by a man I never met. It doesn't matter to me that you aren't him."

"He is the reason *I* cannot be with you," Ash repeated, more forcefully. "Not why no one can be with you."

His face was utterly unreadable, as closed and expressionless as she'd ever seen. She looked at his hands instead. That was how Ash betrayed emotion, she knew.

Right now his left hand was clenched tight over the scar on his right forearm, knuckles white. His nails dug so deep that she feared he was about to slit his own wrist.

She reached out to him, to make him break that shaking grip, but he jerked away.

"Do not—" He stopped, closing his eyes for a moment and taking a deep breath. "Don't touch me. You would not want to, if you knew what I have done."

And suddenly, she did. It was an impossible, ridiculous conclusion, but she knew, *knew* that it was right.

"You knew my mate," she said.

He had the face of a dead man, gray and frozen. Very slightly, he nodded.

It was like a candle kindling in her mind, throwing new light on piles of shadowy memories. Innocent, perplexing mysteries about him, suddenly illuminated.

Suddenly made monstrous.

"You." She could barely force the words out past the hurt and betrayal tightening her throat. "You had something to do with his death."

"I did not kill him." His hand twisted on his wrist. The old scar stood out stark white against his tanned skin. "But I might as well have done. In any event, I am the reason you don't have a mate."

"How?"

He flinched as though the word had been a gunshot. "You know that I was imprisoned, once."

She did, though he'd never explained how on earth anyone could have shackled the Phoenix. It had taken her over a decade to tease out the barest facts—that he'd been a captive of a secret military program in America, that he'd grown up there, that he'd eventually escaped and sought asylum in England.

"Your mate was there." His eyes met hers for a fraction of a second. "Do not ask me how I know. There are things I cannot—*will not*—tell you. But he was there. And when I destroyed that place, I also destroyed your future. Your happiness. And so I destroyed us. What chance we might have had."

She felt cold inside, cold as ice. She picked up her glass, draining the whiskey in a single swallow. It might as well have been water. The burn didn't touch the numbness in her chest.

She'd never told anyone the date of her mate's death, the exact moment when she'd felt that shock of loss. She wouldn't have been able to stand having people creep around her, pitying, uncertain of the correct protocol. She'd always pretended it was just another day.

But now she realized that Ash had always been there. No matter whether the date fell on a weekday or weekend, he'd made sure she wasn't alone at that hour.

He'd *known.*

"All this time," she said, through the ringing in her ears. "*All this time*. Would you ever have told me, if I hadn't forced the issue?"

"No." His tone was flat, final. There was no hint of apology in it.

Distantly, she wondered if she should be angry. If she should throw him out, ban him from her life, never speak to him again.

But he was still *Ash*, her friend. Even now, with her soul raw and bleeding, she simply couldn't believe that he would ever hurt her. That he *could* hurt her.

"You didn't tell me for a reason," she said slowly, things connecting in her head. "And not just because you didn't want me to hate you."

He stopped breathing. She'd never seen anyone so utterly motionless.

"Do you hate me?" he said, after a moment.

"I don't know yet," she said, honestly. "This is—it's—damn it, Ash, talk to me! Tell me why you didn't tell me this before."

He stared down at his knees. "Because I knew that it would bring you nothing but pain. And I could not bear to hurt you any more than I already had."

She digested this for a moment. "I have questions."

He straightened his spine, shoulders setting. He looked like a prisoner facing a firing squad. "As I said, there are things I cannot tell you. But I will answer what I can."

A million questions whirled through her mind. She rubbed her palms across her face, trying to organize her racing thoughts.

"Did you know him well?" she asked.

"I thought I did." He made a sharp, hollow noise, somewhere between a laugh and a gasp of pain. "The older I get, the more of a stranger he becomes."

"Who was he?"

He looked at her, and said nothing.

"You won't even tell me *that*?"

"I will tell you nothing," he said softly, "that would only hurt you."

Ash had been held captive. He'd never spoken about what had happened to him, but she knew it had been brutal. An experience so traumatic that it had frozen him into the man he was today.

Her mate had been part of that. And Ash did not want to tell her anything about him. Because it would only hurt her.

"Was he…" The word *evil* stuck in her throat. "Was he…complicit, in what happened to you there?"

He didn't say anything for so long that she thought he wasn't going to answer. But just as she opened her mouth to ask something else, he said, "Yes. For a long time. He meant well. But yes."

No, her swan cried in her soul. *No. Our mate was good and strong and kind. He would not hurt anyone, not ever, except to protect and defend. He was our* mate.

But bad people could have mates too.

If she'd found him…would she have been horrified? Tried to redeem him, to pull him away from that dark place?

Or would her animal's instincts have overpowered human morals? Ash had said her mate had had his reasons. Would she have listened to them? Found her own excuses?

Would she have become one of Ash's tormentors too?

We would have stood by our mate, insisted her swan. *Never left him. Always loved him, always, forever.*

"You're absolutely certain he was my mate," she whispered.

"He knew who you were. He knew your name."

"How?"

Ash shook his head again, silent.

Swans weren't the only type of shifter to have special powers relating to finding their mate. But the thought that her mate might have been a *shifter,* one of their own kind, and yet still been part of whatever evil organization had tortured Ash…somehow, that only made it all worse.

"Why didn't he come for me?" she asked. "I came to find him. I crossed half the world in search of him. If I'd found him, would he have turned me away?"

"I think," Ash said, with a catch in his voice, "that would have been the only way to keep you truly safe. He stayed away to protect you, Rose."

"Do you think he was right?"

"Yes." He met her eyes at last, and there was nothing but raw, bleak honesty in those dark depths. "God forgive me, but yes. He kept you safe, in the only way he could, and even now I cannot hate him for that."

She hid her face in her hands. It was too much, too fast. Her swan still said *no, no, no,* even as her human mind had to accept the truth of Ash's words. She didn't know how to feel.

"I wish you hadn't told me," she said, muffled.

"I never wanted to." She heard him stand. "But now you understand. Goodbye, Rose."

And she knew that she would never see him again.

CHAPTER 12

PAST

20 years ago…

Go back, go back, go back.

Blaze had a lifetime of experience in ignoring his beast. He ignored it now, flying steadily against the frantic pull urging him in the opposite direction.

Rose hadn't wanted to leave him. No matter that she wasn't safe as long as they were together. No matter that he was the Phoenix, while her own animal had no defenses against the predators stalking them. If he'd let her, she would have stayed at his side and guarded his back to her last breath.

He'd cheated, in the end. Used her fierce, compassionate heart against her.

"Rose," he'd told her, cupping her angry, tear-streaked face in his hands. "We know how to free the other shifters now. I have to go back."

It had been the one argument he'd known she wouldn't be able to counter. And she'd had to admit that she would only be a liability on this mission. She'd snuck into the warlock base once—and the mere thought of how she'd endangered herself for him still froze the blood in his veins—but this was no longer a matter of stealth and subtlety.

He wasn't going to infiltrate the base.

He was going to destroy it utterly.

He'd thought that his beast would revel in the prospect. But strangely, the fire fought him. He had to force every wingbeat, when normally he would have been able to arrow across the sky as fast as thought.

Go back, go back, go back.

He ground his beak, his talons clenching on nothing. Our animals are wiser than us, Rose had said to him, but there was no sense in the urgent tug of his beast's instincts. No matter how they screamed at him that he had to be at his mate's side to protect her, his rational mind knew better.

Corbin could track him. Until the warlock was dead, he couldn't risk being near her.

He glanced up at the sun, judging the time. By now, she should have reached the airport. Soon she would be safely away, back to her own country. A warlock could theoretically open a portal even to England—though the effort expended would drain even a powerful shifter to the point of death—but why would they? Without his betraying presence at her side, the warlocks had no way of knowing where she'd gone.

He knew it was right for them to separate. He knew it was the only way to keep her safe.

But still: *Go back, go back, go back.*

He'd expected to hear the wail of sirens the instant he came in sight of the base. But no alarm came. No soldiers patrolled the high, wire-topped walls; no robed figures ran to meet his assault. Even the door to the menagerie hung open, unguarded.

The base looked deserted.

Suspecting some kind of trick, he dove fast as a missile, a wave of fire billowing before him. Barracks and labs burst into flame...but no one came running out.

He swooped lower, more slowly, still alert for any attack. His eagle-sharp eyesight scanned the base, and his unease grew.

Every last vehicle was gone, leaving behind only deep ruts in the dirt road. Even that could have been a decoy, to tempt him into coming down to investigate further...but there was no fooling his psychic abilities. If there had been people present in the base—no matter how well concealed—he would have sensed the fires of their souls.

They were gone. They were all gone.

Abandoning caution, he landed outside Corbin's private residence, a stately manor house set within formal gardens. The front door hung ajar. It creaked in the wind caused by his fiery aura, swinging further open.

He shifted back into human form, recklessly. Even *that* didn't prompt an attack.

He'd never been into the mansion before. The cells, the labs, the training grounds—those were the parts of the complex that he knew. Not this, Corbin's private domain.

His feet left blackened footprints on the marble floor as he stalked through the deserted rooms. The library still had books scattered across the shelves, but many volumes were missing. Desk drawers were pulled out, clearly having been emptied of any important contents.

Corbin had departed in a hurry. But not in a panic.

The High Magus had been able to sense him coming. He'd had time to execute an evacuation plan. Blaze has a sick certainty that there wouldn't be a single clue left anywhere in the complex that might hint where the warlock had gone.

The trail was cold. He had no idea how to find Corbin.

He couldn't protect his mate.

Helpless fury from exploded out of him, torching the remaining books. Every window shattered, shards of glass lancing outward. The heat of the inferno swirled around him, but the fire offered no comfort.

He'd been certain that Corbin would face him rather than flee.

He'd thought that the half-hearted attack earlier had just been a ruse to draw him back here—if Corbin had seriously been trying to take him by surprise, he wouldn't have sent such weak warlocks. A wolverine, an ocelot, a wolf...those were all the types of creature that were given to mid-ranking Adepts, not the more experienced senior warlocks, the Magi.

He'd been expecting a trap. The base was heavily fortified, the best place Corbin could pick to make a stand. Blaze had been bracing himself for the fight of his life. Dozens of powerful warlocks acting together would have been a challenge even for the Phoenix.

Why had Corbin run? Why hadn't he made use of all the weapons at his disposal? Why hadn't he unleashed—

And Blaze realized that he'd made a terrible mistake.

Go back, go back, go back.

"I'm *going* back, stupid swan," Rose snarled under her breath, trying to concentrate on the road. "Shut up and let me drive!"

She'd made it approximately ten miles before her swan's incessant nagging had made her do an abrupt U-turn. Now she drove as fast as she could down unfamiliar backcountry lanes, following the pull of the mate bond. It was more urgent than ever.

"Shouldn't have listened to him," she muttered to herself, taking switchbacks at unwise speed. If she crashed and burned, it was all going to be *his* fault. "So distracted by that pretty mouth, didn't realize what horsefeathers were coming out of it. Argh! Why do you have to be able to fly so fast, you overgrown oven-ready chicken?!"

Thinking up ridiculous insults for her noble, protective, and above all *idiotic* mate was all that was stopping her from succumbing to stark terror. She'd let him sweet-talk her into this stupid plan to separate. And now he was flying straight into a trap.

The warlocks captured him once. Of course they can bind him again!

But not if *she* was there. She'd freed him once, after all. And the warlocks who'd attacked them earlier hadn't made any attempt to bind either of them. It was like their magic was a sick, twisted version of the mate bond. It had no strength in the presence of the real thing.

But she had a horrible, horrible certainty that protection wouldn't work at a distance. And that Corbin had manipulated them both like puppets to separate them.

A sign flashed by, warning of another sharp bend coming up. Much as her swan screeched for more speed, it wouldn't do Blaze any good if she crashed and burned. Reluctantly, Rose took her foot off the accelerator.

That was all that saved her life.

Between one breath and the next, the world outside the car windows went white. Her tires slid on sudden ice. Too shocked even to scream, Rose reflexively spun the steering wheel, turning into the skid.

If she'd been going any faster, she would have gone straight off the edge of the road and over a cliff. As it was, the car slid sideways into a tree with a bone-rattling *crunch.*

Shaken, bruised, it took Rose a moment to work out whether or not she was dead. The airbag had gone off in her face. She struggled free of its enveloping folds, beating down the collapsing fabric. Breathing hard, she stared out the cracked windscreen.

That can't be right.

It was snowing. In July. In *California.*

Not just a little snow, either. A full-on blizzard had fallen out of the clear blue sky, whiting out the world. She couldn't even see the end of her car's hood, let alone the road. Her breath steamed in the suddenly freezing air.

Her breath steamed in the suddenly freezing air.

The warlock base. Blaze's cell. The *other* cell.

"Oh no." Her fingers had gone numb. She scrabbled at her seat belt, frantically trying to release the catch. "No, no, no..."

The wind scratched over the car. It sobbed and whined, like a starving dog.

It spoke.

"Hungry."

Rose screamed as the windscreen imploded in a shower of glass. Branching antlers the color of ice stabbed through, nearly impaling her.

Rose made the fastest shift of her life. Her swan-self slid free of the seat belt as the monstrous antlers withdrew. With the speed of terror, Rose hurled herself out the shattered windscreen, leaping over the creature crouched on the buckled hood.

Polar bear, some oddly calm corner of her mind thought. *But no, polar bears don't have antlers—*

Whatever it was, she thought for one heart-stopping second that it had grabbed her. The blizzard seized her outstretched wings, shaking her like a dog with a chew toy. She tumbled head-over-tail feathers, completely out of control.

Something smacked her out of the air. She smashed to the frozen ground, sliding, fetching up against something warm.

Legs.

"I've got the shifter!" Still half-stunned, Rose couldn't resist as human hands grabbed her ankles, hauling her into the air. "Huh, it's smaller than I—what the hell? It's just a swan."

"I don't care what it is, hurry up and bind it!" yelled a second voice. Dangling upside-down, Rose had a confused glimpse of ice-blue light swirling around upraised hands. "I can't hold my beast for much longer! I have to get it back to its cage before it breaks free!"

"I *told* the High Magus you were too weak to handle the wendigo," the first man snapped. "*You* should be the one who has to shackle himself to this overgrown duck."

"You really want to try to transfer familiars *now*? Just bind the damn bird! Unless you want to explain to the High Magus that you were too proud to carry out his orders?"

The first man heaved an irritated, put-upon sigh. "I swear, if any of you bastards dare to laugh about this..."

He switched to some foreign language, chanting out words that ran over Rose's skin like ants. One of his hands groped for her right wing.

Unfortunately, the brief exchange had given Rose's head time to clear.

"Just a swan?" Her beak turned the words into angry hisses and ear-splitting honks. The warlock howled as her wings smashed into his arm. "*Just* a swan?!"

Finding himself unexpectedly holding a very large, very awake, and very *angry* swan, the warlock made a very unwise decision.

He let go.

Birds were descended from dinosaurs. In this form, Rose was a lot more closely related to a velociraptor than a human being.

The warlock screamed as she attacked him, shattering his leg with a single blow. She charged straight over his fallen, writhing form, wings spread, aiming for the second warlock. He back-pedaled frantically, chanting something. Blue light crackled around his weaving fingers.

Rose's iron-hard beak hit him, full force, square in the crotch.

Apparently not even a warlock could do magic under those circumstances.

The dancing sparks faded into nothing as he folded around himself. And from behind Rose, that winter-wail voice spoke again. A different word, this time.

"Free."

Rose cowered into the snow as a frost-white shape bounded over her. Foot-long claws like shards of ice extended. The warlock never stood a chance.

Rose took one slow, careful step back, then another. The creature didn't react, fully occupied with its prey. She crept back another pace.

A scrabble of sudden motion made her freeze. The other warlock was madly trying to flee on hands and knees, sobbing, his broken leg dragging through the mounting snow.

"No," he cried, as the creature's antlered head jerked up. "Nooooo—!"

His scream ended as bone-colored jaws closed. Red drops scattered across the snow, steaming.

Rose held very still.

A long white tongue ran over the lipless maw. The creature's head wasn't just bone-colored—it *was* bone, a stag's long, eerie skull. The spreading antlers were wider than Rose's car. Icicles clung to the branching tines.

The antlers dipped, as the creature nosed along the ground. Nothing remained of the two warlocks but a patch of red-stained snow. The monster licked it up hungrily, crouched on all fours. Its body was bigger than a bear, but lean as a wolf. Rose could count every rib through its ragged white fur.

Rose edged back another step.

The skull-head turned. Cold blue fire burned in the empty eye sockets.

"Still hungry," whispered the wendigo.

There was no hope of fleeing. Even if the howling wind hadn't made flight impossible, a swan couldn't take off from a standing start. All Rose could do was face the beast head-on, refusing to flinch.

Blaze's beautiful, beloved face filled her mind. If she was going to die, at least he would be her final thought—

Fiery wings swept around her, hurling back the blizzard's cold. The wendigo howled in fear, leaping away from the burning feathers.

The Phoenix's eyes were twin suns, incandescent with rage. Outside the vast arc of his wings, snow hissed into billowing clouds of steam. Every feather blazed white-hot—but where Rose crouched, in the heart of that protective embrace, she felt nothing but a pleasant, gentle summer's warmth.

The wendigo was an indistinct white blur amidst the swirling veils of steam and snow. All Rose could see clearly were the bright, cold lights of its eyes, fixed on the Phoenix.

The blizzard picked up, making the edges of the Phoenix's flame-feathers flicker. Winter winds whined and begged.

Hunt, then. The Phoenix's searing voice wasn't aimed at her; Rose only caught the edges of the thought, like smoke rising from a distant fire. **But only your rightful prey.**

The wendigo's vast antlers dipped. It bowed, low to the ground.

Then, in a swirl of snow, it was gone.

In moments, the sky cleared to brilliant blue. Tentatively, a bird chirped, and was answered by another. Sunlight and summer returned, as if nothing had happened. Churned mud—and, of course, the crashed car—were the only signs of the attack.

Adrenaline deserted Rose, pulling her back into her human skin. Strong arms caught her as her knees buckled.

"Rose, *Rose.*" Blaze held her as tightly as if he feared she might melt away like the snow. "I was nearly too late. If you'd been farther away, if you'd gone to the airport like we agreed...I was nearly too late."

"I worked out it was a trap." She clung to him just as fiercely, needing to reassure herself that he was truly there, hot and solid under her palms. "But I thought it was for you, that they were going to try to bind *you* again!"

"No. Corbin knows I'm too strong for that. He has to be touching me in order to bind me, and I'd kill him before he finished the spell." He made a sound that was half-laugh, half-sob. "It's not me that he's after now. He wants *you*. To make me surrender myself voluntarily."

"Don't you *dare* do that," she said forcefully. "Not ever, no matter what, you hear me? But how did they know where I was? Were they following me?"

"They don't have to. That's what I worked out, why I raced back. Remember what the warlock, the one with the ocelot, started to say? 'You can't hide from us. You *or* your...'" Blaze didn't finish the sentence, instead burying his face in her hair. "Rose, I was nearly *too late.*"

"You weren't," Rose said again, though she was beginning to suspect he wasn't going to break out of this spiral of guilt for a while. "But I still don't understand."

"Corbin can track the Phoenix. And you're bound to me, to the Phoenix, sharing its fire." His hands gripped her shoulders. She could feel him shaking. "Corbin can find you too."

CHAPTER 13

"Wait."

Ash didn't want to. He needed to be gone, somewhere, anywhere. He should never have returned to her at all.

He had only ever brought her pain. The only way to avoid hurting her even more was to remove himself from her life entirely. The best thing he could do was to go, now, and never look back.

"Wait," Rose said again.

He could not ignore his mate's command.

He stopped with one hand on the door handle, not looking round at her. "You should let me go, Rose."

"Not until you answer one final question." He heard her get up, coming toward him.

Even now, after all he'd done to her, he knew he would not be able to withstand the sweet fire of her touch. He was forced to turn to face her, before she could reach out and burn away the last of his resolve.

She didn't reach out to him, but she was still close, too close. He pressed his back into the closed door, trying not to feel the heat of her body. He focused on the tears gleaming against her ebony skin so that he would not see the lush softness of her half-parted lips, or fall into the endless wonder of her eyes.

"Did you..." Rose paused, her throat working as she swallowed. His fingertips yearned to trace that long, elegant column. "Did you ever truly care for me? Or was it just guilt?"

His own throat burned. He wasn't sure whether he wanted to laugh or cry. Everything that he'd done to her, and *this* was what she asked?

"I never just *cared* for you," he said. Her eyes widened, but he hadn't finished. The words spilled out of him in a fierce, desperate torrent, bursting free at last. "I love you, Rose. I have loved you from the moment I first saw you. I will always love you. I came here, I stayed here, because I could not bear to be apart from you. I love you."

She searched his face. "Even though I'm not your mate?"

"I am not your mate." She still didn't notice the subtle correction. "But you are my everything."

She nodded, once, as though she'd come to some private decision. "I don't want to be alone."

Of course she didn't, not after everything he'd dropped on her tonight. Even now, his heart lifted a little at the prospect of being able to serve her in some small way.

He reached for his work-issue cell phone, holstered as always on his belt. "I could call Hayley, or—"

Her look stopped him mid-sentence.

"Ash." Very deliberately, she hooked a finger through one of his belt loops. "You are an *idiot*."

This seemed very likely. His mind had gone completely blank. He stumbled forward as she pulled him into her arms.

"But," he started, and then completely forgot whatever he'd been about to say as her free hand curved around the back of his neck.

"Shut up, Ash," she whispered, drawing him down.

Her mouth pressed against his, silencing him. And she was warm and welcoming and *his mate*, and it had been so, so long since he had been home.

He closed his eyes, sinking deep into the sweet taste of her. Her lips parted for him, without hesitation, just as they'd done all those years ago. She was still just as bold and fierce, claiming his tongue with hers, her fingernails digging into the back of his neck. He cradled her face, fire racing through him as his fingers spanned the familiar, proud line of her jaw, the fine arch of her cheekbones.

He tightened his grip, holding her still as he broke the kiss. Even pulling away the barest inch felt like ripping his soul in half all over again. He burned with the need to fall back into her heat again.

"Rose," he gasped, barely able to draw enough breath for words. "I took everything from you."

Her eyes met his. "So give me something back."

Her strong fingers were still hooked into his belt loop; she pulled him closer, pressing her hips against his. The shock of that contact undid him completely.

No more restraint. No more second thoughts. *She* was his only thought now.

The Phoenix rose in his soul, unrestrained, ravenous. His body rose too, fast and hard. Rose's eyes flew open.

"Oh my," she gasped into his mouth. "Ash, this is probably the point where I need to tell *you* something. I'm a virgin."

For a second, he was utterly baffled—and then his heart lurched.

"You never, in all these years..." He choked the words off before he said too much. His thumb brushed over her mouth, lightly, wonderingly.

"You're my first," Rose said, her midnight skin taking on a warmer hue as she blushed furiously. "And, um, that doesn't feel like novice-sized equipment."

He was her first. Again. Which meant that he was her only.

He kissed her hard, deeply, until she was limp and liquid in his grasp, head tipped back, hands fisted in his shirt. His mate. His Rose. His first and only, as he was hers, always, forever.

"What was that for?" she gasped, when he finally had to come up for air.

"You." He scooped her up in his arms. "For being more than I will ever deserve."

She bit his lower lip lightly. "Don't you dare start that again. You'd better be carrying me to the bedroom."

He was. The guilt that had bound him for so long was crumbling into ash, burned away by the fire she'd lit within his blood. Once again, she'd freed him—with a word, with a touch, with her love.

He had come back to her, and he would never leave her again.

He laid her carefully, so carefully, on the bed. He stretched out next to her, propping himself up on his side so that he could kiss her again, slowly, lingering.

They had never had the time to be slow, before.

But he'd had twenty years to dream.

Her temples, the dimples in her cheeks, the secret, sensitive spot behind her ear—he worshipped them all. Her skin was even softer than he remembered, traced with fine lines around her eyes and mouth. Beautiful lines, tracks of joy and grief and wisdom. Her soul had shaped her body, over the years. She had become more *herself*.

She touched the corner of his eye. "Ash," she whispered.

He brushed his tongue over her fingertips, tasting the salt of his tears. "Joy. They're for joy. Rose, oh *Rose.*"

She arced up to him as he worked his way down the glorious line of her neck. He was dizzy with the scent of her, near drunk on the taste of her skin. Need pulsed urgently through him, but it was different from the unstoppable, feral drive that had gripped him at their first mating.

She was already his mate. This was about *their* desires now, not their animals' instincts.

And, oh, he desired her, with the intensity of a thousand suns. He would burn for her always, never dimming, with a fire as eternal as the Phoenix itself.

Knowing that, he could take his time.

One by one, he undid the buttons of her blouse, holding his breath as he exposed her inch by inch. She rolled to let him pull the soft fabric free from her body. He skimmed the white straps of her bra, sliding them down over the soft curves of her shoulders. A slightly awkward moment, Rose giggling and wriggling while he fumbled with unseen hooks—and then she was bare to him at last.

All the breath sighed out of his lungs. He drank in the sight of her rich curves, the proud, dark peaks of her nipples. Her breasts were fuller now. They would overflow his palms with their lush bounty. Just the thought made him clench his hand in the bedclothes, struggling not to lose control.

"You are more beautiful than I—" He very nearly slipped and said *remembered.* "Than I dreamed."

Rose's eyes were wide and dark, hazed with desire. She folded her arms behind her head, arching her back in blatant invitation.

That *did* break his control. He buried his face in her richness, groaning at the softness, the fullness, the unbearable perfection of her nipples. He teased the buds with tongue and fingers and palm, savoring the way they swelled and hardened under his touch. His own hardness grew too, until his thighs tightened with the effort of holding back. It was agony, sweet agony, but the delicious sounds he won from Rose's gasping mouth were satisfaction enough.

"Ash!" she cried out, head flung back, hips lifting. "*Ash!*"

He'd gone by that name for two decades, and yet now it rang false in his ears. He silenced her mouth with his own, sliding his palms down over her stomach, under the tight waistband of her skirt. They both groaned as he found the softness of her curls, already damp for him. Her hips pressed up into his hand, her knees spreading, but the angle was wrong; he couldn't reach any further.

She pushed at his shoulders, though her mouth didn't release his. He braced himself on one forearm, lifting just high enough for her hands to be able to dive between them. She unzipped her skirt, shoving it down past her hips with an impatient wriggle. The motion ground her thigh against his rigid length, and he almost lost control there and then. He had to roll away, gasping, fighting against his surging need.

Rose very nearly undid his efforts by straddling him. She'd stripped off her skirt and panties, leaving her gloriously, maddeningly bare. He caught her hips, stopping her a scant inch above him.

"I've waited a long time for this," he said hoarsely. His muscles shook with the effort of holding her away rather than pulling her down. "I don't want it to be over too fast."

He jerked as she deliberately canted her hips, brushing against him through his pants. Rose grinned wickedly down, smug delight sparking in her eyes.

"I should make you wait longer, since you made *me* wait so long," she said, leaning forward. "But I'm not that patient."

She claimed his mouth as her fingers worked down his shirt buttons. White-hot sparks flashed across his vision as she ran her hands over his bare chest. Oh, her hands remembered him, even though her mind didn't. They knew exactly where to touch him, and how, until he was gasping underneath her, every muscle knotted.

Blindly, he reached up, pulling her down. With a twist, he captured her underneath him, pressing her into the soft covers. Every inch of him was on fire. Her bare skin against his was relief and fuel combined; ecstasy that only sparked greater hunger. He slid down her body, planting feverish, open-mouthed kisses across her stomach and thighs.

"Oh," she gasped, legs falling open for him. "*Oh.*"

There she was at last, better than memory, better than dreams. He slid under her legs, hooking her ankles over his shoulders, so that he could gaze at her. His hands cupped her soft buttocks, lifting her up a little, exposing every rosy, gleaming fold. He breathed in her exquisite scent, uniquely *her.*

Her thighs quivered around his neck, tensing. "Ash?" she said, with a catch of uncertainty.

If she had still been connected to him, she would have known his hesitation for what it was—a moment of overwhelming, dumbstruck awe at her magnificence. She was offering him a priceless gift. It was only fitting that he treat it with reverence.

But she couldn't read his soul. He couldn't surround her with his feelings, so that she knew as deeply as he did her perfection and magnificence.

All he could do was show her.

He bent his head, sliding his tongue through her slick folds. He relished her taste, her soft sounds of pleasure, the way she opened and bloomed in response to his touch.

He circled her sensitive bud, sucking, teasing. Even as she cried out in ecstasy, her hips bucked up against him, demanding more. Oh, that was Rose, his Rose, open with her desires, boldly claiming her due. Delighted by her urgency, he slid two fingers into her welcoming depths.

Her thighs clenched hard around his head, as hard as her body around his fingers. The hot pulse of her fulfillment filled him with fierce satisfaction.

She gasped as he crooked his fingers, her inner walls still trembling with shuddering flutters. He would gladly have wrung wave after wave of pleasure from her, but she pulled away.

"I said I'm not patient, Ash." Pushing him off, she sat up, flushed and gleaming with sweat. "Don't make me wait any longer."

He was so hard that it was a struggle to undo his pants. He couldn't bite back a groan as his length sprang free from the confining fabric at last.

Rose drew in a soft, sharp breath. A little tentatively, she reached out. He jerked at the first brush of her fingers, wetness beading his tip. Every shy touch was exquisite agony as she explored him.

He caught her wrist as she started to wrap her fingers around him. "*Rose.*"

She stopped immediately, withdrawing her hand. "Not good?"

Again, that slight catch of uncertainty in her voice. He wished with all his soul that she could feel what he felt, the effect she had on him.

"Too good," he said gently, bending to kiss away the worried crease in her brow. "Rose, my Rose. If only you could see yourself through my eyes."

Her smile dazzled him. "No more waiting?"

"No more waiting," he breathed.

She might not be able to read his soul, but he could read hers. Imperfectly, through the old, blackened scar between them, but he still didn't need words to know her desires.

He stretched out on the bed, lying on his back. Once again, she straddled his hips—but this time, there was nothing between them. He caught her hands, bracing his arms. Supporting her steadily, holding still, despite the inferno raging through his blood.

Slowly, maddeningly, her wet heat enfolded him. She took him with painstaking care, biting her lip in anticipation of pain. He clenched his own teeth, staying silent even though he longed to reassure her that he wouldn't hurt her, couldn't, never would again.

"Oh," she gasped, as she stretched around him. "*Oh.*"

She took all of him easily, so easily. He couldn't hold back any longer as her depths embraced him. He thrust upward, fingers clenching around hers, burying himself in her welcoming warmth.

She cried out his name as he filled her utterly. He thrust again, and again, her body moving to match his, picking up the same driving need.

He pulled her down to him, wanting her closer, skin to skin. He held her tight in his arms, her breasts to his chest, her breath in his mouth. In her and around her, bodies united into one.

It wasn't enough.

Even as her back arched, even as she screamed his name, even as he emptied himself into her, it wasn't enough. They were as close as two people could be, yet she was still agonizingly untouchable. What should have been an open bond between them, bright and strong, lay scorched and black and dead.

He poured into her, longing for her, straining to reach her across that old, charred scar—

Her half-lidded, ecstasy-glazed eyes snapped open. She stared down at him, her lips shaping a single, impossible word.

"Blaze."

CHAPTER 14

PAST

20 years ago...

Blaze lay awake in the dark, watching Rose sleep. Even exhaustion couldn't drain the tension from her body. She huddled against him, one arm thrown over his waist, her face pressed into his side. Every now and then her fingers twitched, clutching at him as though to make sure he was still there.

He stroked her hair, sending gentle reassurance down the mate bond. "It's all right," he whispered. "Sleep, Rose. I'm here. You're safe."

It was a lie. She would never be safe.

Not while she was his mate.

A soft beeping noise made him start. A light on the hotel phone was flashing, next to a label saying *Front Desk*. Rose stirred fretfully, mumbling something.

"Shh," he murmured, tightening his grip on her. "It's nothing. Go back to sleep."

Rose sighed, relaxing again. It took him a second to pull back his own fire to the point where he could pick up the phone without melting the handset. He fumbled with it, getting it the right way round on the second attempt.

"Mr. Blaze?" a voice said apologetically in his ear. "Sorry to disturb you, sir, but I have a call for you."

He rubbed his aching eyes, trying to concentrate through the haze of exhaustion. "A call? For me?"

"Yes, sir. He asked for you by name. Would you like me to put him through?"

He suddenly felt cold, despite Rose's warm body pressed against his. "Yes."

A click.

"This is a demonstration," said a familiar, icy voice.

Rose flinched in her sleep. He held very still, gripping his emotions tight to stop them from spilling down the mate bond.

"Corbin," he said.

"You are at the Hilton at Sacramento Airport," the warlock said, in the same factual, level tone. "Evidently booked in under your own name. You traveled there today at speeds which suggest a car or taxi rather than flight. Is that sufficient to convince you how closely that I can track you, or shall I continue?"

Blaze forced himself to breathe calmly and evenly. "Tell me my mate's name and animal."

The briefest of pauses. "Her identity is irrelevant. I can scry her easily, always, thanks to the bond you have foolishly forged with her. By linking your souls, you have sealed her fate."

The tightness in his chest eased a little. Corbin still didn't know who Rose was. It wasn't much, given that the warlock could still find her by magical means, but at least they didn't need to worry about more mundane methods.

"What do you want, Corbin?" Blaze asked.

"That should be self-evident. Your willing submission."

"Never. You have no leverage. You lost the wendigo, your best weapon against me. You don't even have the element of surprise. You won't have another chance at my mate."

"Still letting your beast think for you," the warlock said. "Really, Blaze. Do you really think you can guard her every minute of every day? I can tell that she is sleeping at this very moment. I will know the instant that *you* surrender to exhaustion—careful, now. You'll wake her, if you don't control yourself."

His fingers dug into the softening, scorching plastic of the phone handset. He clenched his teeth, pushing the fire back down.

"If you harm her," he breathed, "if you *touch* her, I will destroy you. If it takes my entire life, I will obliterate you all."

"Yes," Corbin agreed, not sounding at all concerned. "And your mate would still be dead."

"*You'd* be dead. This is a stand-off. You have just as much to lose."

"Don't tell me what I have left to lose," Corbin snarled, his cultured manner dropping away to reveal the seething hatred beneath. "You have already taken everything from me. I did the impossible, I bound the Phoenix, I was a *god*. You cannot imagine what it is like, to hold such power only to have it ripped away. I want it back. *I will have it back.*"

Corbin fell silent. His breath rasped in Blaze's ear.

"And if I cannot," the warlock added, after a moment, in much more his usual measured, controlled tones, "then I will take everything from *you*. I will teach you what it means to be empty inside, to lose what you hold most dear. You cannot hide from me. You cannot run. No matter how long it takes, I will kill your mate."

Rose struggled out of sleep, pulled by a persistent, nagging feeling of wrongness. She felt cold, despite the blanket carefully tucked round her. The space next to her on the bed was empty.

"Blaze?" she said, jerking upright.

She relaxed a little as his mind brushed against hers, soft and fleeting as a kiss on her forehead. Nonetheless, something felt...off. He wasn't far away, yet his presence in her soul was dim and subdued, like a banked campfire.

"What's wrong?" She sat up, glancing at the bedside clock. It was mid-morning. Golden light filtered through the closed curtains. "What are you doing?"

He didn't pause in gathering up their few possessions. "Packing. I talked to the concierge. There's a flight to London in a few hours. He helped me to book you a ticket on your card."

"What?" Rose flung back the sheets, suddenly wide awake. "But we still haven't worked out how to sneak you onboard the plane!"

He zipped up the suitcase, his back to her. She couldn't see his face. "I'm not coming."

She scrambled out of bed, glad that she'd been too tired to get undressed. She grabbed his arm, trying to pull him round to face her. He resisted, shoulders hunching, not looking at her. His muscles were like iron under her fingers.

"Blaze. *Blaze.*" She didn't have a chance of moving him against his will. She ducked under his arm instead, popping up on the other side so that they were face to face. She lifted her chin, refusing to let him evade her glare. "What's going on?"

For a moment he just looked at her, expressionless, mouth set in a flat, unreadable line. She reached for him down the mate bond, but she might as well have stretched up to try to catch the sun. She could still feel him, still see him, but she couldn't touch him.

Then he let out his breath in a sigh. His arms closed around her, gathering her close. His head dropped to rest on hers.

"Corbin called," he said into her hair. "He knows we're here."

"So?" His heartbeat thrummed through her body, rapid and agitated. She stroked his back, trying to calm him. "We already knew that he could track us."

"He made threats. Against you. Rose, I have to hunt him down." Blaze pulled back, hands on her shoulders, holding her at arm's-length. "As long as he lives, you aren't safe."

"He was trying to scare you, Blaze. It's just another trick to try to split us apart. He can't touch us as long as we stay together."

Blaze shook his head, his mouth twisting in agony. "I can't protect you. Not by staying at your side. Rose, Corbin still doesn't know who you are. If I…if I stop him from tracking you magically, he won't be able to find you."

Rose blinked. "You can do that?"

"I can. I worked out how, while you were sleeping."

Blaze didn't look like a man who'd found a way out of a trap. His expression reminded Rose of the people she'd seen fleeing the raging wildfires—numb, blank-eyed, clutching a few irreplaceable treasures tight in their arms. Abandoning everything, to save what they most loved.

She gripped his arms, hard, fingers digging into his taut muscles. "Blaze, what aren't you telling me?"

His chest jerked with a spasmodic, painful catch. "It…it will hurt you. Terribly. But just for a moment."

She couldn't help flinching away from him. "Not my swan! Don't take my swan!"

"No!" He looked horrified, as though it hadn't even occurred to him that she might think he would burn her animal. "That would change *you*, who you are, your very nature. I could never do that."

"Then what are you proposing to do?"

His eyes squeezed closed for a second, as if in pain. "I can't explain it. There isn't time, the taxi will arrive any minute to take you to the airport…*please*, Rose. This is the only way I can keep you safe. Trust me."

Our mate, her swan whispered in her soul. *He is our mate. We need to be with him.*

But that was an animal's instinct. She pushed her swan aside, forcing herself to consider the situation with human logic.

Blaze was right. The current situation was untenable. He'd been half-mad last night with guilt, and the warlocks had barely managed to touch her. If something worse *did* happen…it would destroy him.

She couldn't be responsible for that. Couldn't consign her mate to a life of paranoia and fear, always looking over his shoulder, always having to be on guard to protect her.

If they were ever to find true happiness, she had to let him go.

Nonetheless, Rose hesitated. "You said it would hurt."

His fingertips traced the side of her face, soft as a feather. "Only for a second." His mouth curved in a strange, wavering smile that didn't reach his eyes. "Then everything will be the way it was before. You won't even remember it happened."

"And afterward…when it's all over, you'll find me again? We'll be together?"

He hesitated. "Rose, Corbin will still be able to track me. If I can't find him, if I can't eliminate the threat, you'll be in danger if I'm with you."

"I don't care," she said fiercely. "Promise me you'll come back to me, no matter what. *Promise me.*"

He leaned his forehead against hers. "I promise," he whispered, very softly.

She took a deep breath, setting her shoulders. She was so scared she was shaking, but this was *Blaze,* her mate. Her life, her heart, her soul.

For his sake, she could bear any pain.

"Okay," she said, her throat dry. "Do it."

Scrunching up her face, she braced herself for—she didn't know what. Fire, flames, sweeping agony.

She wasn't prepared for his mouth to press against hers, fierce and desperate. He kissed her with even more passionate intensity than he had during their mating, as if claiming her anew. All her fear and apprehension melted away in that irresistible heat. She leaned against him, pressing up into his mouth, certainty filling her as bright as the mate bond itself.

No matter what, she was his. He was hers. Forever.

His hands slid down from her face to her shoulders. Gradually, reluctantly, he pushed her away. Even as he stepped back, he bent to keep his lips on hers, lingering as long as possible.

When he finally released her, she wobbled. She had to brace herself on her suitcase to keep standing. Her lips felt hot and flushed, her mind reeled, her whole body tingled…but she didn't feel any different.

He'd *said* she wouldn't remember.

"Is it over?" she asked uncertainly.

Blaze had backed away as far as the door, never turning. He

fumbled for the door handle, never taking his eyes off her. Every muscle in his body was strung tight, as though he was having to fight himself to stay where he was, to not stride back to her. Black flames burned in his eyes.

"I will always love you," he said.

The door closed behind him.

No, no, no! cried her swan. *Go after him, he needs us, he is our mate!*

Rose forced herself to turn away from the door. Scrubbing her hand across her eyes, she made herself look at the paper he'd left on top of the suitcase. A printout of her flight times and itinerary. This time tomorrow, she'd be back in England.

Without him.

"Just for a little while," she said out loud, to the empty room. "It'll just be for a little while. He'll come back. He promised."

And then—

Her scream ripped the remnants of his soul into tattered shreds. Blaze slid down the closed door, fists clenched, biting his lip so hard that blood ran over his chin.

He had to hold back his own howl of agony. He couldn't let her hear him, couldn't let her know he was there.

She *didn't* know he was still there.

She couldn't feel him any more. She never would again.

But he could still feel *her*. The one thing he couldn't burn was his own mind. Despite the smoking, blackened chasm between them, she was still his mate.

He knew the depth of her pain. Could sense her confusion, her terror. Could sense how she sank to the floor, clutching her head, fragments of scorched memories whirling through her mind like burning leaves.

"My mate, my mate, *my mate!*" Rose screamed, and he knew that she didn't even remember his name.

She didn't remember him at all.

It felt like every bone in his body was broken. He made himself stand anyway. Made himself walk away from the terrible sounds of his mate's grief.

Even though she didn't know who he was, she still wept for him.

But not forever. She would mourn the mate she'd never known, but eventually, she would move on. She would find happiness. She would heal.

He never would.

He'd burned the mate bond.

There was nothing left but ash.

CHAPTER 15

She stared down at him, and it was like she could suddenly see through time. She saw him twenty years younger—hair sandy-brown without a hint of gray, face unlined by grief. Still solemn, still controlled, but with his fire burning close to the surface, lighting his features with warmth and power.

She knew that face. Knew his name. Knew who he was.

"You're Blaze," she said, numbly.

His face reflected her own dumbstruck disbelief. For a moment, he just gaped up at her, eyes wide with shock.

Then he whispered, "You remember." His open-mouthed astonishment transmuted into pure, shining joy. *"You remember!"*

He was still holding her, still *inside* her. She leaped off him as if he'd burned her, scrambling backward from the man who was suddenly, terribly, not her Ash.

"No, Rose, wait!" He sat bolt upright, reaching out to her. "I know this must be confusing, but—"

"Don't touch me!"

He stopped at her shriek, hands freezing in mid-air. She scrabbled further away from him, chest heaving, until her back pressed against the wall. Her head was like a shaken snow globe, whirling with fragments of memories.

Memories that she'd forgotten.

"You made me forget you." She clutched her head, trying to make sense of the flashing images. "You burned my memories, you burned my *mind*. You made me forget you!"

"It was the only way." His hands were still outstretched, fingers open toward her, trembling. She'd never seen his face so raw and unguarded. His eyes shone with an emotion too deep to name. "I had to burn every trace of myself from your mind. It was the only way to stop Corbin from being able to find you. It was the only way to keep you safe."

She huddled into a ball, shaking with shock. "I would rather," she said, her voice muffled in her arms, "have died."

"It was the only way to keep you safe," he said again. "Rose, oh, *Rose*. You truly remember me?"

She scrunched her eyes shut against a barrage of impressions—a frost-covered window, a blazing inferno, walls of a building falling away from rising wings. The scent of scorched cloth, the sweet burn of his touch. Cinnamon and cream, a laugh, fire turning snow into steam. His voice in the dark. The heat of his mouth.

Blaze.

Her mate.

"My mate," she said out loud.

"Yes," he breathed. "My mate, my Rose, *yes.*"

Not our mate! Her swan's scream split through the chaos in her mind. Its furious wings beat back the old memories, fighting them, refusing them. *Our mate is gone, our mate* left us, *this is not him! Not our mate!*

Her throat felt sliced open. She couldn't speak, choked by pain. She *remembered,* remembered what he'd been to her. Remembered how bright and fierce he'd burned in her mind, how he'd lit up her entire soul.

Now...her heart was a barren, charred wasteland. And it had been for twenty years. She'd huddled over cold ashes, and thought herself content, because she'd forgotten she'd ever known fire.

She lifted her head, looking at him. The young man she'd loved so passionately, the older one she'd loved no less deeply. She saw them both at once. Blaze reignited in Ash's careworn face, hope burning bright in those eternal eyes.

She jerked her gaze away, unable to bear the sight of him. Sliding off the bed, she snatched up their discarded clothes.

"Get dressed," she snarled, hurling his uniform at him. "And get out."

He caught his garments, but made no move to put them on. "Rose, you remember me. That should be impossible, I was *sure* it was impossible, but my fire touched you just now, and you *remembered—*"

He stopped abruptly, his breath catching. The joy transfiguring his stern features faded, turning into horror.

"Ten years." He scrubbed his hands over his face, hiding his expression. "I wasted ten years."

"Twenty." Rose could barely do up the buttons of her blouse, her fingers were shaking so much with rage. "*Twenty* years, Ash—Blaze—oh, for heaven's sake, what am I supposed to call you now?"

He dropped his hands again, emerging looking gray and weary. "Ash will do. That's how everyone else knows me, after all. And I couldn't have returned to you earlier. I had to hunt down the warlocks, had to make sure none of them were alive to follow me to you. It took me a decade."

More fragments of memory flurried up in her head—cages, despair, an ocelot's spotted fur. She remembered her own righteous fury, how she'd burned to bring the warlocks to justice. Her own raw, young passions washed over her, disconcerting in their intensity. When had she stopped feeling things so deeply?

When he burned our mate bond.

"Well, at least one good thing came of this," she muttered. "I'm glad you destroyed all those evil monsters."

His mouth tightened. His fingers crept up to rub the old scar around his right wrist. "I didn't. I never found Corbin."

She stared at him. "But you came back to me."

"I'd made a promise," he said, very quietly. His shoulders dropped in a long sigh. " I *shouldn't* have come back to you. We never found a trace of him, not in all those years."

"We?"

"I didn't hunt alone." He hesitated. "Do you remember the wendigo?"

A blizzard in July. Icicles and antlers. She flinched. "You teamed up with *that* thing?"

"He...wasn't what he seemed." He shook his head. "In any case, we killed every warlock from the base, tracking them down one by one. Except for Corbin. Ice—the wendigo—was certain he had to be dead. He wanted to give up the hunt. And I...I'd reached a point where I couldn't bear another day without you."

He looked away, down at the clothes still draped across his lap. He absently smoothed a thumb over the fire service crest embroidered on his sleeve. "I didn't mean to stay. I just wanted to know that you were well. That you'd made a life for yourself, like you'd dreamed. So I came to England. I found your pub."

His voice went soft. "And when I walked through the door, you smiled at me, whole-heartedly, as though you'd been waiting for me all that time. Even though you didn't know me."

She remembered the first time she'd seen him—no, not the first time, oh, this was far too confusing—she remembered when she'd first laid eyes on *Ash*. How she'd looked up at the door just before he opened it, though she hadn't sensed anyone approaching. How her stomach had given an odd little flip at the sight of his tall, quiet form, even before she'd seen his face. How her swan had said *not our mate*, the way it always did...but how her heart had said otherwise.

That wasn't a new memory. She'd worn that one smooth, reliving it night after night. Trying to decide if she was just being fanciful, or if she really had felt that strange, bright spark when their eyes met.

Now she knew that she had.

Even now, his broad shoulders and defined arms lit an undeniable heat low in her belly. She tried to look at his hands instead, but that was even worse. She couldn't help remembering how those strong, callused fingers had caressed her inner thigh...

She swiveled on her heel, clearing her throat. "Will you please put some damn pants on?"

To her relief, she heard a rustle of cloth. She pretended an intense interest in smoothing out creases in her skirt, determinedly not looking.

When she risked a peek, Ash was sitting on the edge of the bed, buttoning his shirt. And he *was* Ash now. It was like he'd put on that still, silent persona along with the uniform. She couldn't see Blaze anymore in his shuttered, frozen face.

Somehow, it was even more difficult to talk to him now that he was fully dressed. Sitting next to him on the bed would have been far too intimate, so she leaned awkwardly on her dresser instead. She folded her arms.

"If Corbin was still out there, why did you stay?" It came out aggressive, accusing. She didn't care. "After going through all this to keep me safe, I'm surprised you risked hanging around."

"I shouldn't have." Ash didn't look at her, still concentrating—or, she suspected, pretending to concentrate—on doing up his cuffs. "But I found I couldn't leave. Not again. I told myself that I wasn't endangering you, not as long as I was careful not to get too close to you. None of the warlocks knew your name or appearance, after all. I tried to keep my distance from you so that even if I was being watched, the warlocks would have no reason to suspect anything."

That's why he'd kept his distance from *everyone*, Rose realized. Why he'd maintained a level of reserve even from Alpha Team. If he showed that he cared for anyone, the warlocks could have used them as a hostage.

"Do you think you *are* being watched?" she asked.

He shook his head. "No. Otherwise I wouldn't have..." He made a vague gesture, indicating both himself and her. Then he let out a short, ironic laugh, rubbing his forehead. "And quite likely would have gone another twenty years certain that I'd destroyed our bond past repair. I truly am an idiot."

"We agree on one thing, at least," Rose muttered.

"Rose." He dropped his hands again, fists clenching. He looked at her at last, eyes burning with intensity. "What I did was unforgivable. I know that. But if there's a chance, no matter how small, that it can be undone—"

His cellphone went off.

Rose had never heard Ash swear before. Even Chase would have been impressed by the way he blistered the air now. His hand automatically flew to his cellphone, but he checked himself before drawing it out of its holster.

"No, go ahead," Rose said as he hesitated. She sighed. "I know that's your work ringtone."

He snarled out a last bitter profanity, but answered the call. "Fire Commander Ash."

The words *This had better been an emergency* hung unspoken in the air. From the way Ash's face went utterly expressionless, it was.

"Understood," he bit off curtly. "On my way."

"I take it something's burning," Rose said as he slid his phone back into his belt.

He nodded, standing up. "Apartment block. It's giving even Alpha Team trouble." He hesitated. "Rose—"

"Of course you have to go," she interrupted him. She grimaced, pinching the bridge of her nose. She still had a literal headache from the new memories jostling for her attention. "And to be honest, I really need some space from you right now. You've had twenty years to come to terms with this. I haven't."

He let out his breath as if he'd been punched in the gut. Before she knew what was happening, she found herself pressed back against the wall by his hard, scorching body. His hand cupped the side of her face —infinitely gently, but with a leashed strength that took her breath away.

"I will never walk away from you again," he whispered, lips brushing against hers. "*Never.*"

Then he was gone.

Our mate is gone. Her swan keened in grief. *Not our mate, not anymore. Our mate is gone.*

The room seemed suddenly cold and barren. She couldn't bear to even look at the rumpled bed, let alone make it.

She fled to her living room, but that was just as bad. The two chairs opposite each other, the two empty glasses on the table, even the pictures on the walls...everywhere she turned, she was reminded of him.

Memories glittered in her mind, sharp and jagged, threatening.

"Tea," she said out loud, to fight back the rising whispers. "That's what I need. A nice cup of tea."

That was what you did when the world was falling apart around you. You made tea.

The first step down the darkened staircase nearly undid her—she stumbled, suddenly seeing another staircase, a descent into the unknown. She caught herself on the banister, clenching her fingers around smooth, worn wood.

Not cold metal. She wasn't back there. Wasn't searching through that terrible prison, feeling the pull of the mate bond with every beat of her heart...

"Tea," she said again, her voice thin and panicky in the dark.

Her swan wrapped comforting wings around her. Holding onto her animal like a child clutching a teddy bear, Rose staggered to the kitchen.

Mug, kettle, teapot. The familiar ritual was soothing. This was something she could do without thought.

She couldn't think. Didn't want to.

She wrapped her hands around the hot mug—

His heated palm pressing against her own, fingers intertwining—

—and dropped it.

China smashed on the tiled floor. Scalding liquid splashed, only just missing her bare feet.

Her swan hissed at the crowding memories, driving them back. Rose drew in a deep, shuddering breath. Then she knelt to pick up the shattered pieces.

She was just wiping up the last of the spill when she heard the front door creak open. Her heart lurched—but then she caught a swirl of jumbled emotions from whoever had entered the pub. It couldn't be Ash. She'd never been able to sense him.

Except, of course, she *had*. Twenty years ago, he'd been the *only* person she could sense. He'd changed that, changed everything. She'd gained her strange empathic power at the exact moment he'd scorched her soul. Ever since she'd lost the mate bond, her flailing mind had been desperately trying to connect with someone, anyone, everyone...

She shuddered away from the realization. She could have reached out with her empathic sense to identify her visitor, but she abruptly never wanted to use her twisted ability ever again. Hastily scrubbing her hands across her face to dash away the betraying tears, she rose.

"I'm sorry," she began as she went into the main room of her pub. "But I'm closed tonight—Wayne?"

She wasn't entirely sure for a second it *was* him. His back was curled in a painful-looking hunch, his stiff hands nearly at the same level as his knees. His shabby hat hid his eyes, but couldn't conceal the distorted line of his jaw. Jagged, protruding teeth forced his mouth into a permanent, half-open snarl. Drool trickled down his matted, graying beard.

"Wayne, what's happened?" Rose hurried round the bar, reaching out to him as he swayed. "Sit down. You need a doctor, a shifter doctor, right now. I'll call Hugh."

"No!" It came out as more like a bark than a human voice. "Rose...I'm sorry."

He raised his head, and Rose gasped, recoiling. Wolf eyes shone yellow in his half-shifted face, filled with shame and agony.

"Run," Wayne gritted out, his fangs cutting his lips. "*Run!*"

Too late, she saw his bared right arm...and the intricate tattoo twining around it.

Bristling black runes, edged with crimson where they cut into his skin...

She knew those marks. *Now* she knew them.

She tried to turn, to flee, but her feet were stuck to the floor. Scarlet ropes of light twisted around her ankles, holding her fast. Wayne moaned in pain as the glowing coils rapidly spread to bind her whole body.

Her swan beat inside her heart, but the magical cage held her trapped in her own skin. She couldn't shift, couldn't move so much as a muscle.

The front door of her pub creaked again.

A man stepped through. He was tall and lean and old, with thin white hair brushed back from a high forehead. Behind his scholarly spectacles, his gray eyes were cold as a winter sky. Blood-red light wove around his left hand, the runes running up his arm glowing with power.

She'd never seen him before...but she knew who he was.

"The Phoenix's mate," Corbin said. "We meet at last."

CHAPTER 16

"Report," Ash snapped, the moment his boots touched the ground.

"It's a bloody mess," Hugh said succinctly, not glancing up from his patient.

Ash cast a practiced eye over the scene. The entire ground floor of the low-rise apartment block was aflame, thick black smoke pouring out of heat-shattered windows. A fire of this magnitude turned out the whole department—three full crews were already battling the spreading blaze. Behind Hugh, several other paramedics were frantically triaging a dozen shaking, shocked victims.

Fortunately, all the non-shifters present were far too preoccupied to have noticed his abrupt arrival. The current officer in charge—a solid, capable, and completely human firefighter—had his back turned, busy barking orders into a radio. Ash knew that he could be trusted to coordinate the mundane efforts to douse the flames.

But the officer didn't know about the *other* efforts.

Ash reached out with his mind. **Report,** he said again, but this time not out loud.

The storm-swift swirl of Chase's mind touched his. **Griff and I have cleared the upper floors. We've been flying people out.**

"Which is why I've got six casualties down here having screaming meltdowns because they were swooped through the air by invisible monsters," Hugh muttered under his breath, clearly eavesdropping on the telepathic conversation. "We're going to have a lot of clean-up later."

Ash repressed a grimace. He always hated having to wipe the memories of ordinary people who'd witnessed Alpha Team at work. **Chase, is the building clear?**

No. Chase's tone was uncharacteristically grim. **I can sense two people trapped on the second floor. They're completely surrounded by fire, we can't get to them even with protective gear.**

Ash broadened the psychic channel. **Daifydd?**

"Here." Dai's soft Welsh voice came, unexpectedly, from next to one of the ambulances. He waved off the paramedic who'd been working on him, coming over. Soot streaked his face. One side of his uniform jacket was in blackened tatters.

"I already tried to reach them." Dai indicated the nasty burn showing through the scorched hole in his turnout gear. "You can see how well that went."

Long habit kept Ash from showing any alarm. But now he knew why he'd been summoned so urgently. As a red dragon shifter, Dai was immune to any normal fire. For flames to be able to scorch even him...

"Are we dealing with a rogue dragon here?" he murmured, pitching his voice low in case any of the nearby victims were more alert than they seemed.

Dai shook his head, mouth set in a worried line. "It's too intense even for dragonfire. Could be hellhounds, I suppose, but...something about this doesn't feel right, Commander. It's not behaving like any fire I've ever seen. And John can't call down the rain."

Ash picked out John's towering form, backlit by the fierce orange glow. The sea dragon appeared to be busy laying hose for the front line firefighters, but Ash knew that his real focus was on an entirely different task. He was too far away to be able to make out the words John was singing, but he could tell from the tense line of his shoulders

—not to mention the fact that the sky was still clear overhead—that the sea dragon's magic was not going well.

Ash decided not to break John's concentration for now. The first priority had to be to rescue the trapped victims. After that they could worry about containing and eliminating the blaze.

"I will clear the way," he told Dai. "Are you fit to carry the victims out?"

Dai's jaw tightened with pain as he flexed his burned arm, but he nodded. "Ready when you are."

Ash released his control.

The Phoenix burst from his soul, brighter than the inferno. Hugh shielded his eyes with a muttered curse, though none of the nearby humans reacted. Mythic shifters could always see each other, but in this form he was invisible to mundane eyes unless he willed it.

He preferred to be discreet when he had to use his powers. It wasn't exactly desirable for the regular firefighters to see their Commander stroll unprotected into a burning building, after all. He had a hard enough time enforcing safety regulations as it was.

He swooped through the air, passing unseen over the heads of the firefighters still struggling to control the flames. They glanced up uneasily, feeling his heat even through their safety gear. Dai pushed past them, taking advantage of the distraction to enter the building unnoticed. The dragon shifter disappeared into the billowing smoke.

The fire whispered to him like a lover. He knew better than to try to resist.

Instead, he spread his wings wide, embracing it.

A team of firefighters scattered, falling back, as the fire leaped up anew. His own burning feathers flared too, echoing the triumphant flames. The inferno's fierce hunger was just a pale echo of his own. To transfigure dull matter into light, to blaze bright in the darkness, to *burn*...

Ash focused his will—but not on the fire.

He didn't control fire. He never had. All he could control was himself.

That was what no one had ever understood, not even Corbin. He was the Phoenix, and the Phoenix was the flame eternal, and so he *was* the fire.

He forced down his own raging desires, and the inferno grudgingly died down as well. He calmed himself, and the flames calmed too, allowing Dai to sprint through them.

It was harder than normal to hold onto his control. At first he thought it was just due to his unsettled mind…but it wasn't just the intoxicating memory of Rose's body against his that was making it difficult to maintain his discipline.

Dai was right. This fire *was* strange. It fought him, hissing in malice. It sent out sparks into his soul, trying to rekindle his own destructive instincts. It was as if it had a will of its own.

Or as if someone else's will was driving it.

Someone else's will *was* driving it. A will that he recognized.

How could he not, when it had bound his own for so long?

Hurry, he sent to Dai, battling the rage and terror rising in his heart. *This isn't a fire. It's a distraction.*

CHAPTER 17

Rose couldn't so much as twitch a muscle as Corbin walked round her. The warlock's lips pursed as though she was a particularly perplexing piece of modern art.

"Not quite what I was expecting," Corbin said. Rose's skin crawled as his left hand closed around her right wrist. "But you will serve my purpose."

The warlock glanced across at Wayne. "You, on the other hand, are no longer useful."

The tattooed runes on the wolf shifter's arm flared red hot. Wayne's half-transformed maw gaped wide in a howl of agony—but only briefly.

Held motionless by Corbin's magic, Rose couldn't even close her eyes. All she could do was watch, helpless, as Wayne collapsed in on himself, shriveling as though all his vital fluids were being sucked dry. Within seconds, he was nothing but a handful of ashen dust.

Corbin drew in a sharp breath as Wayne's empty clothes crumpled to the ground. He closed his eyes for a moment, like a smoker savoring the last drag of a cigarette.

Then his thin mouth twisted with dissatisfaction. "How quickly it fades."

The runes on his left arm were indeed dimming, turning back into mere inked lines on his skin. The glowing ropes holding her were fading away too. She could move her fingers, her toes. She tensed, straining against the slackening restraints—

But before she could break free, Corbin's hand tightened around her wrist. "Let us see what *you* contain, Phoenix's mate."

A searing pain wrapped around her arm, but it was nothing compared to the agony that ripped through her soul. It felt as if the warlock had cracked open her chest, plunging his hand into her heart. Her swan shrieked in terror as the warlock's will closed around it like a fist.

Corbin's eyebrows rose. He looked at her as though only truly seeing her for the first time. "So strong. Interesting. Though perhaps I should not be surprised."

He opened his hand again, releasing her arm—but not his grasp on her mind. Wrong, *wrong*, to have someone else touching her animal, touching her *soul*. This wasn't the mate bond, a willing sharing of strength. This was someone reaching in and *taking*, greedily latching onto her swan like some vile parasite.

Corbin held up his left hand, flexing his fingers experimentally. Rose gasped as a thousand needles bit into her right arm. Her swan thrashed in panic, only cutting itself further on the sharp-edged runes binding it. Every beat of her heart felt like it was pumping her blood into someone else's body.

"*Very* interesting," Corbin murmured, studying the smoky, pitch-black darkness winding around his fingers.

Rose fell to her knees, gripping her burning wrist. The runes were barely visible against her deep black skin, but she could feel every sharp edge pressing into her flesh. Her swan keened, trembling.

"I advise you not to fight," Corbin said in a disinterested tone, as though it made no difference to him whether she did or not. "You will only hurt yourself. I am the only man ever to bind the Phoenix, after all. Holding *you* is child's play in comparison."

Rose licked her dry lips, struggling to form words. It was hard to think with her swan's distress shaking the foundations of her mind.

"You've made a mistake," she croaked out. "I'm not his mate."

"Indeed not." Corbin leaned against the bar, considering her thoughtfully. "Not a flicker of fire within you. He truly did destroy your bond. Well. I suppose any animal will chew its own leg off to escape a trap."

"That's right." Rose drew on all her pent-up feelings of betrayal and anger, praying that they would give strength to the lie. "There's nothing between us. You're wasting your time. He won't come for me."

Corbin's mouth curved in the thinnest of smiles. He turned away from her, facing the door.

"He will," he said. "He has."

Rose had seen Ash in his shifted form before. She'd seen him freed, soaring across a summer-blue sky. She'd seen him unbound, rising in fury from the prison that had held him.

But she'd never before seen the Phoenix truly unleashed.

The old oak door exploded as if hit by a meteor. The entire front wall of the pub simply vanished, stone vaporized instantly by unimaginable heat.

He came like a falling sun, like the wrath of heaven, like the end of the world. Even shadows burned away to nothing before him. He filled the room with white-hot fury, his wings curving round to trap Corbin in a circle of flame. The great beak opened, blasting the warlock with a wordless, blistering shriek of rage.

The warlock tipped his head back, facing the Phoenix without flinching. The edges of his robes smoldered. "We will speak when you can do so as a man rather than a beast, Blaze."

Fire swirled, condensing down into human shape. Ash stood there, backlit by the inferno. The flames were so bright that he was just a dark silhouette, face hidden.

"Release my mate," he said.

"No," Corbin replied, quite calmly.

Rose tried to move, to call out, but the runes bit into her arm. Corbin didn't so much as glance at her, but her jaw locked tight, bound by the warlock's will. All she could do was watch.

Fire spread behind Ash like wings unfurling. "Release my mate *now.*"

"Or what, Blaze? You'll burn me?" Corbin shook his head. "If I die, she dies with me."

"Not if I free her first."

"Go ahead." The warlock stepped to one side, sweeping his hand in Rose's direction in invitation. "There she is. I can't stop you. Burn her animal."

No! Rose screamed silently, as Ash's head turned in her direction. *No, kill him, kill us both. Take my life, but don't take who I am.*

Ash stood there, motionless. Corbin laughed.

"I knew you would not be able to do it," the warlock said, with an ugly, gloating smile. "There is only one option left, Blaze. Even I can only bind one shifter at a time. So who will it be? Her, or you?"

The flames died, all at once. In the sudden darkness, she heard Ash speak.

"Me."

No, no, no! Rose cried out in her mind—and then, as the bindings around her swan loosened and fell away: "NO!"

Too late. The runes wrapping her right arm shimmered and faded as the warlock released her. The sudden lack of pain such an intense relief that every muscle in her body went limp. For a moment all she could do was gasp for breath, as though she'd been drowning.

"Yes, yes!" Fire flared again—not Ash's pure white flame, but demonic hellfire. It twined around Corbin's upraised hand, illuminating his face with a baleful orange glow.

The warlock flung his head back, expression transfigured in bliss. "My power, mine again at last, *yes!*"

Rose tried to push herself back up, to fling herself at the warlock while he was still distracted, but her limbs were still shaky with shock. She had to clutch at the bar just to stay on her feet. She groped for something to throw at the warlock. A pint glass, a bottle, *anything*.

Soft laughter froze her hand.

It didn't come from Corbin.

Runes wound around Ash's forearm, on top of the old scar. He'd fallen to his knees at the warlock's feet, hands braced in the rubble, head hanging. Blood slicked his wrist, spreading across the blackened floor.

Yet still he laughed.

Corbin's arms dropped from his exultant pose. He frowned down at Ash, brow creasing in suspicion. "What?"

Slowly, as if fighting against a great weight, Ash raised his head. "You've made a mistake."

Corbin crooked his fingers, and Ash jerked as though struck across the shoulders with a barbed lash. "You cannot fight my will. You are mine again."

"Yes." Ash's teeth bared in a triumphant, agonized smile. "But *they* aren't."

Red scales filled the hole in the wall. Rose instinctively ducked, shielding her head, as an enormous horned head shoved through the charred stones. Emerald, cat-slit eyes narrowed as they focused on Corbin.

"Now, Dai!" Ash shouted.

"*No!*" Rose screamed, as the red dragon drew in its breath.

Panic gave her strength. She ran forward, flinging herself in front of the opening jaws.

The dragon's eyes widened. Its mouth snapped shut, smoke gouting from flared nostrils as it choked back its flame.

"Rose, *move*!" Ash shouted. "Get out of the way!"

Rose held firm, not letting the red dragon get a clean line of sight on the warlock. With a growl, Dai drew back. A glimmering white shape leaped through the gap instead, pushing past Rose. The unicorn leveled its horn at Corbin, the gleaming length bright as lightning.

"No, Hugh!" Rose flung her arms around the unicorn's neck, grabbing hold of its sweeping mane. "If you kill him, Ash dies as well!"

The unicorn's head jerked up. It stared at Ash, ears flattening. One silver hoof stamped the ground in indecision.

"Just *kill him!*" Ash's voice cracked in desperation.

"Rose." John's deep voice shook her bones. His huge hands closed over her arms, lifting her away as easily as if she was a child. "You must go."

"No, no, no!" Rose tried to scramble back the moment he released her, but a gleaming black wing barred her way. *"Chase!"*

The pegasus snorted, nudging her toward the hole in the wall. Then it swung round, flanking John. A great golden griffin guarded the sea dragon's other side, lithe and powerful. The red dragon's horned head loomed above them all, lips drawn back from razor-sharp fangs. The mythic shifters fanned out, trapping Corbin.

"We will give you one chance, honorless worm." Even though John was still in human form, he looked no less dangerous than his shifted comrades. "Release our Commander, or you will live long enough to beg for a clean death."

"Alpha Team," the warlock murmured, as though John hadn't spoken. His gray eyes swept over the threatening shifters, pausing on each one in turn. "Dragon. Pegasus. Griffin. Sea dragon. Unicorn. You brought them all."

Corbin raised both hands. Ash's breath hissed between his teeth as the warlock's runes lit up.

"Don't be foolish, Corbin." Ash's left hand was clenched on his right wrist. Blood ran over his fingers in a steady stream. "Even with my power, you cannot hope to defeat them all, not together. Not with me fighting your control with all my will."

"Correct," the warlock said, light gathering in his palms. He spread his fingers, each one outlined with eye-searing fire. "I could not."

He slashed his hands down.

Ten glowing rents opened in the air.

"You didn't come alone," Corbin said, smiling, as dark-robed figures surged through the portals. "Neither did I."

CHAPTER 18

He awoke shivering. It had been so many decades since he had last been cold, for a moment he thought the ground was shaking. But no—*he* was shaking, his bones like shards of ice. Only the barest embers of eternal flame glimmered in the darkness of his soul.

"You are awake," said a familiar, hated voice. "Good. I feared that I had tested the limits of even the Phoenix."

With great effort, Ash managed to raise his head an inch off the concrete floor. Iron bars crisscrossed his field of view.

Corbin sat at ease just outside the cage, foot crossed over one knee, a glass of ice water in his hand. The warlock had swapped his customary heavy black robes for ones made of silk, loose and flowing. Despite his light garments, a faint sheen of perspiration beaded his lined brow.

It's hot, Ash realized. The cage was set in a garden courtyard, the walls obscured by overgrown vines. A fierce tropical sun blazed high overhead in a perfect azure sky. Dimly, he was aware of its heat beating down on the back of his neck, but it didn't touch the cold filling him.

Corbin had never drained him so far before. He felt weak and shaky, as if waking up from a fever. Everything after Corbin had used his power to summon the other warlocks was a confused blur. All he could remember was fire, screaming, black wings cutting through rising smoke…

"Where?" he rasped.

"It seemed appropriate to celebrate our reunion by taking a once-in-a-lifetime vacation." Corbin sipped his drink. "I am impressed, Blaze. Transporting so many people halfway around the world would have killed any lesser shifter outright. And yet you have recovered even faster than I calculated."

"No." Painfully, Ash pushed himself to his feet. He had to grip the iron bars to remain standing. "Where is she?"

"Ah, yes." The warlock smiled thinly. "You burned your mate bond. You cannot sense her, can you?"

Corbin was wrong. Even though Ash had scorched Rose's side of the connection to charred ashes, there was no power on earth—not even his own—that could destroy his love for her. She would always be his mate.

Ash concentrated, turning inward. In his weakened state, the mate bond was dim as a distant candle, but she was *there*. She burned resolutely in his heart, a single point of defiant light.

He sagged against the bars in relief. "I can sense enough to know that she is safe. You don't have her."

The faintest flicker of annoyance flashed across Corbin's face. The warlock quickly stifled it, but Ash knew that Corbin had hoped to use false threats against Rose to keep him obedient.

"The swan is irrelevant," Corbin said, rising. The cage door opened at his touch. "Let me show you what I *do* have."

Ash clenched his jaw as the binding bit into him. He allowed it to pull him after the warlock. No point in wasting his limited strength fighting it now. He had to be patient, and wait for his moment.

The courtyard was bigger than Ash had been able to see from within the cage. It was overgrown with creepers and weeds, but it looked like it had been some kind of private menagerie at some point. The high stone walls were lined with cages and enclosures; some large enough for a bear or big cat, most designed to hold smaller creatures.

Corbin led the way down the row. A black-robed warlock sat cross-legged on the ground outside large cage a little way off, hunched over a laptop. Every now and then he let out a delighted giggle.

"Progress?" Corbin asked the man.

The warlock lifted his head. His eyes gleamed pure gold, without white or pupil.

"I can see *everything*," he said dreamily. "Patterns in the data. Connections I never imagined. It's so obvious now. Give me a week with this power, and I will see the very fabric of the universe."

His words washed over Ash. His attention was fixed beyond the warlock, on the dark interior of the cage.

"Griff," he breathed.

The griffin lay sprawled on the floor, wings splayed like broken fans. Many of the long golden feathers were charred and blackened. His eyes were closed, but his beak gaped open, his furred sides heaving for breath. His talons clenched spasmodically, raking grooves into the concrete.

Ash tried to contact him telepathically, but ran into the thorns of the binding. He couldn't reach beyond his own mind. All he could do was clench his fists futilely on the bars imprisoning his friend.

"Yes, yes, very nice," Corbin was saying to the other warlock with a touch of impatience. "Anything *useful*?"

The warlock shrugged. "Oh, I've already worked out how to increase the potency of our binding spells tenfold. Child's play." His golden gaze drifted back to his laptop screen again. "It's all so *obvious*. Why did I never see it before?"

"You didn't have the right source of power," Corbin said. His lips thinned as he glanced at the unconscious griffin. "Ensure that you ration yourself, and give your familiar time to recover. It is a unique resource, not to be spent too quickly."

"Yes, High Magus," the warlock said vaguely, lost once more in his research. "I just need to see a little more..."

Corbin let out an irritated sigh, but didn't reprimand the man further. He went on, and the binding forced Ash to fall into step behind him.

He already knew what they would find in the other cages.

John would have filled the entire courtyard in his native sea dragon form. Even in his human shape, he couldn't stand straight in his cage. But that didn't stop his frantic, maddened pacing, back and forth, hunched nearly double in the tiny enclosure. From the bruises striping his face and bare arms, Ash guessed that John must have thrown himself at the iron bars until forbidden to do so by his warlock.

The sea dragon's indigo eyes met his, half-feral and agonized. John sang something in his own language, three chords of pure misery.

Ash's heart constricted. John had already lost human speech. The sea dragon had been born to the freedom of the entire ocean, his soul more dragon than man. To be cruelly bound to an alien will, constrained and tied down…he would go mad even faster than a land shifter.

"Hold on, John," Ash whispered as Corbin dragged him past. "Hold on."

Dai was in the next cage, also in human form. He seemed to be holding out better than John, though he sat huddled with his arms around his knees, muscles knotted. At the sight of Ash, he scrambled to his feet, hastening to the front of his cage. The black runes of his binding stood out stark on his forearm.

"Commander." Dai's eyes were cat-slit and emerald, blazing with dragonfire. "Are you all right?"

Ash reached out to him, but they both jerked back, simultaneously dragged away from each other by their respective bindings. Dai hissed in pain, red scales rippling down the sides of his neck.

"No shifting, beast," ordered a nearby warlock, without looking round. Bright orange flames wove around his upraised hands, gathering into a flaming sphere. Without warning, he hurled the fireball—not at Dai, but at another warlock across the courtyard.

A wall of water sprang up. The fireball hissed harmlessly into steam. The second warlock laughed as the wave splashed back to the ground.

"That all you got?" he taunted his colleague. "I told you a sea dragon would be more powerful. But noooo, you had to have the fire dragon."

The first warlock dropped his hands, looking disgruntled. "My familiar's still fighting me. Yours is just more docile. Once I've got mine properly tamed, *then* we'll see who's more powerful."

A little way off, a dark-haired woman lounging against another cage rolled her eyes. "*Boys*."

The water warlock caught sight of Corbin, and his smirk vanished. "High Magus!"

"Having fun?" Corbin asked acidly.

The first warlock whipped around. He straightened to attention, going pale. "Just, ah, practicing, High Magus. Like you told us to."

"I ordered you to learn the capabilities of your familiars," Corbin said in icy tones. "Not to attempt to vaporize each other. I am aware that the power is intoxicating, but if you cannot comport yourselves with dignity, there are plenty of acolytes eager to take your places. No matter how strong your familiars, I am quite capable of stripping them from you. Do not think to test *my* power. Understand?"

Both warlocks hung their heads. "Yes, High Magus," they mumbled in unison.

Corbin fixed them with his stare for a moment more before turning to the dark-haired woman. "I trust you have been using your time more productively, Magus Serena?"

The witch smiled. Shaking back the sleeve of her robe, she held up her left hand. Her runes lit up with a starlight glimmer. Pursing her lips, she whistled a short, liquid trill.

An emerald hummingbird darted out of the overgrown creepers, its tiny body flashing jewel-bright in the sunshine. It flew in an unnaturally straight path straight to the witch's hand, as though reeled in by an invisible fishing line. Its pinprick claws clutched her fingertip.

The woman stroked the trembling ruby throat. "Pretty thing," she said fondly. "So intricate. So delicate."

Pursing her lips again, she blew out a soft puff of breath, ruffling the brilliant feathers.

The hummingbird went rigid. It tumbled off her hand, instantly dead.

"So easy to break," the witch said. The ground around her feet was littered with limp little bodies. She laughed, casting a scornful eye over at the two male warlocks. "And you fools thought this familiar's power could only be used to *heal*."

"Very good," Corbin said, as the two warlocks glared daggers at the witch. "Though I remind you that I need you to be able to drop beasts *without* killing them."

"I will keep practicing, High Magus." The witch glanced into the cage behind her. "But this one has a strong will. It is difficult to maintain a light touch on the spell while also forcing enough power out of him."

Behind her, inside the cage, the unicorn's head hung low. Its white flanks trembled, lathered with sweat. Blood crusted the black runes winding around its right foreleg. Nonetheless, its ears were flat back against its skull, sapphire eyes blazing with hatred.

"You have a few days to break him," Corbin told the witch. "We cannot risk delaying longer."

"I understand, High Magus." Turning back to the captive unicorn, the witch reached through the bars. The unicorn twitched, but was forced to hold still as she caressed its quivering neck.

"Pretty thing," the witch crooned. "Perhaps I'll braid your mane."

"Ash!"

He jerked at the sound of his name, managing to turn before Corbin's will could tighten on him. Across the courtyard, Chase pressed against the bars of his cage, spitting out a chewed wad of fabric. The pegasus shifter's mouth was bloodied and bruised. The torn remnants of a makeshift gag fluttered around his neck.

"Ash, I know where we are!" Chase yelled frantically. "It's—"

Chase choked mid-sentence, as though a noose had tightened around his neck. He dropped to the ground, thrashing.

Corbin looked at the sky in utter exasperation. "How is that creature *still talking*?"

"Sorry, High Magus!" Another warlock ran up, out of breath. "I swear—I only left—for a second!"

"For Merlin's sake, Barry, how hard can it be to lay a simple mute spell?" the witch said in irritation.

"He keeps breaking my command!" Black lightning sparked between the warlock's fingers as he fought to control the struggling Chase. "And that's the third gag he's bitten through. *You* try shutting him up!"

The witch tilted her head. "Well, I could fuse his vocal cords. Or permanently paralyze his tongue…"

"Not until you have better control of your own familiar," Corbin said. "And Adept, *you* must master the pegasus shifter. His powers are essential to ensure our success."

"Yes, High Magus." The warlock made a final throttling gesture, and Chase collapsed into unconsciousness. "I can do it. I just need a little more time."

"Time is our most limited resource." Corbin swept them all with his flinty gaze. "Even with my spells of concealment, our presence here will not go unnoticed for long. It is essential that you master your beasts. By any means necessary."

His underlings bowed or nodded or muttered acknowledgement. The group split up, each warlock going back to his or her own familiar.

"Come," Corbin said, without looking round at Ash. The binding tightened around his soul, leashing him to the warlock's will. "We have work to do."

CHAPTER 19

"What's happened?" Hayley strode into the council chamber with a sleepy toddler on each hip and an expression that could have killed a man at twenty paces. The two towering sea dragon knights escorting her looked positively cuddly in comparison. "Rose, what's going on?"

"Give her some space," Connie said, without looking up from sponging Rose's arms. "Ivy, can you pass me that ointment?"

The wyvern shifter shook her head, her hands tucked under her armpits. She was being careful to stay well back from everyone else in the crowded room, especially the children. "I can't, I'm not in control of my venom. Not with Hugh—" She broke off, biting her lip.

"Here." Virginia plucked the tube from the first aid kit, tossing it to Connie. "Do you need bandages too?"

Rose hissed as Connie started dabbing the antiseptic cream on her burns. "Not that bad," she croaked. "Don't fuss. No time."

She had to stop to cough. Her throat still felt full of smoke. She'd had to fly through the burning roof of her pub in order to escape. Even in the confusion of the fight, she'd barely managed to evade capture. There had been so *many* of them.

She took a deep breath, trying to stop her shaking. She'd flown straight to Neridia and John's private seaside villa. It was the most secure place in the city—quite possibly in the entirety of England—thanks to the dozens of sea dragon knights who made up the Pearl Empress's honor guard. Even now, she could hear the muffled sounds of clanking armor and shouted calls from the warriors securing the perimeter. Everyone would be safe here.

But the warlocks had taken down *Alpha Team…*

"Daddy!" Hayley's son Danny shot out from behind his mother, making a bee-line for Reiner. The boy leaped into the lion shifter's arms, burying his face in his chest. "I can't feel Da in my head anymore, he's not there, he went away!"

"I can't feel Alpha either, my son," Reiner said, rubbing Danny's back. He exchanged a worried glance with his sea dragon mate Jane. "Something's interfering with the pride bond. But he didn't go away. Someone took him."

Hayley looked like she would have thrown up her hands, if they hadn't been filled with her clinging children. "How does anyone kidnap a fully-grown griffin? Or, or a dragon, or the *Phoenix*, for crying out loud! Rose, your message didn't make any sense."

No matter how much Rose tried to get a grip on herself, she couldn't stop trembling. She felt cold, bone-deep cold, like her heart had frozen solid.

"Someone should find some beds for the little ones," she managed to get out. "It's very late."

"Rose," Hayley started, but stopped as Virginia put a hand on her shoulder.

"Little pitchers have big ears," she murmured, with a significant glance down at her own daughter Morwenna. The three-year-old was staying close to her mother, but her wide emerald eyes were skipping from face to face, clearly trying to interpret the adults' expressions.

"We'll take them," Reiner said, catching his mate's eye. Letting Danny slide down to the floor, he took the twins from Hayley. "Rory, Ross, we're going to have a sleepover! Won't that be fun?"

From the way the twins' faces crumpled, they weren't entirely convinced.

"I'll shift and we can all wrestle," Reiner hastily added, turning the incipient wails into happy giggles. "Come on, Danny, you too."

Danny hung back, his brown eyes fixing on Rose. "Is my Da in danger?"

"Da goes into danger every day," Hayley said firmly, before Rose could find words. "But he always, *always* comes back to us. You know that."

Danny nodded, his mouth firming. "Then I'll be alpha for the little ones until he gets back. Come on, Wenna. I'll protect you."

"I *dragon*," Morwenna said indignantly. She drew herself up to her full height, which put her about on level with Danny's elbow. "Protect *you*."

Jane smiled, coming forward gracefully. "Well, I'm a dragon too, but not a big, fierce, fire-breathing one. Perhaps you would come and help guard my hoard?"

"Go with your Auntie Jane," Virginia murmured, sending Morwenna off with a pat on her backside. With a last defiant glance at Danny, the little girl took the turquoise-haired sea dragon's hand.

Neridia motioned the ever-present guards to close the doors again after the children had left. "Now we may speak plainly. Rose, what has happened?"

Rose had finally managed to stop her teeth from chattering, though she still shook with cold. She looked around at them all. "You can all still feel your mates?"

"I can sense John," Neridia confirmed. "But I can't *reach* him."

"Dai's further away than I've ever known," Virginia said. "I can't tell where he is, but I can feel that he's furious."

"So's Hugh," Ivy said. She swallowed hard. "And he's hurt."

"I think Chase is as well," Connie said, her face pale beneath her flaming red hair. "He's barely there. I think he's unconscious."

"Griff is knocked out too," Hayley said. "And he's..." She took a deep breath, as though needing to steel her nerves to get the words out. "It feels like something's pulling him apart. As if his lion and eagle have separated and are fighting again."

"It's not that," Rose said, and Hayley's shoulders slumped with relief. "But he *is* being pulled apart. They all are. We have to get them back, quickly, now. Or they'll lose their minds, their very souls. We have to get them back!"

She realized that her voice had risen shrilly on the last sentence. Her heart thudded against her ribs like a bird battering against a cage.

They could all sense *their* mates. But she couldn't sense Ash. Had no idea if he was all right, or in agony, or already dead...

"Rose, dear heart," Neridia said, crouching down. Even kneeling on the floor, the sea dragon Empress was still taller than Rose sitting down. "We *will* get them back. I have every warrior in the sea poised to move at my command. But you need to tell us exactly what's happened."

Rose ground the heels of her hands against her eyes. Her memories were a shattered mosaic, sharp-edged new shards pushing everything she'd known into foreign shapes. How could she begin to explain, when she barely grasped it herself?

But she had to. Ash needed her, *now*.

She dropped her hands, meeting their eyes again. There was only place to start, really.

"First, I need to tell you all how Ash and I met," she said.

"Wait," Virginia said, holding up her hands. "I'm still trying to grasp this. Ash is your *mate?*"

"Yes. No. It's complicated." Rose gratefully accepted a glass of water from Neridia. Her throat felt lined with sandpaper after telling her tale. "He *was*. But like I said, he burned our bond."

The mates all exchanged glances. "He offered to do that for me, once," Neridia said. "When I was still afraid of my destiny."

"Yes, and I put a flea into his ear for even suggesting such a dreadful thing." Rose sipped her drink, remembering that night. "The irony is overwhelming."

"That—that—" Connie appeared to be searching for a strong

enough word. "That *man!* Oh, when we get him back, I'm going to kill him with my bare hands!"

"I think that's my line," Ivy murmured. "Though maybe you *should* do it. My venom would make it too quick."

Despite everything, Rose found herself with an obscure urge to defend her ex-mate. "He did it to protect me. It was the only way."

"Considering what happened the moment you two *did* get back together, it seems that he was right," Virginia said with a sigh. "Evidently these—what did you call them? Wizards?"

"Warlocks," Rose supplied.

Virginia wrinkled her nose, as though it pained her scientific mind to have to admit to the existence of such things. "These warlocks must have been spying on him all this time. Just waiting for something they could use against him. No wonder he was always so distant."

"Poor Ash. It does explain a lot." Hayley glanced round at the others. "We're still going to beat him like a piñata, right?"

"Definitely," Neridia said, with a dangerous gleam in her sea-blue eyes that did not bode well for Ash's continued health.

"Well, before we can kick him as he so soundly deserves, we have to *find* him," Virginia said pragmatically. "I think we can assume that the warlocks will have taken them all to the same place. If we can find one of them, we'll find them all."

"If he *was* still my mate, my swan would be able to lead me to his location," Rose said. "But he's not, and I can't. None of you can track your mates?"

They all shook their heads. Rose's heart fell, although she hadn't really been expecting any other answer. Most mated couples could tell where each other were over short distances, but it generally only worked within a mile or two.

"Swans aren't the only type of shifters who can find people, though," Hayley said thoughtfully. She glanced at Connie. "Could one of Chase's relatives help?"

"I already thought of that," Connie said. "He's much too far away. Even a pegasus can't locate people over this sort of distance."

Neridia smiled. "I think I know someone who can."

~

"The Phoenix?" said the Master Shark, his image rippling on the surface of the wide silver bowl of sea water.

Rose had met the man in person once before, just after Neridia had ascended the Pearl Throne. Then, he had been a hulking, glowering, silent presence, clearly only dragged into her pub by the direct order of his Empress. Even her empathic sense hadn't been able to penetrate the ironclad armor around his soul.

Now, however, he looked...different. The harsh, craggy lines of his face were smoother, more relaxed. His previously marble-pale skin had a faint tan. He even appeared to have put on a little weight which wasn't entirely muscle. He was no less broad and looming, but somehow considerably less terrifying.

Of course, Rose had to concede, it would be difficult for *anyone* to appear menacing while wearing a neon pink Hawaiian shirt with a startling pattern of cheerful cartoon sharks.

"Yes," Neridia said to the Master Shark. She had her fingers submersed in the scrying pool, using her sea dragon magic to talk to him across thousands of miles. "I know that shark shifters can scent power like regular sharks are drawn to blood. Could you track the Phoenix?"

"A *dead* shark could do that," the megalodon shifter said dryly. "But yes, I can do so over greater distances than most. A shifter of that power, I could sense from halfway around the world." He turned his head, his gray eyes going a little distant. "I can taste his smoke even now, though only faintly in this form. Give me a short while, my Empress, and I will find him for you."

"Grandpa Finn, Grandpa Finn!" A young boy appeared in the shimmering image, leaping up onto the Master Shark's back like a monkey. "Why are you standing in the lake? Abuela said we couldn't swim straight after lunch—oh! Hi, sea lady!"

The Master Shark looked pained. "*Your Majesty*, Manny."

"Your Majesty," the boy echoed dutifully. He peered over the Master Shark's shoulder, his dark eyes bright underneath his mop of curly black hair. "Are you and Big John gonna come see us again soon?"

"I hope so, Manny," Neridia said, with only the faintest of catches in her melodious voice. "But first I need to borrow your grandpa for a bit. Give my love and apologies to your grandma, okay? Finn, I'm sorry to have to pull you out of retirement like this."

The Master Shark shrugged the boy off his massive shoulders, dunking the delighted child into the lake. "I always stand ready to serve, my Empress."

"Be careful," Neridia warned. "Just find them, and report back. The last thing we need is for the warlocks to get you too."

The Master Shark grinned, showing double rows of jagged, razor-sharp teeth. Suddenly he was just as menacing as the last time Rose had met him, Hawaiian shirt or no.

"They might find me a difficult catch to land," he said. "But I shall heed the warning. I am already near the Sea Gate you created for me. I shall go through to the open ocean, and shift, and then the hunt shall begin. Expect to hear from me shortly."

Neridia withdrew her fingers from the scrying pool. The image on the rippling surface of the water blurred back into their own reflections.

"So now what can we do?" Connie asked, her hands cradling her rounded belly protectively.

"There's no point in making plans without information." Rose looked round at them all. "So now we rest, while we can. And wait."

It was agonizing.

Neridia ordered guest beds made up for all of them, but no one felt much like sleeping. Ivy paced round the perimeter of the council room like a caged tiger, arms folded and shoulders hunched, keeping away from everyone else. Virginia and Hayley drifted in and out, compulsively checking on their sleeping children. Rose made cups of tea that nobody drank. Connie constructed a nest of blankets on the floor, and lay staring at the ceiling. Neridia dozed in a chair next to the scrying pool, one hand limp on the rim of the bowl.

The first morning light was brightening the windows when the pool began to glow. It was so dim that at first Rose thought it was just a trick of the dawn. But no—the water rippled with a faint, silvery radiance, brightening and fading in a steady rhythm.

Rose sat up quickly, dumping Connie's feet off her lap. "Neridia!"

The sea dragon Empress awoke with an unladylike snort, her hand splashing into the basin. They all crowded around as the silver glow steadied.

The Master Shark's craggy face looked up at them from the water. "I found him. I went through the Sea Gate intending to start the search at Atlantis, but the Phoenix's blood-scent dragged me out at quite a different location. And not one I would ever have expected."

"Where?" They all said it at the same time, their voices overlapping.

"A place I know well. But I cannot imagine the warlocks are there for the same reason I was." The Master Shark looked grim as death. "My Empress, we must move quickly. They are on the island of Shifting Sands."

CHAPTER 20

Shifting Sands. We're on the island of Shifting Sands.

Ash had never been here before himself, but Chase's cut-off sentence combined with the unmistakably tropical climate had allowed him to work out their location. Chase had once won a vacation at the all-shifter resort here, as a finalist in some ridiculous 'Mr. Shifter' pageant. The pegasus shifter had waxed eloquent—even more so than usual—about the many delights of the island for months afterward.

He'd even mentioned that there was a disused villa on the far side of the island, well away from the main resort. It had once been the private residence of the island's previous owner, a man who had kept a secret zoo of imprisoned shifters. Justice had caught up with the collector; the captives had been liberated, and no one had used the place since.

Ash was fairly certain that Corbin was using it now. He also suspected that Corbin had known the previous owner—he certainly sounded like a man whose interests would have aligned with those of the High Magus, even if he hadn't been a warlock himself. Corbin seemed just a little too familiar with the layout of the dusty, abandoned mansion.

And Ash had a growing, terrible certainty that he knew why Corbin was here.

The warlock had been using his power to portal in dozens more warlocks throughout the day. But *these* warlocks had all come alone, without familiars. The runes around their left wrists had just been flat black ink, the tattoos not yet shimmering with power. They'd all had hungry, eager expressions. Ash had seen people like that before.

Acolytes. Trained in binding shifters, but not yet with familiars of their own.

And across the island, there was a whole resort full of shifters, unguarded and unaware…

"More," Corbin demanded.

Ash clenched his teeth, feeling the warlock's will probing at him like a dagger between his ribs. He kept his own mental walls high and tight, as blank as his face.

He had years of experience in hiding his soul. He'd sat night after night in Rose's pub, watching her from the corner, and never revealed his feelings.

He used all that hard-earned discipline now. The binding cut into his arm like red-hot wire. He couldn't stop the warlock from drawing power from him, but he could at least slow the torrent.

The warlock held up one hand, studying the orange light jumping fitfully over his runes. "This childish defiance is pointless, Blaze. You are only hurting yourself."

Despite Ash's resistance, Corbin's fingertips still burned with flickering flames. They glowed bright in the dim, shuttered room, reflecting in the glassy eyes of the stuffed animal heads on the walls.

Corbin rubbed his hands over each other, as though smoothing lotion into his skin. As the fire faded, so did the age spots and wrinkles lining his old flesh. His swollen knuckles straightened and strengthened.

Corbin let out a long, pleased sigh. He opened and closed his hands experimentally, his fingers moving more smoothly now.

"Twenty years will take some time to undo," he said, admiring his own rejuvenated flesh. "It was the one spell I could not perform with any lesser shifter. Even I can only be reborn in Phoenix fire."

He'd never wondered, before, why Corbin had never seemed to change. When Ash had been a child, Corbin had just been a towering, god-like figure. Even as he'd grown, he hadn't really noticed that Corbin didn't age. When you were in your twenties, everyone over the age of forty just fell into the vague category of *old*.

But now that *he* was in his forties, it was painfully obvious in retrospect that Corbin had never aged naturally. Ash cursed himself for not realizing exactly why Corbin had been so fixated the Phoenix. No wonder the warlock had pursued him across twenty years and two continents.

If he'd known, he would never have allowed himself to grow so complacent. He would never have assumed that the warlock had given up or died.

He would never have gone back to Rose...

Even as he thought it, he knew it was a lie. He'd *known*, at some deep, dark level, that he was putting her in danger just with his presence. He simply hadn't been able to stay away from her. He never *would* be able to.

His only hope now was that the same was true for her.

Corbin settled himself on a moth-eaten velvet sofa, crossing one foot over his knee. The warlock tilted his head to one side, regarding him with an inscrutable expression.

"A break, I think," Corbin said. "To refuel the fire."

The agony faded as the warlock closed the connection between them once more. Ash sucked in a gasping breath, sweating despite the cold still deep in his bones. He fell to one knee, bracing himself on the dusty floorboards with a splayed hand.

Corbin's newly agile fingers tapped thoughtfully against the arm of the sofa. "You did not use to fight me this hard, Blaze."

"Release my men," Ash said hoarsely, "and I'll stop."

"A noble offer." Ash bit back a grunt as Corbin flexed his will, the binding digging deeper for a second. "But I think not. No matter how you resist, I can still take what I need, albeit a little more slowly than I might like. And as for your men…I have use for them."

Ash knew exactly what that use was. Corbin needed the power of Alpha Team to capture more shifters. Ash could see the shape of the warlock's plan as clearly as if he'd could read Corbin's mind.

Chase's powers to locate and identify all the potential familiars. Griff's to spot and close off any avenue of escape. John's to summon a monsoon, providing cover for the attack. Dai's fire to panic shifters out of the resort. Hugh's power, inverted, used to paralyze rather than heal.

And his own fire, the unstoppable force of the Phoenix, to eliminate any shifters still able to resist.

Then Corbin would have even more warlocks serving him. Warlocks bound to powerful familiars, mythic shifters, alpha predators. Nothing would stop him from sweeping on to another hidden shifter community. And another, and another, and another…

All Ash could do was try to delay him. Rose was clever and fierce and she'd *escaped*. No doubt she was already in the company of the other women. Virginia, Connie, Hayley, Neridia, Ivy—none of them would rest for a second while their mates were in danger.

The women would find them. Ash didn't know how, but he knew, bone-deep, that they would.

He had to give them time.

"The more you tighten your grasp, the sooner I'll escape you." With an effort, Ash lifted his head, meeting Corbin's narrowed eyes. "You can't afford to drive me too hard, Corbin. You know what will happen."

He'd seen it himself, time after time, during those long years in the base. It went against everything in a shifter's wild, primal nature to be leashed to a warlock. The older and more powerful the shifter, the sooner the binding drove them insane. And then, it was a quick, short spiral into death.

He'd been the only one to ever last more than a few short years. He'd been brainwashed, his own will bent and warped to support

Corbin's instead of fighting it. That has been the only thing that had allowed him to endure.

Now, though…now, he knew better.

"I can already feel the madness rising," he said, which wasn't actually a lie. The Phoenix *was* mad, mad with rage, its seething flames gnawing at his control. "Drain me too far, and my beast will consume my human mind, and my body shortly after that. You had to wait twenty years to claim your prize. At this rate, you risk losing it again in a matter of days."

"Yes," Corbin said slowly, drawing out the word. "That is a pity. I had hoped that you would settle tamely back into harness. It will be aggravating to have to track down and capture the next Phoenix."

He stared at the warlock.

Corbin raised his eyebrows. "Did you think that you were my first, Blaze? I have been doing this for a very, very long time. You are correct, most of you don't last long. But you…oh, you were perfect. Orphaned and abandoned, so pathetically eager to be wanted. So starved of love that you took my hand without question."

A very, very distant memory flickered in his mind. Not so much a recollection as an impression—bars across an uncurtained window, moonlight, a hard, lonely cot. A shadow, a hand, a voice: *Come. You belong to me now.*

"Rare, very rare, for the Phoenix to choose so young and malleable a host," Corbin mused, as Ash crouched in frozen shock. "Small chance of it ever happening again. That was all that stopped me from simply having you killed, these past few years. I was on the verge of doing so anyway, and accepting the risk that the next Phoenix might prove even more difficult to capture, when you very kindly revealed your weakness to me."

The warlock leaned forward, gray eyes glittering. "Since you are so keen on self-sacrifice, Blaze, you might care to consider that you are all that is standing between me and the *next* unfortunate soul to host the Phoenix. I would not be so eager to go mad, if I were you."

Corbin sat back again. "I know what you are doing," he said conversationally. "You are trying to delay me. You pin your hope on the thought of rescue. Who is it that you think will come? How do you think they will find you?"

"You took the mate of the Pearl Empress. You cannot begin to imagine the powers she has at her command."

"Oh, but I can," Corbin breathed, an avaricious light gleaming in his pale eyes. "Beasts of the deep, legends from out of time, power to delight any warlock. Let her send her armies. My acolytes shall bind her warriors, and her forces will become my own. Abandon your futile thoughts of rescue, Blaze. I have won. I was always going to win. Accept that, and submit to my will."

"So confident." Ash met the warlock's eyes. "Just as you were twenty years ago."

The barb hit home. Corbin's nostrils flared in anger, his mouth pinching.

"And you still have the same weakness." Painfully, Ash straightened, drawing himself up to his full height. He looked down his nose at the warlock. "It is you who should surrender, Corbin. There is a flaw in your plan, and it is not one that can be covered. You know that. I know that. And there is another who knows it too."

"Bluff," Corbin snarled. "A good attempt, Blaze. But I have studied the Phoenix for hundreds of years. I know how your powers work, even better than you do yourself. When you burned the mate bond, you burned yourself from her mind. She does not—cannot—remember."

"She does not need to. She is my mate. I told her everything."

Corbin laughed scornfully. "More lies. I have spied on you for a decade, Blaze. You didn't tell her anything. You let her eat her heart out pining for you, to the point where even I was fooled. Oh, you cracked in the end—driven by jealousy, no doubt—but you cannot persuade me that you spilled all your sordid secrets in a single night. She *doesn't* know. I am quite certain of that."

The punch of the warlock's will took him by surprise. His head snapped back, spine arching as cold, intangible claws raked through his soul.

"And by holding your tongue you have sealed your fate, and that of all your friends." Corbin's taunting voice sounded distant, muffled by the agony roaring in his ears. "Just think, Blaze. If you had been honest with her, she would have known how to defeat me. How does it feel, to be the architect of your own doom?"

He bit his tongue, the iron taste of blood filling his mouth. With every ounce of will, he fought, holding his fire just out of the warlock's reach.

And as he fought, he prayed.

Remember, Rose. Remember.

CHAPTER 21

"The Knights of the Third and Fourth Water shall form defensive lines here." The Knight-Commander—a handsome man with blue-green hair and eyes who, at a mere six foot two, was distinctly short for a sea dragon—indicated a point on the map shimmering on the surface of the scrying pool.

Rose tried to see around the massive, armored forms crowding around the basin. Peering past a sea dragon warrior's steel-clad elbow, she saw that the Knight-Commander was pointing at Shifting Sands Resort itself. The beach was mapped in exquisite detail, but the actual buildings were just vague blobs. Neridia's powers as Pearl Empress only allowed her to view areas directly adjacent to water.

"The shark warriors shall be here." The Knight-Commander spread his hand over a patch of water. "Waiting in the lagoon, in case reinforcements are necessary."

A slim, pale woman—a Great White shifter, one of the leaders of the sharks—showed her serrated teeth. "We are not children, to be kept away from battle. We can fight just as well as any dragon."

"Restrain your bloodlust," the Knight-Commander answered coolly, meeting her challenging gaze. "We must maintain some forces in reserve, as a last-ditch defense. The warlocks clearly fight without honor, so we must be prepared for them to mount a counterattack on the resort. The civilians at must be protected at all costs."

The assembled knights nodded seriously. There were a dozen of them, representing various subsections of the sea shifter forces. Rose wasn't quite sure on the distinctions between the different orders. There was clearly some sort of hierarchy, but they all looked equally fearsome to *her*.

To a warlock, however...

Wriggling through the crowd, she worked her way around to Neridia. The sea dragon Empress stood with her fingers in the basin, maintaining the view of the island while her officers debated strategy. Rose tugged at her arm.

"Remind them not to let the warlocks too close," Rose whispered. "They *mustn't* underestimate how dangerous they are."

Neridia nodded, straightening up again. "My captains," she said, addressing her forces. "In the coming battle, all warriors—no matter what their role—must fully understand the danger. The enemy must be kept at arm's-length. If they lay a single hand on you, they can bind you to their will."

"Surely honor shall be our shield—" a sea dragon knight began.

"It *won't*!" Rose interrupted. Some of the warriors glared at her coldly, clearly not appreciate a mere civilian raising her voice at a council of war, but she ignored them. "It's not a matter of honor, or willpower, or anything else. If they touch you, they'll have you. I should know, one of them bound *me*. And he controlled me, utterly, mind and body. I couldn't do anything to resist."

A couple of nearby knights exchanged significant glances. She knew what they were thinking: *Well, of course* she *wouldn't be strong enough to break free.*

"Listen," she said, desperate to make them understand. "It wasn't anything to do with the fact that I'm just a swan, not a mythic shifter, or even a warrior. Warlocks bound John Doe, one of your own kind!"

"The Royal Consort was taken unaware," a looming warrior rumbled. "We shall not be."

"Don't be arrogant," Rose snapped. "A warlock bound the *Phoenix*, for crying out loud. Do you honestly think yourself stronger than him?"

"As I understand it, he bowed his neck willingly to that leash," another knight interjected, with a distinct note of disapproval. "Trading himself for you."

"That was the *second* time they got him. He was bound by them before, for years and years. He only managed to break free because...because..."

She trailed off. She had a very clear mental image of the Phoenix rising in fury from the warlock base, twenty years ago, but she was still struggling to put her shattered memories in the correct order. What had happened just before that?

"Peace, honored captains," Neridia said, with a hint of steel. The muttering knights instantly fell silent. "You will all heed Rose's warning. And if any *do* fall, others must take care. Remember that any warlock with glowing tattoos must be captured, not killed, or else their bound shifter will perish as well."

"But the shifters *can* be released?" a knight asked anxiously. Rose knew that he was one of John's friends; they often came to her pub together.

"We know that a warlock can relinquish their hold over their shifter, if they so choose," Neridia answered. Her jaw set. "Once we have taken the warlocks captive, we shall ensure that they do so."

Rose had a sudden recollection of spotted fur shifting into a woman's naked skin. She swallowed hard, feeling sick. If Ash broke loose from Corbin, he could *definitely* free the other shifters. But the cost, oh, the cost...and even if any of Alpha Team *did* choose to gain freedom by sacrificing their animals, would Ash be able to bring himself to do it?

It won't come to that, she tried to reassure herself. *It can't come to that. We'll find another way.*

After all, Ash had freed himself, twenty years ago...

Neridia was still talking, gesturing at the map. "There is a Sea Gate already established near Shifting Sands. Once we depart Brighton, we will be able to use the gate network to reach the island in short order. After we have come through the Gate, I shall—"

"Your Majesty!" the Knight-Commander exclaimed. A mass intake of breath marked the sea dragons' shock at his rudeness in interrupting the Empress. "You cannot be contemplating joining the assault?"

"My mate is there," Neridia said, simply.

"But in your advanced condition," the man indicated her gravid belly, "you cannot shift. Even with your powers, you will be vulnerable."

"My mate is there," Neridia said again—and this time, it was not the woman who spoke, but the Pearl Empress. The hair rose on the back of Rose's neck at the power in her voice. "And so I shall be there."

"And me," Ivy said fiercely, from the back of the room.

"No," the Knight-Commander said, shaking his head. "I may not gainsay my Empress, but I will not bow to anyone else's whim. The battlefield is no place for the inexperienced."

"Tough, because I'm going too," Virginia said firmly.

"Me too," Hayley agreed.

"And me," Connie said, glaring up at all the sea dragons towering over her. "Just try to stop us."

The Knight-Commander's mouth opened and closed soundlessly, like a fish. He appeared to be on the verge of having a stroke.

"Connie, you're pregnant," Neridia pointed out.

"So are you." Connie folded her arms over her prominent bump, setting her feet. "At least I'm not in danger of actually giving birth mid-battle."

"If we take you, Chase is going to kill us all the instant we rescue him." Ivy looked around at Virginia and Hayley. "That goes for you two as well. Do you think Dai and Griff would want you to put yourselves in danger? Neridia and I are shifters, but you're all just human."

"Which means the warlocks can't bind us," Virginia countered. "If anyone should be staying behind, it's you and Neridia."

The Knight-Commander beamed at her like she was his new best friend. "A very compelling argument. Your Majesty, I urge you to reconsider. What if a warlock binds *you*?"

"I am the Pearl Empress—"

"And as we have heard," the Knight-Commander sketched a small bow in Rose's direction, "even the most powerful of shifters can be taken by these fiends. If you will not consider yourself, consider your unborn child. What if a warlock can bind *him*, even while he lies in your womb?"

"He's got a point," Hayley said, looking worried. "Neridia, maybe you should stay behind."

Neridia bit her lip, a crack appearing in her imperial manner. One of her hands spread in front of her stomach in an unconscious protective gesture. "But I *have* to be there..."

Memory clicked into place.

"Yes," Rose said loudly, cutting across the rising argument. "We all do."

"For the love of sweet little fishes..." the Knight-Commander muttered. He looked as though only military discipline was keeping him from beating his head against the nearest wall. "Honored ladies, I must remind you that I am in command here. *None* of you shall join the assault. My authority on this matter is final."

"No, it isn't." Rose looked past him, to Neridia. "Your Empress calls the shots. And I'm going to have to ask her to trust me."

CHAPTER 22

He'd never thought that he would ever miss his old cell, but this new cage had him thinking wistfully of that stark, spartan room. At least it had had a bed.

Ash slept anyway, curled on the concrete floor with the single blanket Corbin had given him wadded up under his head. It was an old knack, perfected during the ten long years that he and the wendigo had hunted warlocks across the globe. When you were a fugitive, you learned how to snatch rest where you could.

You also learned how to sleep lightly. He was fully awake even before he knew what had disturbed him.

He lay still, feigning sleep, but let his eyes open the merest crack. The stars still gleamed through the bars of the cage overhead, though the fading hue of the sky suggested that dawn could not be far off. He held his breath, listening intently.

"...Only a small force, High Magus."

The voice was distant, but coming closer. The speaker was the warlock who had bound Chase, if he was not mistaken. And evidently, Corbin accompanied him.

Quickly, Ash wrapped himself in the blanket. Subduing his inner fire as much as possible, he curled tighter, pretending to shiver. In truth, he'd recovered enough strength that the chill night air couldn't touch him. But better for Corbin to think him still weak.

"I counted four," the warlock continued. "All sea dragons, I am certain of it. They made a brief stop at the resort, then started swimming around the island, following the coast. I couldn't maintain the spell for long, but it looked like they might be heading for that small cove near us, the one with the waterfall."

"An advance party, I suspect." Corbin sounded unruffled. "Scouting out our defenses. Well, they will not be returning back to the main force to make any report. Are the acolytes ready?"

"I have selected suitable candidates, High Magus." That was the witch, the one bound to Hugh. "Our most talented and worthy, who I predict will be able to easily bind the shifters. They are most eager to acquire familiars at last."

"We will take six with us. Some spares, in case any fall before all the beasts are subdued." Corbin let out a dry chuckle. "A little competition will spur the acolytes to perform better, in any case."

From the sound of it, Corbin had nearly reached his cage. Ash braced himself, and was unsurprised when the binding bit into his arm.

"Up," Corbin ordered.

Ash pushed himself to his feet, taking care to move sluggishly, as though still exhausted. In truth, not all of his stiffness was feigned. He had been much younger the last time that he had slept so rough. He rolled his shoulders, wincing, before stepping out of the cage.

A small floating sphere of witchlight orbited Corbin, illuminating his glittering gray eyes and hungry expression. He was clearly looking forward to the coming fight. As well as the witch, he was accompanied by four other warlocks, all of whom Ash recognized. They were the ones who had bound Alpha Team.

"Magus Serena," Corbin said, turning to the witch. "Are you also in readiness?"

The witch hesitated. "This assault has come a little earlier than anticipated, High Magus. I am still mastering the finer points of my familiar's power. If you wish me to come, I shall, but..."

Corbin shook his head. "No. Sea dragons are too rare and valuable a prize to risk accidentally killing them. You shall remain here to guard the other acolytes. Even without you, we have a more than sufficient strength to deal with such a small force."

"Er..." Griff's warlock cleared his throat. His agile hands twisted together nervously. "My familiar has not yet recovered consciousness."

Corbin sighed in irritation. "I *told* you not to draw so heavily on the griffin's power, Adept. Let this be a lesson in how critical it is to conserve your familiar's strength."

The remaining three warlocks exchanged glances. To Ash's secret delight, matching expressions of guilt spread across their faces.

Corbin had noticed too. His tone sharpened. "Adepts. Are *any* of your familiars fit for this fight?"

Dai's warlock studied his shoes. John's discovered a sudden interest in astronomy.

Ash stood still and silent in the shadows, unnoticed, but fierce jubilation beat through his veins. Even caged and tormented, Alpha Team were not yet defeated. They were fighting their warlocks, no matter how it ripped their minds and souls.

Corbin, you fool, he thought, watching the warlock's expression darken. *You always did try to grasp more than you could hold.*

"Y-you *ordered* me to use my familiar's power, High Magus," Chase's warlock stuttered. "A-and the pegasus shifter is much more willful than I anticipated. He fights so hard, so relentlessly...I can only force him to submit by driving him to the brink of exhaustion."

"And that's just a glorified pony," Dai's warlock said quickly. "I'm trying to tame an actual *dragon*. No one could do it in a day."

"And yet, here I stand with the Phoenix leashed to my will," Corbin said, in his iciest tones.

All three warlocks winced.

"But you are the High Magus," John's warlock ventured, with a sycophantic, ingratiating smile. "You have more power than all the rest of us combined. We can only dream of attaining a fraction of your mastery."

Corbin's taut shoulders eased a little. He'd always liked flattery. "True enough. Well. Perhaps you weaklings *are* unnecessary for handling such a small force."

Corbin cast a quick, assessing glance at him. Taking a risk, Ash relaxed his guard a little, not resisting as the warlock's will probed at his fire.

Whatever Corbin had sensed, it appeared to satisfy him. He cast a pointed glare round at the rest of the group. "*My* familiar is well-rested, and more than capable of supplying sufficient power for this task. Let you all take heed, and do better managing your own creatures."

Ash let out his breath. He didn't know what Rose was planning... but dangling such a small, tempting target in front of Corbin had to be bait to lure him out.

And it had worked.

Too late, he realized that Corbin was still watching him. He schooled his face to blankness, but the warlock's eyes narrowed.

Corbin stared at him for a long, excruciating moment, then turned to Chase's warlock. "Adept. Did your spell detect any other shifters, closer to our location?"

The warlock gulped at finding himself in the spotlight of Corbin's attention again. "N-no, High Magus. Just the ones who were already at the resort, and the new small force swimming round the coast. No others."

"And they were definitely all sea creatures?" Corbin pressed. "No others? Say, a swan?"

The warlock looked baffled. "Not unless it can breathe underwater."

"Very good." A small, smug smile curved Corbin's thin mouth. "Gather the acolytes at the front gates. I shall be there shortly, and portal with them to the cove."

The warlocks and witch bowed, scattering. Corbin waited until they were all out of sight.

"So," he murmured, for Ash's ears only. "You told her everything, did you?"

Ash avoided the warlock's gaze, clenching his jaw. Corbin let out a short, ugly bark of triumphant laughter.

"I knew you were lying." Corbin turned away, snapping his fingers as if commanding a dog to heel. "Come. Victory awaits."

Ash bowed his head, letting his shoulders slump as if in despair. But in the secret depths of his soul, he gripped a bright, unquenchable spark.

Rose has a plan. She remembers. She will come.

Holding fast to his faith in his mate, he followed the warlock.

CHAPTER 23

I could have done with one of these twenty years ago, Rose thought, gripping the pearl around her neck in a sweaty hand.

She'd been worried about how they were going to sneak up on the mansion—she didn't know what sort of magic the warlocks had at their disposal, but she had to assume that they had *some* way of detecting approaching shifters. But it turned out Neridia had an answer to that problem.

"These pearls of concealment will hide us," she'd said, opening a casket in her treasury. "The Master Shark made them many, many years ago, for himself and my father, so that they could sneak out from court and adventure together. One of them kept *me* safely concealed for many years, until I was ready to accept my destiny. I am certain that even warlocks will not be able to penetrate their power."

Despite Neridia's confidence, Rose hadn't been entirely convinced that any mere pearls—even ones as big as grapes—could really be magic. But it seemed the sea dragon had been right.

After Neridia's knights had dropped them off at Shifting Sands Resort, there hadn't been any sign that the warlocks had detected their arrival. They'd been able to meet with Scarlet, the resort manager, who had provided them with a staff vehicle and detailed instructions on how to get to the old abandoned mansion. She'd also introduced them to a strange, shy woman who'd peered at them through tangled, white-streaked hair.

"I know how you can get in," she'd whispered, and Rose's heart had bled at the fragile, trembling bravery radiating from her. "Where the cages are. You have to stop the tattooed men. They're giving the island bad dreams."

Rose didn't know what Gizelle had meant by *that,* but however strange her manner, her information had been accurate. Following her advice, they'd been able to sneak through a hidden crack in the high walls surrounding the property. Now they crouched behind thick bushes in the overgrown garden, eyeing the mansion itself.

"There's the side gate," Virginia whispered, her breath tickling Rose's ear. All six of them were huddling close together to make sure that the magic of the pearls covered them all. "Gizelle said the menagerie is right through there."

"I can sense Chase," Connie said. "He's definitely in there. Can everyone else feel their mates too?"

A pang went through Rose as everyone—apart from herself—nodded. She would have given anything to be able to reach Ash.

Not our mate, her swan said. It arched its neck, feathers bristling. *But we will still get him back.*

"Any word from the decoy group?" she asked Neridia.

The sea dragon's blue eyes went distant as she communed telepathically with her warriors. "Nothing—wait! The Knight-Commander says there are people on the beach. He's certain he just spotted Ash."

"It worked," Hayley breathed, looking relieved. "Corbin took the bait."

"Remind them not to engage the warlocks," Rose said anxiously. "This really isn't the time for a glorious charge."

"Don't worry, I picked my most sensible men for this task." Neridia made a slight, rueful face. "Well, as sensible as honor-sworn knights can be. But in any case, none of them will do anything rash.

They're pretending they haven't seen the warlocks. The Knight-Commander says they'll try to draw them further away down the coast, but he fears Corbin will quickly become suspicious when they don't land."

"Then we'd better not waste a second." Ivy cracked her knuckles. "I think it's time to stop being subtle."

There was a pause, and Rose realized they were all looking at her to give the command. She could feel their emotions—fear, yes, but mostly iron-hard determination. They were ready.

She stood up straight, lifting her chin. "Let's get our mates."

Ivy grinned like a shark. Without another word, she sprinted in the direction of the side gate, her green-streaked hair flying behind her.

Halfway there, she jumped. Her curvy body shimmered, lengthening and shifting. Emerald wings caught the air.

A shout of alarm rose from somewhere inside the mansion, but the wyvern was already opening its jaws. It breathed out a thick white cloud of acid. The side gate disintegrated, wood shriveling and falling away.

"Come on!" Rose yelled, hauling Neridia up.

It was probably the slowest attack in the history of warfare. Neridia and Connie did their best, but since they were carrying four babies between them—one due to make an appearance any day—it was more of a waddle than a charge.

But with a rampaging wyvern clawing down the walls, the warlocks were far too preoccupied to even notice the small group of women. The startled shouts turned into screams as Ivy disappeared through the hole she'd made.

Rose helped Connie over the smoking stones, leaving Virginia and Hayley to haul Neridia through. A sudden glare of light made her flinch. Spots danced across her vision as a searchlight beam swept across them.

The circle of light swung wildly across the courtyard, fixing on Ivy. The wyvern's scales glittered like cut emeralds in the harsh white glare.

"Dragon!" someone yelled from on top of the walls. "It's a dragon! Someone bind it!"

Dozens of running footsteps converged on them. Rose sensed a thick, black fog of greed and hunger.

"Ivy, get out of the light!" Rose yelled, dragging Connie forward as fast as she could.

The wyvern whirled, but with only two legs, it was clumsy on the ground. It couldn't escape the pinning stare of the searchlight. It breathed out a blast of acid, forcing the first group of warlocks back, but more lunged out of the shadows behind it. One robed man leaped, snatching at the wyvern's folded wing.

"Ivy, *watch out!*" Rose screamed.

The wyvern abruptly disappeared. The warlock's fingers closed, not on scales, but on Ivy's bare wrist.

"*Got* you," the man crowed—and then his eyes widened. His mouth worked, soundlessly.

"Surprise, asshole." Ivy twisted free as the warlock collapsed. She pushed up her sleeves as he collapsed. "Anyone else want to try?"

A couple more warlocks took her up on the offer. They very quickly discovered that there was a very, very big problem with binding a shifter whose skin could sweat deadly venom.

In the space of seconds, the tables were turned. Ivy's teeth bared in a feral grin as she chased fleeing warlocks in a lethal game of tag.

"Not too fast, Ivy!" Rose hurried after her, the others at her heels. "We have to stay together—"

Rounding an empty cage, she found herself face-to-face with a robed man. He yelped, cringing—and then his eyes widened as he realized she wasn't Ivy.

"There's more of them!" the warlock yelled at the top of his lungs. "More shifters!"

Fast as a snake, he grabbed for her arm. Sheer terror froze her in place as his fingers brushed against her skin.

No, no, no! Her swan beat its wings in panic. *Not again!*

Then she was stumbling, falling, as Connie shoved her out of the way.

"Not her!" Connie cried, offering her own arm. "Take me instead!"

The warlock didn't need to be invited twice. With a snarl of triumph, he seized Connie's wrist.

Nothing happened.

The warlock blinked. He stared down at his own hand as if it were a gun that had just inexplicably misfired.

Which meant that he wasn't looking when Hayley brained him over the head with a rock.

"That's for my mate," Hayley growled as he collapsed. She stomped across his prone body, not being too careful about where she put her feet, and pulled Rose up again. "Come on, we're nearly there!"

Rose gasped, adrenaline still making her heart vibrate like a hummingbird. Dizzy, she tried desperately to orient herself.

The courtyard was a madhouse of searchlights and screams. Ivy darted in and out of the shadows, her deadly touch dropping warlocks like flies. Virginia and Connie supported Neridia, helping her over the uneven ground as they searched for their mates.

Rose's breath seized in horror as a warlock lunged at the three women. Either he was more observant than his colleague, or just luckier, because he ignored the two humans. Barging Connie aside, he grabbed for Neridia.

Neridia's chin lifted. She gazed down at the man with regal poise.

The warlock made a strange gurgling noise. Releasing the sea dragon, he sank to his knees, clawing at his throat. A gush of water spewed from his mouth.

Calmly, the Pearl Empress stepped round him, leaving him to drown on dry land.

"Hugh!" Ivy cried out. Abruptly abandoning the warlock she'd been pursuing, she whirled—and froze.

Rose tried to turn to see what she was looking at—but stumbled on feet that suddenly seemed like blocks of wood attached to her legs. Numbness spread up her limbs. Beside her, Hayley gasped, apparently paralyzed as well. Out of the corner of her eye, Rose could see that Neridia, Hayley and Virginia had been caught too.

"I have them!" A woman with long, flowing black hair strode into Rose's field of view. Shining silver runes wound up her left arm.

And behind her...

Ivy made a high, keening sound, like a trapped animal.

"Oh, no," Rose whispered.

The unicorn hobbled painfully behind the witch, all grace lost. Its left foreleg was matted with dried blood. Every time the silver, cloven hoof touched the ground, its white flanks shivered with pain.

But it still carried its head high, refusing to be bowed. Even though all the light had been snuffed from its horn, its eyes still burned with unquenchable spirit.

Spotting Ivy, the unicorn called out, a fierce, clear cry. They both strained for each other, but neither could break their invisible bonds.

Hugh wasn't alone. Griff was there too, in griffin form, towering over a slender warlock with a narrow, scholarly face. Beside Rose, Hayley caught her breath in a sob of pain. The griffin's head turned, eagle eyes widening as it saw her.

"Virginia!" Dai shouted. He was in human form, supporting John Doe.

Seeing his own mate, the sea dragon shifter broke into a frantic, staccato song in his own language, more like organ music than speech. Neridia sang something back, her voice breaking with yearning.

"Will you shut that animal up?" the robed woman snapped at one of her colleagues. "I can't hear myself think."

The man made a jerking gesture, and John Doe's song cut off. Dai tried to speak again, but was silenced by his own warlock. In the abrupt hush, the witch swept the courtyard with a scornful stare.

"Panicking like chickens," she said scathingly, to the men who'd been fleeing for their lives mere moments ago. They crept sheepishly out of the shadows, hanging their heads—though Rose noticed that they all still stayed well away from Ivy. "Anyone would think you'd never seen a shifter before."

"We *haven't* seen one like that before, Magus!" one of the chastised men protested, pointing at Ivy. "It's some kind of dragon, but—"

The witch rolled her eyes. "I'm not interested in feeble excuses.

Just hurry up and bind the wretched creature, before the High Magus returns and sees this mess."

Several of the acolytes stepped back. The one the witch had picked out went pale. "B-but, Magus," he stuttered. "No one can touch it. Everyone who's tried, well..." He trailed off, gesturing helplessly at the collapsed forms scattered around the courtyard.

The witch tilted her head, looking interested. She walked closer to Ivy, dragging Hugh along behind. Ivy's jaw worked as though she wanted to spit, but the witch's magic held her motionless. All she could do was glare at the woman in pure hatred.

"Interesting." The witch tapped a fingernail against her lips for a moment, evidently thinking. Then her mouth curved in a smile. Silver light shimmered around her fingers as she reached out to caress Ivy's cheek. "But no great obstacle. I shall simply neutralize its venom—"

The witch stopped. An expression of great puzzlement spread across her face.

She looked down at the gleaming horn protruding from the center of her chest.

"The unicorn is loose!" a warlock screamed.

"Yes!" Rose shouted in triumph, as the magic holding her abruptly disappeared. "*Yes!*"

She'd gambled everything, based on a single, newly-recovered memory. A recollection of a gun, swinging up to point at her...and the Phoenix, exploding out of his cell in response.

And she'd been right.

Nothing could stop a shifter from protecting his mate.

Chaos erupted as Hugh flung the witch's limp body aside. Warlocks scattered in all directions, desperate to escape the rampaging unicorn. The black binding around its foreleg had completely vanished. Its horn flashed like a blade, sparks trailing behind it. Ivy shifted into her wyvern form again, fighting back-to-back with her mate.

"No!" the warlock next to Griff howled as a couple of acolytes tried to grab Ivy's wing. "That's a mated pair! Don't try to bind them, you fools!"

"Hit them with everything you've got!" Dragonfire swirled around a warlock's upraised hands. Dai snarled in rage and pain, clutching at the runes around his wrist, but he clearly couldn't stop the man from drawing power from him. "All of us, together, on the count of three!"

John's knees buckled as his warlock summoned a crackling ball of lightning. Griff writhed like a cat trying to escape a harness as his warlock too drew power from him.

"One!" Dai's warlock shouted. All three took aim at Ivy and Hugh. "Two! Thr—"

Virginia, Hayley and Neridia stepped between the warlocks and their targets. The women linked hands, forming a human shield.

Griff's warlock's eyes widened as he realized he was threatening his shifter's mate. "Oh, sh—"

He didn't get to finish the sentence. The griffin's gleaming golden beak snapped shut, silencing him forever.

And suddenly the courtyard was very, *very* full of dragon.

John's huge, finned tail swept his warlock, a dozen acolytes, and quite a lot of the nearest wall into oblivion. Dai vaporized his own warlock with a single, precise blast of fire, then ducked his head. Virginia scrambled up onto the dragon's neck, clinging onto his curving horns. John picked up his own mate, cradling her protectively in webbed feet.

"Chase!" Rose shouted, looking around frantically. "We have to find Chase!"

Connie was already running, awkwardly, arms supporting her pregnant belly. Leaving the dragons to finish destroying the last few warlocks, Rose pelted after her. They ran down the row of cages.

"You!" Connie yelled in fury. "*Get off my mate!*"

A warlock was frantically clutching at Chase's mane, trying to scramble up onto the pegasus's back. At Connie's shout, he fell off. Chase danced away, snorting, black hooves striking sparks on the flagstones.

The warlock scrambled to his feet, making a grabbing motion at thin air. Chase bucked and twisted, as though caught on an invisible leash.

"He's mine," the warlock gabbled. His hands were upraised defensively, but no magic snapped around his fingers. "I know who you are, I know how this works. As long as I don't touch you, he can't break free. And you can't touch me, or he'll die. You've got no choice but to let me go."

Rose hesitated...but Connie didn't.

Without breaking stride, Connie kicked the man squarely in the balls. As he folded over, she shoved past him. Her hand touched Chase's gleaming hide.

The runes around the pegasus's foreleg flared—and vanished.

Chase kicked the warlock too. Only this time, in the head. The man flew ten feet through the air and hit a wall with a very final-sounding *crunch.*

Rose's breath whooshed out of her lungs in relief. "How did you know that would work?"

"I didn't," Connie gasped. She wrapped her arms around the pegasus's neck, burying her face in the sweeping black mane. "Oh Chase, *Chase.*"

The pegasus shimmered, shrinking into human shape. Chase enfolded his mate in a fierce hug, leaning his forehead on the top of her head.

"I'm all right." His voice was hoarse and rasping. "The others?"

"We're here," Hugh said from behind Rose. "Except Ash."

She turned, and saw him limping toward them, Ivy at his side. All the others were there too. John and Griff were back in human form, holding hands with their mates. Dai was still in his dragon shape, alert for any danger.

"Come here so I can heal that," Hugh said to Chase. The unicorn shifter looked exhausted, but he still reached for Chase's wounded arm. "I've already fixed up everyone else. You and Griff have to fly our mates out of here, the rest of us will try to free—"

Dai roared a warning. They all ducked, the men instinctively grabbing for their mates, as the red dragon's wings swept protectively around them.

Fire exploded against the tough crimson webbing. The dragon

roared again, this time in pain. For the flames to burn through even his scales...it could only mean one thing.

"It's Corbin and Ash!" Rose hurled herself to the front of the group, spreading her arms wide. "Everyone get behind me!"

"What-?" Griff started.

"No time to explain, just do it!" Virginia hammered her fist against her mate's armored scales. "Shift, Dai! You're too big a target!"

Dai shrank back into human form, just in time. Another fireball blasted through the space his head had just been. Both his arms were blistered and burned. Hugh grabbed him, his hands lighting up with a silvery glow to heal the wounds.

John tried to step in front of Rose, his knightly oaths no doubt demanding that he shield them all with his own body, but Neridia pulled him back. All the women were yanking at their confused mates, hauling them into a corner of the courtyard and forcing them to crouch down.

Left alone at the front, Rose spread her arms wide, trying to make herself as big as possible. All around, the menagerie was burning. Fire leaped from shattered timbers and licked along tangled, overgrown creepers. Heat washed across her face, but she held firm.

In the shifting orange light from the inferno, she faced down Corbin.

The warlock was still backlit by the fading glow of a portal. His left hand gripped Ash's right wrist, fingers spread, digging cruelly into the black runes of the binding.

Ash was on his knees, one hand braced against the ground, the other painfully twisted up by the warlock's iron grasp. Blood poured down his right arm. Rose knew he was fighting Corbin with every ounce of will, but he couldn't stop the warlock from drawing on his power.

Hellfire snaked around Corbin's tattooed runes. The warlock raised his free hand, searing flames gathering around his clenched fist. The seething red light illuminated Corbin's twisted, outraged face. It was the expression of a man watching all his plans crumble into ash, a man with nothing left to lose. Hand crackling with power, he stared straight at her.

Rose met his hate-filled eyes without flinching.

Yes, she silently willed him. *Do it.*

She wouldn't be able to get out of the way, she knew. If Corbin threw that incandescent fireball at her, it was possible that not even the Phoenix's power could call it back.

But whatever happened to her...Ash would be free.

With a snarl, Corbin opened his hand—but not to attack her. Instead, he swept his arm round in a wide, horizontal arc. A wall of fire cut between them, leaping up to shield the warlock and his familiar. Through the roaring flames, Rose caught a glimpse of him turning away, starting to sketch glowing lines in mid-air.

A portal.

"He's going to get away!" Hayley cried out.

Virginia caught Dai as he tried to surge forward. "No! It's too hot, you won't make it!"

The magical fire burned white-hot, so intense that their shadows stood out stark and black behind them. The flames curled and writhed like a nest of snakes. They stretched unnaturally, forming a dome, completely enclosing Ash and Corbin.

For a moment, Rose saw Ash's face through the inferno. He was looking right at her, as if nothing else existed in the world.

He was her mate. And she knew, *knew,* that he would never hurt her.

"Rose, *no!*" Connie screamed.

Too late. She was already running, flat out, dodging their attempts to grab her.

Without hesitation, she hurled herself into the flames.

CHAPTER 24

Time slowed. Through the inferno and the red agony hazing his vision, he saw Rose leap. She seemed to hang in mid-air, as if taking flight. Her expression was as serene as her swan, calm and still and utterly unafraid.

Her eyes locked onto his. He could look through them straight into her soul. Perfect love, perfect trust. Even after everything he'd done.

They were mates, and nothing could ever keep them apart.

He threw himself against the binding, barely feeling the bite of the runes. The flow of power reversed, surging back into his veins.

"*No!*" Corbin howled.

The binding was just a fraying thread around his soul. Distantly, he could sense Corbin pulling frantically at it, but the warlock's leash was powerless in the face of the mate bond.

Ash reached out. His love wrapped around Rose, shielding her from the fire. The flames rippled around her, parting easily, harmlessly.

He caught her outstretched hands. Her fingers intertwined through his.

The binding stretched, strained...and held.

Rose stared down at the blood-streaked runes, mouth opening in horror. She gripped his hands harder, as though she could physically yank him out of the warlock's power. He could sense her trying to reach him down the mate bond...but there was nothing for her to grasp. Just cold ash, where there should have been a link between their souls.

He could enfold her in his power, but she couldn't reach him in return. And without *her* power, *her* strength, he couldn't break free of the binding.

Behind him, Corbin started to laugh. "Oh, you fools. You poor, poor fools. Now you're *both* mine."

Corbin made a swirling gesture with one finger. A glowing collar appeared around Rose's neck. Her hands flew to her throat, eyes widening in panic.

Fire rose in his soul—but the warlock's will clamped tighter around him. Though the binding was frayed almost to the point of breaking, it still held him. He fought as hard as he could, but the moment of shock had shattered his control. Power drained away from him, gathering in Corbin's hands.

"That's better," Corbin crooned, sounding amused. The warlock turned away, raising his hands again to sketch the lines of a portal. "I'm not hurting her. I'm just bringing her along...as surety for your good behavior."

Distantly, Ash was aware of roars and shouts coming from outside the dome of fire covering the three of them. Shadows moved on the far side of the flames—Dai, Chase, Griff, John, Hugh, all desperately trying to find a way through. But they had no equipment, no gear, nothing to protect them from the intense heat.

He couldn't make a path through the fire for them as he had for Rose. Though she'd loosened the binding almost to the point of breaking, he couldn't calm himself enough to calm the flames. Not when *she* was in such terrible danger...

The Phoenix raged in his soul. His chest was filled with its incandescent fury, so strong that the strained binding could barely constrain him. If he could just stretch it a little further, enough to burn Corbin—

He couldn't. Even the weakened binding wouldn't let him harm the warlock. It trapped his fire within the confines of his body.

And he realized there was one thing he *could* burn.

Please, Rose desperately begged her own innermost heart. *We have to reach him, we have to save him,* please!

But still her swan keened, in denial and despair. *Not our mate!*

Ash had been right. It didn't matter that she knew he *had* been her mate. It didn't matter how desperate she was to save him. It didn't even matter how much she loved him. No matter how her mind screamed *yes,* the deep, animal center of her heart knew the truth.

He wasn't her mate.

She couldn't free him.

She'd failed.

Ash raised his head. His jaw had been clenched as he fought Corbin's will, but now his agonized expression relaxed. He looked strangely relieved, as though he'd finally put down an unimaginable burden. His eyes were deep and clear as he gazed into her own.

His mouth shaped three final words.

I love you.

Then he collapsed.

"NO!"

Corbin's shriek echoed her own. The pulsing light around the warlock's hands went out like a blown candle. The fiery shield covering them spluttered and faded.

The warlock's magic had died...along with his familiar.

She was barely aware of Alpha Team bursting through the dwindling flames. In all the world, the only thing that mattered was Ash's still, silent body.

He lay utterly motionless. All the lines of care and worry were finally smoothed away. His face held the slight, faint trace of a smile.

To save her, he'd burned the only thing he could. The last thing remaining to him.

His own life.

Her knees hit cold stone. She couldn't breathe. Didn't *want* to breathe. Her lungs burned, but how could she draw in air, when he never would again?

A dark-clad form crashed into her, knocking her to the ground. She gasped, time starting again. Corbin's frantic, contorted face was mere inches from her own. Somewhere, someone was shouting, dragons were roaring—but she knew in a sudden moment of icy clarity that they weren't going to reach her in time.

Corbin's cold, bony hand clawed at her wrist.

And then—

The Phoenix rose.

Unbound from mortal flesh, it was invisible, the pure essence of fire. Untouched, untouchable, it soared upward, outward.

Free, free at last! It blazed brighter than the rising sun, rejoicing.

But no fire could burn without fuel. The spirit that had fed it for so long was dwindling now, drifting away like smoke. The Phoenix gripped that fading spark in incandescent talons, refusing to let the soul slip away just yet.

It needed that soul to sustain its immortal flame for a little while longer. Just until it found a new host, a new spirit to fuel its own. Then, and only then, could it release the ashes of the old to finally find rest.

It was time to be reborn.

The Phoenix spread its spectral wings wide, encircling the world. Souls flared in answer, shining like scattered stars. Bright souls, strong souls. Age, race, gender—such things were irrelevant. It was the deepest essence that mattered. A steadfast will, a true heart.

A thousand worthy souls beckoned to the Phoenix.

It chose.

—Fire filled her.

It struck through her like white lightning. The flame poured into her, until she felt that she must blaze with it, shining like the sun.

Corbin shrieked, recoiling, his hands burned and blistered. He tried to scrabble away, but now it was her turn to hold fast.

The force inside her *knew* the warlock. It burned with a deep, powerful emotion. Not rage, or hatred, but something pure and bright and utterly without mercy.

Justice.

He had brought pain and suffering to countless lives. He should not exist.

And so, as easy as thought, he didn't.

She unmade him, burning him right down to component particles. Wordless satisfaction radiated from that foreign force in her soul as the smoke drifted away. In a million ways, a million lives, the atoms that had once been the warlock would find new purpose. All matter danced in the endless cycle, constantly changing, eternally reborn.

Just like the Phoenix.

There was still a tiny spot of blackness in the blazing whiteness within her. Her swan nestled in the heart of the inferno, dwarfed by the fiery wings enfolding it. Yet it opened its own ebony wings wide in a welcoming embrace.

Oh! her swan called out fiercely. *Oh, at last, at last! You came back, as we knew you would, at last you are back!*

Her swan knew the incandescent power filling them. Knew *him*.

"Rose!" Virginia seized her shoulders, ashen with terror. "Are you all right? Did Corbin hurt you?"

"No," Rose said. Her voice sounded strange in her own ears. Some part of her expected it to be much deeper. "I'm fine." A pure, delighted laugh bubbled up from the center of her being. "Everything's fine."

"Rose…" Virginia swallowed, hesitating. "Ash is, is…Hugh's working on him now. But it's not looking good."

Rose put her hand on Virginia's, squeezing it. "It's going to be fine."

Virginia was still eying her worriedly, as though concerned she had gone mad with shock. Rose wished she could reassure her, but time was running short.

Very carefully, she stood up. Walking with the Phoenix inside her felt a bit like trying to balance a tray of full, brimming pint glasses. Power threatened to spill out with every movement.

She heard Connie suck in a gasp. "Her *feet*. Look at her feet!"

The scent of scorched rock rose in her wake. Dai put out a hand—to support her, to stop her, she couldn't tell—but snatched it back. The red dragon shifter stared at his burnt fingers.

"Hugh," she said softly. "Stop."

The unicorn didn't move. Its forelegs were bent, whole body bowed low, every muscle tense. The silver radiance of its horn was too bright to look at directly. The sharp point rested directly over Ash's heart.

Yet his chest stayed still. Despite the healing power pouring into him, there was no flicker of life. His open eyes gazed into eternity, empty and peaceful.

"Hugh," Rose said again. She held out a hand, moving closer. "It's all right. You can stop now."

The unicorn flinched from her burning aura. It stumbled back, head hanging in exhaustion. With a shimmer of light, it shrank back into Hugh.

"I'm sorry," he said, his voice cracking. Ivy hurried to support him, wrapping comforting arms around her mate. "There's nothing I can do. He's gone."

"I know." Rose sank to her knees next to Ash's body. "Don't worry. It's going to be all right."

He was still warm. She cradled his head in her lap, smoothing back his graying hair. Her fingertips traced the beloved lines of his face.

Now, she said, to her swan.

Her animal hesitated. It huddled down as though protecting an egg. *But he is ours. Our mate.*

Yes. Rose stroked her animal, coaxing its black wings open. *And we need to put him back where he belongs.*

Reluctantly, her swan stepped back, yielding. Carefully, Rose gathered up what her animal had been guarding.

A spark, a mote, nearly lost in the Phoenix's eternal flame. But to her, it burned brightest of all.

Bending down, she pressed her lips to his.

And breathed Ash's soul back into his body.

CHAPTER 25

The Phoenix's fire streamed out of her, following Ash's soul like the tail of a comet. She let it go gladly, releasing the borrowed power. No matter how glorious it was, she was comfortable with her own self. She had no desire to be permanently transfigured into something different.

Yet not all the power left. A bright, fiery thread remained, stretching out from her soul. She could *feel* it, deep in her heart, a bond that would never be broken again.

Underneath her palm, Ash's chest rose. He drew in a slow, calm breath, as though he'd merely been sleeping. His hand came up to cup the back of her neck, pulling her further down, deepening the kiss.

"He's alive!" Hayley squawked.

Rose pulled away, laughing, as everyone crowded around them. "All right, all right, get back or he won't *stay* alive!"

She flapped her hands, shooing Alpha Team away. Five anxious firefighters were *far* too many muscles to try to cram into one small space. "The poor man's been dead, for pity's sake. Let him catch his breath."

Hugh elbowed through the crush, kneeling next to Ash. "Don't move. I need to check you over."

"I am quite well." Ash tried to sit up, but was firmly shoved down again by the paramedic. With a slight, wry smile, he submitted to Hugh's quick, practiced inspection.

"Well." Hugh sat back on his heels, somehow managing to look simultaneously jubilant and exasperated. "In my professional medical opinion, this man is definitely alive."

"He doesn't need your help?" Neridia said, her voice high and tight.

"As I said, I am perfectly fine." Ash pushed himself up at last, waving away half a dozen outstretched hands. Even the place where his binding had been was just an old, pale scar, completely healed.

"Good." Neridia paused, catching her breath with an odd, guttural grunt. "In that case…Hugh, could you please help *me?*"

"Neridia, are you in *labor?*" Rose exclaimed.

"I…" Neridia swayed, doubling over. John surged to her side, supporting her in his strong arms. "I think…I need…*Hugh!*"

The paramedic leaped to his feet. "Right. No need to panic," he said, though his expression did not entirely match his words. "It's your first baby, we have plenty of time to get you somewhere more comfortable. There's no danger of anything happening until the contractions are two minutes apart."

"Hugh," Neridia gritted out, through clenched teeth. "That was ten minutes ago."

Hugh's face went as white as his hair. "Bloody hellfire, woman, why didn't you *say?!*"

Caught in the throes of another contraction, Neridia could only shoot him a look. It was, however, a very eloquent one.

"My mate, my heart, all will be well." A reassuring melody wound around John's words, filled with harmonics of love and comfort. His face was rigidly calm, but Rose could sense the panic beating against his ribs. "Shield-brother, time grows short. What should we do?"

"Not be here!" Hugh raked both hands through his hair, looking around wildly as though hoping a fully stocked ambulance might drop from the sky. "She can't have a baby in the middle of this!"

The menagerie was a blasted wasteland around them. Many of the iron cages were twisted and wrecked, melted by fire or acid. Soot swirled through the air. Scattered fires still burned around the edges of the courtyard.

Rose raised her eyebrows at Ash. Catching her meaning, he nodded, then glanced casually around.

The flames winked out, all at once.

Ash exhaled. "Better?"

"It's an improvement," Hugh growled. He was busy running glowing hands over Neridia's stomach, his brow furrowed in concentration. "Though 'not actively on fire' is a pretty low bar to clear."

"I've changed my mind," Neridia gasped. Sweat beaded her skin. "I don't want to have a baby. Someone stop it, please."

Virginia and Dai exchanged a wry look. "I remember this bit," the dragon shifter murmured.

"Thankfully, I don't." Virginia took Neridia's hands, rubbing them soothingly. "It's going to be okay, Neridia. You'll forget the pain once your baby's here. I promise."

"Nope. Not doing this," Neridia announced. Despite her matter-of-fact tone, her eyes had gone rather wild and unfocused. "Going for a swim instead."

Head held regally high, she tried to walk off. John lunged to intercept her. He swept her off her feet, holding her fast despite her semi-incoherent protests.

"Careful," Griff warned. "As I recall, the next stage involves trying to take a bite out of you, as punishment for doing this to her."

"I can't be blamed for that," Hayley protested. "I was having *twins.*"

Chase looked at his own mate's pregnant belly, his expression suddenly rather alarmed. "I'm going to need a suit of armor."

"What *we* need right now is a bed," Hugh snarled. "Or at least something more comfortable than a bare stone floor."

"The mansion has not been occupied for some time, but what I saw of it was still serviceable." Ash said. Rose couldn't tell how he did it, but suddenly he wasn't an exhausted man in a filthy uniform, but the *Commander*. "John, help Hugh take her inside."

"Is the ocean there?" Neridia mumbled, her breath coming in fast pants.

"A bath might have to do, honey," Virginia said. She caught Connie's eye. "We'll see what we can manage."

"Do it *fast*," Hugh muttered. "Hayley, with me, please. You can help coach her through this. At least *you've* done this before..."

"Chase." Ash looked at the pegasus shifter as the others disappeared into the mansion. "Fly to the resort as fast as you can, inform them of events. Bring back a medical kit, if you can."

"I'll go too," Ivy volunteered. "I'm even faster. I'll bring back the supplies, while Chase explains everything to the resort manager."

Ash acknowledged this suggestion with a grateful nod. The wyvern and the pegasus shifted and took off into the sky, swiftly vanishing out of sight.

"Griff, Daifydd," Ash said, turning to them. "Search the house for anything useful. Food, clean clothing."

"Towels," Rose put in. "Water, and big pots, so that we can sterilize them."

"I will clean up out here," Ash said, indicating the ravaged courtyard with a slight motion of one hand. "If you find anything inside that needs...disposing of, contact me. Let us not leave any unpleasant surprises for the resort staff, should any come up here later."

Griff and Dai nodded. Without any questions, they headed off.

That just left her and Ash. She cocked her head up at him. "What should I do?"

"You..." Ash's aura of command dropped away like a discarded jacket. He took her hands, pulling her into his arms. "You have already done everything."

She leaned against his chest. "Did you know?"

"That the Phoenix would go to you?" Even without looking at him, she could tell he was smiling. "I had my suspicions. But what you did afterward...that I did *not* anticipate."

"Mmm. If you ever pull a stunt like that again, I'll throttle you." His heart beat strong and steady against her ear. She could listen to that reassuring rhythm forever. "And then bring you back to life so I can kill you some more. Don't think I won't. I can stuff you back in there as many times as I want, you know."

His deep, soft chuckle reverberated through her body. "I will consider myself warned."

"I mean it." She leaned away a little so that she could meet his eyes. "No more sacrifices, Ash."

His expression sobered. He bent down a little, cupping her face in both hands.

"I will never leave you again," he said, his voice low and intense. "My place is at your side. I will always protect and guard and cherish you…as you do me. *You* are my strength. And I will never again be so arrogant and foolish as to forget that."

"Good." Rose tipped her head back, drawing him down to her parted lips. "Don't."

Warmth spread through her chest as they kissed. The mate bond pulsed in her mind, urging her to press closer against him. Even though they were standing in plain sight in the middle of a smoldering battlefield, need roared through her blood.

She'd felt that overpowering, overwhelming instinct before, twenty years ago. In a run-down motel room, just after they'd escaped the warlock base, as she'd bandaged his wounds…

"Ash!" she exclaimed, jerking away in alarm. "I don't think we're fully mated!"

He pulled away a little, brow furrowing. She had a sense of him turning inward, examining the restored connection between them.

"You're right." He didn't sound at all dismayed. Rather, a pleased, wicked heat lit in his dark eyes. His strong hands drew her closer to him, his body hard and hot against hers. "The bond is there, but it's not fully consummated yet. Which means there's something we need to do…"

A scream split the air. Ash let out a muffled, frustrated groan, burying his face in her neck.

She had to laugh, even though her own body ached at the interruption. "One day," she said ruefully, "we might actually be able to have five minutes to ourselves without some crisis interrupting."

He bit her neck lightly, making her toes curl. "I plan to take more than five minutes."

At the moment, she would have taken thirty seconds. But reluctantly, she pushed him away. "Well, right now I'd better go see what I can do to help Neridia. But I *will* hold you to that."

He caught her hand, raising it to his mouth. A delicious shiver ran through her as his breath brushed the sensitive skin of her inner wrist. He planted the softest of kisses over her trembling pulse.

"Soon?" he breathed.

"Soon," she promised.

CHAPTER 26

Soon could not come soon enough.

But no matter how Ash's blood burned with impatience, there were tasks to be done. That was the price of being the leader—those you led instinctively looked to you for guidance, out of habit, out of trust. And a *good* leader never let his team down.

He could tell his men were riding the razor's edge after all that had happened—the false, brittle high of adrenaline that came from sustained, intense stress. If they stopped for a moment, they would collapse.

So he didn't let them stop. He assigned and organized and ordered, with the same calm tone of voice that he'd used through countless fires. He held them together.

And as for himself...he had Rose. Her warmth in his soul was all the strength *he* needed.

There was no further opportunity to speak, let alone do anything else. She was busy, providing a focus for the women as he did for the men, keeping them occupied with bright, cheerful encouragement.

But every time they passed each other in the corridors, they could share a look. A stolen smile, a swift caress. Every glance, every touch, stoked the fire in him higher.

He had waited twenty years. Yet waiting this final day nearly killed him all over again.

He found an outlet for his frustration in personally scorching away every trace of the warlocks. Both he and his inner animal took a deep satisfaction in *that*. He reduced even the iron cages to smoke and cinders. No shifter would ever be trapped here again.

By the time Hugh emerged, exhausted but triumphant, to report that mother and newborn were doing well, both menagerie and mansion were scoured clean. Only blackened stones and a rapidly-dispersing pile of ash showed that anything had happened here at all.

Even once they arrived back at Shifting Sands Resort, there were tasks. Explanations and apologies—unsurprisingly, Chase's version of events had left much to be desired in terms of clarity. It took several hours for Ash to more fully explain matters to Scarlet, the resort manager. She wanted to know everything about the warlocks—especially how to recognize them, and their weaknesses.

"I do not know if the danger is fully passed," he admitted to her. "Their leader is dead, but there may still be others remaining, in hiding. And they know about this place now."

"And now I know about them." Scarlet leaned back in her office chair, a dangerous glint in her eye. "If they come here again...they will regret it."

He almost pitied any warlock who tried to set foot on Shifting Sands in the future. He couldn't tell what manner of shifter the strange, red-haired woman might be, but there was no doubt that she was formidable.

Formidable, and also generous. She waved away his offer of payment for overnight lodgings. "You are our guests," she said firmly. "It's low season, anyway. We have plenty of cottages free."

Then she wrinkled her nose, pointedly looking at his crumpled, soot-streaked uniform. "We also have *excellent* showers."

He took the hint. A discreetly attentive staff member, Breck, showed him to a large, charming cottage , and politely but insistently waited until he handed over his filthy garments. From the way the man carried them away at arm's-length, Ash suspected he was going to burn them rather than clean them.

Which left him trapped in the cottage with nothing but a towel. Shifting Sands might be a clothing-optional resort, but he was very much not a clothing-optional person. Especially not with Rose delightfully, insistently intruding into his thoughts every five seconds.

He took a shower. A very, very cold one.

He was still standing under the pounding water, attempting to scrub the soot from his hair, when he heard the cottage door open. "On the bed, please," he called out, assuming—hoping—it was Breck returning with some form of clothing.

Instead, the warmth of the mate bond shone against his bare back like summer sunshine. "Only if you're going to join me."

He swallowed a mouthful of soapy water, whipping round so fast he nearly lost his balance. Rose smiled wickedly at him from the doorway of the bathroom. A short red dress caressed her curves and brought out the rich ebony of her skin.

"Or if you prefer…" She slid the thin crimson straps down over her soft shoulders. "I could join you."

His mate, his *mate*.

"Yes," he said hoarsely.

He just meant it as yes to *her*—yes, oh yes, always yes—but she took it as invitation. Her dress fell softly to the floor, puddling around her bare feet.

Desire leaped through him at the sight of her. And now, *now* she could feel the effect she had on him. Knew exactly how every inch of her arrested his breath and set his heart to pounding in his chest.

Her smile widened. She sashayed forward like the goddess she was, allowing him to worship her with his gaze. She stepped into the shower…and shrieked, leaping back.

"That's *cold!*" she exclaimed, hugging herself. Gooseflesh rose on her arms. "Ash, why on earth are you taking a cold shower?"

Her indignation was adorable. He found himself grinning, foolishly. "Because I was thinking about you."

She raised her eyebrows at him, an answering smile tugging at her lips. "Was it helping?"

"Not in the slightest."

Her eyes flicked downward. Her smile crooked, delightfully. "So I can see."

He reached for the shower dial, twisting it to hot. At the same time, he let a little of his power rise, heating the air.

"If I promise to warm you up," he murmured, as steam wrapped around them both, "will you still join me?"

"Mmm." She stepped forward. "Close your eyes. You still have soap in your hair."

Part of him—a very specific part—would much rather have pushed her up against the wall then and there. But the sweet anticipation singing down the mate bond told him that she was enjoying taking her time, drawing out the moment. And, truth be told, so was he.

He'd waited twenty years. But he found he could wait a little longer.

He tipped his head back under the hot water, closing his eyes. The hard peaks of her nipples brushed against his chest as she stretched up, and he bit back a growl. She laughed softly against his throat, kissing his collarbone.

"Wait," she commanded. "Let me get you clean first."

Her strong fingers worked through his hair. Her touch was simultaneously provocative and soothing, firing his blood even as his muscles relaxed. He stroked her in return, running his hands over the wet curves of her shoulders, her back, her hips.

Still keeping his eyes closed, he ducked his head. He didn't need to be able to see to capture her mouth. She hummed in pleasure, tilting her face up to him, water running over both their faces.

He kissed the corner of her mouth, her jawline, the hollow behind her ear. "My turn," he murmured.

Reaching for the soap, he lathered his hands. The heady, sweet scent of roses perfumed the air. He stroked her shoulders, down her arms, relishing the smoothness of her skin. He took her hands, cupping them in his own.

"Mmmm," Rose sighed, as his thumbs rubbed strong, slow circles over her palms. Her eyes drifted closed. "That's lovely."

"You're lovely," he whispered, drawing her closer.

He soaped his hands again, this time rubbing the foaming lather over the long sweep of her back. She purred, arching into his touch. He stroked her until every muscle was loose and languid, her body boneless against his.

Her hands moved over him in return. Suds ran down the center of his chest, trickled across his abdomen, dripped lower. He was so hard even that light touch was exquisite torment.

He knew she felt his surging desire. He could feel how every drop of water hit her sensitized skin as well, how his trailing fingers made her own heat rise.

It became a game, to go slowly. To see how slow they *could* go, before one of them snapped. Inch by inch, stroke by stroke, washing each other with painstaking thoroughness. No more darkness between them, no more charred ash and blackened secrets. Just the simple, clean truth of the mate bond.

"Ash," she gasped, her breast pressing into his palm. "Ash!"

His fingers circled between her thighs, dipping into her hot slickness. She broke first, clenching around him as ecstasy swept over her.

The mate bond lay as open and ready as her body, dry tinder awaiting a spark. He could lift her now, slide into her, make her blaze...

He pulled away from her instead, bracing his hands against the shower cubicle. Before, that would have made her hesitate, wondering whether she had done something wrong. But now...now she just opened her eyes again, a rueful smile tugging at the corner of her mouth as she sensed his inner struggle.

"Ah," she said. "You don't want this to be over too quickly."

"I want to be able to do you justice." His breathing was ragged. "Just give me...a moment."

Her tongue ran over her lips. She gave him a look that jerked his shaft to even stiffer attention.

"No," she said slowly. "No, I don't think I will."

He gasped as she wrapped her hand around him. He collapsed back against the tiled wall, momentarily blinded by sensation.

And then her mouth slid over him.

All thought went up in smoke. All he knew was the exquisite heat of her, the play of her tongue, the softness of her lips.

He wound his hand into her hair, hips jerking upward uncontrollably. In mere seconds, he was coming hard, in great, shuddering spurts, emptying himself deep into her welcoming mouth.

Rose pulled back, a satisfied gleam in her eyes. "I have wanted to do that for a *very* long time."

His legs were still shaking. He took her hands, pulling her up, crushing his mouth against hers. He kissed her long and deep, wordlessly telling her everything.

The water abruptly ran cold. Rose yelped. He slammed the dial round so fast the handle snapped off in his hand. He was left holding it, no doubt looking rather ridiculous, as she dissolved into giggles.

"Well, good thing we got thoroughly clean," she said. "Since it doesn't look like the shower will be working again anytime soon."

"I am going to owe Scarlet yet another apology." He balanced the broken handle in the soap dish, for lack of anything better to do with it. "But it was worth it."

Rose had wrapped herself in a towel, but she was still shivering. He went over to her, folding her in his arms, and concentrated.

"Oooooh," she sighed, relaxing as the wave of heat enveloped her. "All right, I forgive you for breaking our shower."

He nuzzled her wet hair, breathing in her delicious scent—the perfumed soap mixing in with the richer, underlying warmth of *her*. "Will you forgive me for not being in my twenties any more?"

She shot him a quizzical look. "*I'm* not in my twenties any more."

"You aren't a man." He gestured downward, rather sheepishly. "You did rather too good a job in there. I may need a little time to recover."

She giggled again, nestling against him. "We have all the time in the world."

CHAPTER 27

Neridia sighed in pleasure, relaxing back against a mound of soft white pillows. "Now *this* is more like it."

If Rose had thought her own cottage luxurious, the one Scarlet has assigned to Neridia and John was positively palatial. Folded-back French windows lined one wall, allowing the salt-tinged ocean breeze to cool the elegant room. Even with the enormous super king-sized bed, it was still big enough to comfortably fit the entirety of Alpha Team and their mates. Potted flowers bloomed on every surface, surrounding them all in a riot of scent and color.

"You've certainly earned it." Rose handed Neridia a lavish non-alcoholic cocktail, so heavily garnished that it was not so much a drink as a fruit salad. "Here. The bartender helped me make this for you. He's very talented."

"All the staff have been so kind." Neridia took an appreciative sip of the drink. "Well, my baby's first few hours may not have been auspicious, but at least he's spending his first night in style."

"Born in the aftermath of battle," John rumbled, pride filling his deep voice. "He will be a mighty warrior."

At the moment, Rose couldn't imagine the tiny bundle growing up to be a mighty *anything*. The sleeping newborn looked small as a kitten in John's vast hands.

The infant's skin was a rich, deep brown, somewhere between Neridia's warm ochre and John's indigo-tinged ebony in hue. His soft bud of a mouth worked in his sleep, dreaming of milk. His thick mop of inky-blue curls gleamed with turquoise highlights.

"Definitely a sea dragon, with that hair," Hayley commented, peering round John's other side. "Have you decided on a name yet?"

John said his son's name. At least, Rose assumed that he had.

"Very pretty," Hugh said, lounging in the corner with what Rose suspected was a rather more alcoholic cocktail than the one she'd given Neridia. "Please tell me there's a translation of that. Otherwise we're all going to have to start carrying around cellos."

"Sea dragon names relate our deeds and lineage," John said, beaming proudly down at his son. "He is the Emperor-in-Waiting, Heir to the Pearl Throne, Crown Prince of the Sea."

The Emperor-in-Waiting, Heir to the Pearl Throne, Crown Prince of the Sea, made a little smacking sound, blowing a bubble.

Griff cocked a wry eyebrow up at John. "Please tell me you aren't going to put that mouthful on his birth certificate."

Neridia laughed. "No. He has an air name too. Joseph, for my father, and Finley, for the Master Shark. Joseph Finley Small."

"Joe." Rose stroked the baby's cheek, marveling at the velvety softness. "He's the most beautiful baby ever."

Griff cleared his throat. "Didn't you say that about *my* wee ones?"

"And my Morwenna?" Dai added, grinning.

"All babies are the most beautiful ever," Rose said firmly. "Can I hold him?"

Carefully, John transferred the infant into her outstretched arms. She cuddled him to her chest, dropping her head down to breathe in his milky new-baby scent. Wistful longing flooded through her.

If things had been different…if she and Ash had never been parted, or had found their way back to each other sooner…

His hand fell on her shoulder. His deep, quiet regret echoed her own.

She blinked hard, banishing unshed tears. She had so much. She wouldn't sorrow for those lost years, the children they might have had.

No, her swan agreed. Its neck arched in sly, secret amusement. *Gather sticks and feathers instead.*

"You know," Chase said thoughtfully, while she was still puzzling over *that* one. "I think we need to come up with a new name."

"Do not listen to this man," Connie announced to the world in general. She spread a hand over her belly. "He is not allowed to name his *own* children, let alone anyone else's."

"I don't know why you keep rejecting my suggestions," Chase said in a wounded tone. "What's wrong with Cainneach, Cionaodh, and Conchobhar?"

Hugh gazed at the ceiling. "Where do we start?"

Ivy elbowed her mate. "I actually kind of like them. They're unusual."

"Spell them," Connie told her. "I dare you."

"Take it from someone named Daifydd," Dai muttered to Chase. "Don't do it."

"Welsh is an unreasonable language," Chase said airily. "Irish at least makes *sense*."

"Unlike yourself." John's bass-deep voice had taken on its darkest, most forbidding tones, but his indigo eyes betrayed his amusement. "May I inquire why, precisely, you are objecting to my son's name, sword-brother?"

"Not *his* name," Chase said, waving a dismissive hand at the baby. "That's perfectly fine, if a little lacking in vowels. I mean *him*."

They all followed his pointing finger.

Ash looked around, then down at himself. "As far as I am aware, I already possess a name."

"A terrible one," Chase informed him, without the slightest hint of shame. "The ladies told us the story. Honestly. From Blaze to *Ash*? You might as well call yourself My-Life-Is-a-Blasted-Barren-Wasteland-of-Nothingness."

"It probably didn't fit on the form," Hugh said, smirking. "Chase has a point. It is a bit angsty."

"*You're* calling someone angsty?" Ivy murmured.

"I'm aware of the irony." Hugh saluted her with his cocktail, his mouth softening into a genuine smile. "In any case, I think that rising from the dead certainly qualifies as an occasion to take a new name. So what shall we call him now, Chase?"

Chase tapped his finger against his lips for a moment. "I suppose Fire Commander Fire doesn't quite work?"

Rose's snort of laughter woke the baby up. She hastily handed him back to his mother. "Not really, no."

"And there would be certain difficulties with yelling 'Fire!' to get his attention," Griff pointed out, his golden eyes gleaming with suppressed mirth. "Especially at the fire station."

"Good point," Chase conceded. He brightened. "Wait! I have it! The perfect thing. Something that says 'fire' without, you know, *literally* saying fire. Flames rekindled, renewed, burning brighter than ever..."

Rose took Ash's hand. "Brace yourself," she murmured in his ear.

Chase pointed finger-guns at him. "Sparky!"

Hugh inhaled quite a lot of his drink. John's huge shoulders shook. Dai and Griff exchanged glances, and burst into howls of laughter.

Ash's poker face was perfect. "Thank you for the suggestion. I shall give it the consideration it deserves."

~

"*Will* you change your name again?" Rose asked him curiously, much later.

They were wandering back from the dining hall, taking a scenic route along the beach. The gleaming white sands were deserted, most of the resort guests still enjoying the sumptuous dessert buffet. To their left, the sun was just touching the edge of the sea, filling the sky with soft shades of gold and orange.

His hand tightened a little on hers. "In truth, I was thinking of it. With your permission."

"Why would you need that?" She leaned her head against his shoulder, enjoying his warmth in the rapidly cooling evening. "Unless you're actually contemplating Sparky, in which case I utterly forbid it. There's a limit to what I'm willing to scream in the throes of passion."

His lips curved. He'd smiled more in the past few hours than he had in the previous *year.* She still treasured every one. She always would.

"Then I shall have no choice but to attempt to reduce you to wordlessness," he teased.

From the way his dark eyes heated, it wasn't entirely a joke. Her body kindled under his intent, hungry regard. She stopped, pulling him down for a long, deep kiss, his hands sliding around her hips.

"Tempting," she murmured against his mouth. "But you don't need to saddle yourself with a terrible name for that. So will you be Blaze again?"

He drew back a little, shaking his head. "Corbin named me that. Ash at least I picked for myself. And over the past ten years..." His fingers traced her lips. "I named myself in bitterness. But every time you said my name, it became a little sweeter. No. I will stay Ash. But I thought I might take a surname at last."

"Now you had *really* better pick something good," Rose warned.

His hand cupped her cheek. "I was thinking...Swanmay. If you will have me."

"Oh," Rose breathed, her throat choking up. "Oh yes. *Yes.*"

Breathless with happiness, she pressed up to him. He laughed out loud in pure joy, lifting her clean off her feet. She wound her arms around his neck, covering his face in kisses.

"Fly with me?" he whispered into her ear.

She nodded, too overjoyed to speak. He let her slide down his body again, carefully, until her feet were back on the warm sands. His fingertips left trails of fire across her skin as he helped her out of her sundress.

Her swan's wings beat eagerly in her soul. Stepping back, Rose shifted.

All the breath left Ash's body. To her surprise, he folded to his knees, never taking his eyes off her. He'd seen her animal before, many times, but now he was staring at her as if he'd never seen a swan before.

"Rose," he breathed, delight spreading across his face. "Look at yourself."

Puzzled, Rose curved her neck—and let out an undignified honk.

Her feathers were no longer plain black. Now every edge burned with golden-red light.

Astonished, she opened one wing, spreading her pinions. That hint of flame flickered around each ebony feather, as though they were about to catch fire.

"Phoenix fire." Ash's trembling hand stroked her plumes. Darting sparks swirled into the air in the wake of his touch. "We both share it now. Oh, my Rose. You are glorious."

No need for an ungainly run-up now; her wings lifted her into the air as easily as thought. With a flash of fire, he shifted as well. He rose with her, trailing flame.

He called out to her, fierce and triumphant, as they spiraled into the sky. Delight surged through her, her feathers blazing even brighter in response. She swooped low, her reflection scattering fire across the sea, and he followed, a burning shadow matching her every movement.

They danced together on the wind, as the sky darkened and the stars came out to watch. With every brush of the Phoenix's wing against hers, every arc of his body, the mate bond burned hotter, until it was a blazing inferno in her soul.

But she wanted more.

She dove again, this time heading for their cottage. She shifted as she flared her wings, returning to human form. No sooner had her bare feet touched the ground, his arms were around her, scooping her up.

Ash's mouth pressed against hers, as hot and hungry as his fire. He carried her inside, kicking the door impatiently closed. The darkness of the cottage closed around them.

"Light," she managed to get out, in between kisses. Her desperate fingers traced his face, his neck, his shoulders, but she wanted to *see* him too. Wanted to devour him with every sense, touch and taste and sight...

He didn't reach for the switch. His hands didn't pause in setting every inch of her aflame, yet light kindled, banishing the darkness. Dozens of white candles crowded every surface, sending up a sweet floral scent.

Rose laughed a little into his shoulder, recognizing that perfume. "Roses?"

"Always," he breathed, kissing his way down her neck. "Always."

There were rose petals scattered across the bed too. Their velvety softness caressed her skin as he laid her down on them. She stretched out, watching greedily as he stripped off his clothes for her. The soft glow of the candles highlighted every line of his body. Honed and hardened, weathered by years, marked by scars...and hers, all hers.

"Ash," she murmured, opening for him.

His strong form covered hers.

And at last, there was no more waiting.

CHAPTER 28

Three months later...

Rose was in the cellar, counting beer kegs, when she heard the door open. It *still* creaked, even though it had been completely rebuilt. The contractor had been embarrassed, but in truth, Rose wouldn't have had it any other way.

"Just a second!" she shouted, scrawling a quick note on her clipboard. She scrambled out of the hatch, brushing herself down, and hurried into the front room.

"Sorry," she said as she stepped around the bar. "But we're actually still closed. The grand reopening isn't until the evening. Come back at—"

She stopped, a chill going down her spine.

The man standing in the middle of the room, gazing around curiously, didn't look at all threatening. He was tall but thin, sinewy muscles strung along his lanky frame. His gaunt, lined face looked tired under his bristling white hair.

But his eyes, when they met hers, burned like frozen stars. Cold hung in the air around him.

"Hello again," said the wendigo.

"Ash!" she yelled.

He'd been upstairs, getting changed from his work shift. He must have been in motion from that first startled jolt of her heart, though, because he burst into the room in mere seconds. His unbuttoned uniform shirt hung askew from his shoulders, the bitter scent of smoke rising from the stained fabric.

He caught sight of the wendigo, and froze. *"Ice?"*

The wendigo's thin smile widened, warming. He held out his hand. "Ash. It's been too long."

Rose beamed as the two clasped forearms, warrior-to-warrior. "You got Ash's message, then. He wasn't sure it would reach you."

"I did. But I thought I would come myself, rather than send back word." He released Ash, turning to her. "I wanted to personally thank the woman who finally put an end to Corbin."

"That was more the Phoenix than me." Nonetheless, Rose shook his hand. His fingers were, unsurprisingly, ice-cold, but his pale blue eyes were warm. "And *I* wanted to thank *you*, for watching over my mate when I couldn't. Ash told me about your years hunting the warlocks together."

"It seems I will be hunting them once more," Ice said, with a hint of a growl. Rose shivered as the temperature dropped noticeably. "I grew complacent. But this time, I and my pack will make sure no seeds of evil remain to take root again." He cast a sly sideways glance at Ash. "I would invite you to join us on the hunt once more, Phoenix, but I think you have other concerns now."

Ash's arm slid around her waist. "I left my mate once. I have promised her that I will never do so again."

The wendigo's eyes glinted. "So you came to your senses at last."

"Will you join us this evening?" Rose asked him. She gestured around at the gleaming, polished interior of the Full Moon. Even though she'd kept as much of the original design as possible, it was still strange to have it all fresh and new. "We're throwing a party tonight, to celebrate reopening. We only just finished rebuilding."

Ice hesitated. "I…am not the sort of shifter that many would welcome."

"Nonsense," Rose said firmly. "*Everyone* is welcome here."

"Stay," Ash put in, smiling. "Please."

Ice shook his head. "If it was just myself, I would. But...my mate is not comfortable in crowds. Particularly not crowds of shifters."

"Your mate?" Rose exclaimed. "Ash didn't tell me you were mated!"

"I was not, when we last parted." A deep, quiet pride lit Ice's haggard face. The chill in the air around him faded. "It turned out that we had nearly crossed paths many times, but we found each other at last. She is outside now."

"Well, call her in!" Rose urged. "I'd love to meet her."

Something crossed Ice's expression—a shadow, a memory. Whatever it was, it was gone too fast for Rose to interpret. Even to her empathic sense, the wendigo was as hard to penetrate as an iceberg.

"You already have," he said.

The door creaked again. A woman slipped through, soft-footed as a cat. She was a little older than Rose, maybe in her fifties, with a diffident, shy manner. Her silver-streaked hair shadowed her face, but there *was* something familiar about her...

"Oh," Rose gasped. She hurried forward, opening her arms. "*Oh.*"

Tears gleamed in the woman's startling green eyes. Without hesitation, she stepped into Rose's embrace, hugging her back tightly.

"I always wondered what had happened to you," the former ocelot whispered into her ear. She stepped back, holding Rose at arm's-length, beaming despite her tears.

"And I you!" Rose could barely speak, she was so choked up. "At least, I did when I remembered—when I got my memory back—oh, I'm glad, I'm so glad!"

Ash had also recognized the woman. He'd faded back a little, his own expression shuttering down. Noticing, the former shifter disengaged from Rose, holding out her hands.

"Do not be sorry," she said. "Some scars cannot be helped. It was the only way."

Ash held still for a moment. Then, slowly, he clasped her hands.

"I am still sorry," he said. "I wish..."

He trailed off, his gaze sharpening. Rose sensed a sudden, strange surge of focus from the mate bond as his eyes flicked from the woman to herself and back again. His fingers tightened.

The woman drew in a short, shocked breath. "What—?"

Rose shielded her eyes as fire flared. Ice lunged forward—but Ash was already letting go of the woman's hands. The wendigo caught his mate as she stumbled.

"What did you do?" he snarled at Ash, teeth lengthening into fangs. If he hadn't been busy supporting his mate, Rose was fairly certain he would have been at the Phoenix's throat. A flurry of snow swirled across the floor.

"Perhaps nothing," Ash said. He'd gone a little pale, looking drained. Without conscious thought, Rose found that she was at *his* side. He leaned gratefully against her shoulder. "I'm not sure. It seemed worth a try…"

"Marietta." Ice brushed his mate's hair back, anxiously studying her face. "Are you all right? Marietta!"

Marietta drew in a deep, shuddering breath, opening her eyes. Something new burned there, a fire rekindled. Her hand crept up, pressing against her heart.

"She's back," she whispered. "*She's back!*"

Her clothes dropped empty to the floor. A sleek golden ocelot leapt into Ice's arms. He started laughing—pure, disbelieving, joyous laughter—as her rough pink tongue licked his face.

Rose stared from the happy couple to Ash. "How did you do that?"

"What was destroyed can be made anew." His arm wrapped around her, holding her as tightly as Ice embraced his own mate. "You taught me that."

~

Rose breathed a deep sigh of satisfaction, looking round the deserted pub. "Now *that's* better."

There were fresh scuff marks on the new floorboards, some from boots, a few from claws. Someone had spilled beer over the upholstery in one of the booths. There was a dent in the polished bar, where a friendly arm-wrestling tournament between the local wolf and hell-hound packs had gotten a little *too* competitive.

From behind her, Ash chuckled. His arms wrapped around her, pulling her back against his chest. "You have an interesting definition of better."

"It was too fresh and new before. Now it feels right." She touched his right wrist. "Sometimes a few scars are necessary."

"Mmmm." He rested his chin on her shoulder, his warm breath tickling her ear. "I am not entirely sure the stain on the ceiling was necessary. Or even how Chase managed to achieve it."

She laughed. "It was certainly a *memorable* keg stand." She turned in his arms, hugging him back. "And party. But it's good to be alone again."

"Yes." His hands slid lower over her hips. "It has been a tiring day."

She pressed against him, grinning at the growing evidence of his arousal. "Evidently not *that* tiring."

"Nonetheless." Ash drew her hair aside, trailing soft kisses down her neck. She sucked in her breath. "I think the tidying up can wait until tomorrow. We should go to bed."

That seemed like an *excellent* idea.

He drew her with him through the rebuilt pub. It was still strange to turn right instead of left, heading up the new staircase. The Full Moon was twice as big as before, and she wasn't yet used to the expanded layout.

Their apartment occupied two full floors above the pub itself. It was light and airy, but cavernously empty. Few of her things had survived the fire, and all of Ash's worldly goods fit inside a single cardboard box.

But they were going to need the space...

"I was thinking," Rose said, tugging him into one of the bare, unfurnished spare rooms. "We should do this one next. Yellow, maybe."

"Yellow?" Ash took advantage of the pause to kiss her again.

"For the walls. And white wooden furniture. A chest of drawers, a bookcase, a nice comfy armchair..."

Ash clearly had other things than interior decor on his mind. She gasped as he pushed her against the aforementioned wall, his body hard against hers.

"And..." Her breathing went ragged as his strong fingers skimmed under the waistband of her skirt. "And a cradle."

He stilled. His hand spread, very gently, across her still-flat stomach. His eyes met hers, pure joy kindling in their dark depths.

"Yes," she whispered, putting her hand on his.

Our mate, her swan murmured, in utter contentment. *Our mate.*

EPILOGUE

Twenty-three years later...

Rory couldn't help grinning as he turned the last corner. As always, the sight of the Full Moon pub filled his chest with warmth—the solid, comfortable instincts of *den* and *safe* and *friends*.

In a way, the old, whitewashed stone building was more home than any of the places he'd lived as a child. He'd grown up in a succession of different, ever-expanding houses—a necessity, given his parents' irritating habit of continually presenting him with new siblings—but the Full Moon had always been a constant in his life.

"So many firsts here," he said out loud, to thin air. "First drink. First kiss. Even my first flight. See up there?" He pointed up at one of the top-floor windows. "Conleth pretended to fall out, so I leaped after him. Didn't cross my mind that *he'd* been flying for a year while I was barely fledged. He got grounded for that. Literally. Took months for his clipped feathers to grow back in. Good times, good times."

The empty space next to him said nothing in response. Not that he'd expected it to.

Rory started to head for the front of the pub, but checked himself. The oak door stood ajar, a narrow beam of yellow light striping the street. Even from a distance, he could hear the mingled laughter and chatter of a party in full swing. The evening was still young, but from the sound of things, the pub was already packed with celebrating shifters.

"Let's go round the back," he said, switching direction. "It'll be less crowded."

A narrow alleyway ran round the side of the pub, barred at the end by a high wooden wall. Rory's grin stretched wider as he threaded his way round the dumpsters.

"Used to come this way all the time when we were kids," he said, looking up fondly at the numerous claw-marks scoring the top of the fence. "We were only allowed into the pub itself on special occasions. Naturally that just made us more determined to sneak in at every opportunity."

Backing away a few steps, he let his animal surge up from the depths of his soul. Golden fur and feathers swept away his skin. The alleyway was too narrow for flight; furling his wings close to his body, he crouched down on his haunches. The claws on his back paws dug into the worn cobblestones.

With a single fluid leap, he cleared the fence. His front talons didn't even clip the top of it. He frowned as he pulled his griffin back into his human body.

"Huh." He glanced back at the fence wryly. "I remembered that as taller."

Nobody replied out loud, but his griffin abruptly sat up in his soul. It tugged at his mind, feathers bristling in anticipation.

Rory laughed at his animal's eagerness. "Of course he's here. Where else would he be?"

He didn't need his griffin's urging to hurry round the building, to the wide courtyard behind the old pub. With the cold of winter not yet giving way to spring, the picnic tables and benches were empty, umbrellas tightly furled. The rose bushes in the decorative stone planters were just bare, thorny sticks. Stacks of empty beer barrels lined one wall, waiting to be shipped out.

One of his earliest memories was playing hide-and-seek in this courtyard garden. Ducking behind barrels, stifling giggles, yelling at the pegasus triplets when they inevitably used their powers to cheat. Everything was just as he recalled. The only thing that had changed was himself.

Well, and one other thing. Rory touched one of the casks in passing, smiling at the bold yellow logo. The stenciled letters underneath proudly proclaimed: *Lionbird Brewery.*

The outer door to the cellar was open. Succumbing to a sense of mischief, Rory slowed down, padding as softly as he could down the steps.

Inside it was cool, the air thick with the scents of malt and hops. A single small light bulb illuminated the racks of casks. In the dimness, Rory's eagle eyes picked out a stocky form kneeling next to one of the fermenting beers.

The man didn't show any sign of having noticed Rory's presence, completely focused on his work. The sleeves of his checked flannel shirt were rolled up, exposing heavily tattooed arms. His strong, square hands caressed the oak barrel as if it was a lover's body. As Rory watched, the other man frowned, rubbing his bearded chin in thought.

Rory folded his arms, fighting down the sappy grin that wanted to spread over his face. "You look like a damn hipster, you know."

His twin didn't even glance up, let alone jump. "I *am* a damn hipster."

"Since when does running a microbrewery means you have to embrace every cliché?" Without warning, Rory lunged, managing to ruffle Ross's hair before his twin ducked away. "What is that, a man-bun?"

"I make artisanal craft beer. Customers expect me to look the part." With dignity, Ross straightened his mussed hairdo. One tawny eyebrow cocked as he looked Rory up and down. "What happened to *your* mane?"

Rory grimaced, running a hand self-consciously over his own short, golden hair. "Had to cut it. Health and safety regs."

"You have safety regulations?" Ross chuckled. "I thought you ran into burning forests?"

"That's why we have safety regulations." Abandoning the banter, Rory pulled his brother into a tight hug. "It's good to see you again."

"And you." Ross hugged him back, nearly cracking Rory's ribs. His brother might not cut firebreaks for up to sixteen hours a day, but he *did* wrestle massive oak barrels for a living. "We were starting to think you weren't going to make it."

"I wouldn't have missed this party if I'd had to fly across the Atlantic on my own two wings."

"Ross!" Rose's voice called from up above. "We're out of Swanfire!"

"On it!" Ross yelled back, releasing Rory. His amber gaze raked over the stacked casks. He hesitated between a couple—both of which looked identical even to Rory's equally sharp eyesight—before hefting one under an arm. "Come on. Everyone's been asking after you."

Rory started to follow his brother up the stairs, then realized the silence behind him had changed slightly. He paused in mid-step, waiting.

Nothing happened.

"Okay," he said out loud. "I'll be back soon."

From the top of the stairs, Ross gave him a peculiar look. "What?"

"Never mind." Rory took the stairs three at a time to catch up. "So the whole gang is here?"

"Everyone except Morwenna and Danny. The baby's due any day now, so they couldn't risk flying out of Valtyra."

Rory shook his head. "I still can't believe we're going to be uncles."

"*I* still can't believe those two really did turn out to be mates. You remember how annoyed he used to get about her following us everywhere?"

"Morwenna knew a long time before he did. It just took her a while to get him to stop seeing her as a little kid." Rory sighed. "Our brother is one lucky man."

"May we all find our mates so easily." Ross shouldered open the door to the main room of the pub. "Rose, look who's here!"

"Rory!" Rose hurried from behind the bar to enfold him in her soft, strong arms. "When did you get in?"

"Just now." Rory hugged her back. "I came straight from the airport."

Like the Full Moon, Rose never changed. Oh, he supposed there had to be a few more laughter-lines around her eyes and a few more silver threads in her hair these days...but she was still *Rose,* as warm and welcoming as ever. He let out his breath, relaxing into her air of deep, wise peace as much as her embrace.

"If you've got time later," he murmured in her ear, "I could really do with some advice."

"I've always got time for my honorary nephews." She drew back, pursing her lips ruefully as she looked around the crowded bar. "Though not literally at this moment. Come talk to me when this quietens down?"

"Thanks, aunt Rose." With a last squeeze, he let her go. "But shouldn't this be your party as much as anyone else's? What are you doing serving drinks?"

"What I love doing," she said, smiling. She bustled off, raising her voice. "All right, all right, I'm coming! Keep your fur on, I won't let you perish of thirst!"

Ross was busy tapping the new cask of beer, with the degree of concentration usually reserved for brain surgery or defusing bombs. Leaving him to it, Rory scanned the crowd. He picked out John Doe instantly—the indigo-haired firefighter towered over everyone else, even the other sea dragons. And where *he* was, you could be sure to find...

"Excuse me. Pardon. Coming through." Rory cut his way through the crowd. Grinning wider than ever, he cleared his throat. "Congratulations, Fire Commander."

The Commander turned. His golden eyes—exactly the same shade as Rory's—crinkled as he glanced down at the rank insignia on his formal uniform.

"One day I'll stop looking around for someone else when people call me that," Griff said ruefully. "Maybe. Hello, son."

Rory hugged him too, rubbing cheeks in the way that lions greeted other members of the pride. The familiar, comforting scent of *Alpha* wrapped around him. His griffin purred in contentment.

"When you called to say Ash was retiring, I honestly thought you were joking," Rory said, releasing his dad again.

"So did the rest of us," said Hugh. The white-haired paramedic was leaning against the wall nearby, a drink in his hand and a slightly bemused look on his face. "I still think this is all just an elaborate way of saving the department from having to pay the cost of his salary. I have a bet on with Ivy that he turns up to work tomorrow morning anyway."

Rory glanced around for Hugh's mate, and found her a little way off, chatting to a circle of wary-looking teens. Rory guessed they had to be her latest group of protégées from her charity for disadvantaged shifters. He made a mental note to find her later. He could do with *her* insight into his current problem too.

"If anyone deserves to enjoy a time of peace at last, it is our former leader," John rumbled. He was wearing gold-inlayed steel bracers and a sword harness over his formal dress uniform. On anyone else, it would have been a bizarre combination, but John pulled it off with ease. The blend of firefighter and sea dragon Knight was just *him*. "He had earned honor enough for a dozen lifetimes."

"Yes, but..." Rory spread his hands, palm-up. "Hugh's got a point. Ash is still the Phoenix. He can't retire from *that*. What's he going to do all day, if not fight fires?"

Beside John, Chase chuckled. There was a little more gray at his temples than the last time Rory had seen him. It gave the pegasus shifter a dignified, statesmanlike air—at least until he opened his mouth. "Oh, I'm fairly certain Sparky will find *something* to fill his time."

Rory followed the direction of Chase's dancing eyes. He was so used to seeing Fire Commander Ash—no, *former* Fire Commander Ash—in uniform, it took him a second to recognize the Phoenix in civilian clothes. Ash stood surrounded by well-wishers, accepting hugs and handshakes with quiet grace. His slight but real smile shone through his reserve like a glimmer of sunlight through clouds.

As Rory watched, Ash lifted his gaze slightly above the heads of the crowd. Across the room, his eyes met Rose's. Just a moment, a glance.

But that look...

Rory looked away, blinking, feeling as though he'd stared directly into the sun. It was the same way his parents looked at each other, even after twenty-five years and five children.

Intense yearning hollowed out his heart. He'd grown up around mated couples, *true* mated couples. Having seen the real thing, he could never settle for anything less for himself.

One day, whispered his griffin, with utter certainty. *We will meet* our *mate. And we will claim her, to treasure and protect, always.*

"Though maybe we can still change his mind," Chase continued, with a wicked sideways glance at Griff. "If we told him our deep and terrible concerns about this new guy who's meant to be replacing him. Anyone want to sign a petition of no confidence?"

"Me," Griff said dryly, as everyone else grinned and shook their heads. "I still think Dai should have got it."

"Not on your life." Dai's amused Welsh voice floated over Rory's shoulder. The dragon shifter came up to the group, mouth crooked in a smile, his arm draped over his mate. "I like charging into burning buildings, not paperwork. You are more than welcome to the boring job of standing back and ordering everyone else around. Hello, Rory. How's life out in the wilderness?"

"Hot," Rory said, clasping his arm in greeting. "You should come join us next season, uncle Dai. Our last big one covered eight thousand acres. Took us three weeks to get it under control."

"Don't let your mother hear you," his dad advised. "She worries enough about you as it is. The less she knows about your work, the better."

"Well, I'll have to tell her a few things." Rory cleared his throat, his face heating. "It's nothing like *your* promotion, but...I made squad boss."

He'd expected smiles and congratulations. He *hadn't* counted on Chase whooping loud enough to make half the heads in the pub turn, then seizing him in a fierce hug. What little breath he had left after *that* was knocked out by John and Dai pounding on his back. Even Hugh joined in, clapping him on the shoulder.

And as for his dad…

His shining eyes said everything. His father's pride wrapped round him like golden wings.

"Like father, like son," Chase said, releasing him at last. "Congratulations! So you'll be leading your own team now?"

Rory nodded, still flushed with mingled pride and self-consciousness. "My superintendent found out what I am. When I told him about Alpha Team, well…" He grinned round at them all. "That's the other reason I'm here."

~

"An all-shifter hotshot crew?" Wystan said.

As expected, Rory had found him lurking in one of the Full Moon's back corridors, away from the crush. From the faint, tight lines of stress across his forehead, he'd needed a few minutes away from the party to regroup and recover. Few people would guess from his unfailingly polite manner, but Wystan was intensely introverted. A large crowd drained his energy rapidly.

"A squad," Rory corrected. "Six people in a squad, three squads to a crew. I'm just a squad boss, not the superintendent."

The corner of Wystan's mouth turned up. "Yet. Evidently leadership runs in the family."

Rory's griffin preened itself at the comparison. *Yes. We will be Alpha of our own pride, just like our sire.* It fell silent for a moment, then added, thoughtfully, *And our territory will be bigger.*

Rory suppressed a snort. *The State Parks aren't our personal territory, you know. It's just our job to protect them.*

Yes, his griffin agreed, serenely unruffled. *That is what an Alpha does.*

Wystan was waiting politely, pretending not to notice Rory's distraction. Any shifter could recognize the signs of someone conversing with their inner beast. Rory shook himself, pushing his griffin back down.

"Sorry," he said, with an apologetic grimace. "Nothing important. So, what do you think?"

"About your idea?" Wystan smiled, his green eyes warm. "It's got a lot of potential. Many shifter talents are more suited for wildland firefighting than urban. But where are you going to find your recruits? You'll never persuade Connor to swap smokejumping for mere ground crew."

"Wasn't planning to. Smokejumpers are reckless. I want shifters with more sense." Rory pointed a finger at Wystan. "So what do you say?"

Wystan's white eyebrows shot up so far, they nearly met his hairline. "Me?"

"Why not? From what I hear, you passed fire academy with flying colors."

Wystan shook his head. "I wasn't planning on actually joining a crew. It was just a stepping-stone to get onto a degree course. I'm thinking of going into fire forensics."

"Come on, you can't just retreat into books and study theory. You need to get *some* experience of what it's actually like to attack a ten thousand acre forest fire with nothing but a chainsaw and a shovel."

"You make it sound so appealing," Wystan murmured.

"You'll love it. Trust me." Rory leaned forward, his own voice dropping into warm, persuasive tones. "We get deployed all over America, to some of the most beautiful and remote areas. Just picture it. Open skies...soaring mountains...magnificent forests..."

"Which are on fire," Wystan finished for him, dryly. He folded his arms, for a moment looking remarkably like his father. "And don't do the voice."

Wystan hadn't been joking about leadership running in the family. Rory cleared his throat, withdrawing that unconscious flex of alpha power as though sheathing his claws. "Sorry. Didn't mean to. Honestly, you *would* enjoy the job. It's a real chance to make a difference, saving not only human lives but animals and their habitats as well. And we spend weeks on end deep in the wilderness. Just the squads. No other people around for miles. Come and try it out, at least. Just for one season."

"Hmmm." Rory could tell that Wystan *was* tempted, despite his self-doubt. The other shifter rubbed his chin. "Even if I say yes...you hotshots are meant to be elites. I haven't even worked on an engine crew. Why would your superintendent agree to hire a rookie?"

"Are you kidding? With *your* qualifications? I already talked to him, and he's as eager to have you as I am. We always need good paramedics."

Wystan's shoulders tensed. "Then you need my father. Not me."

"You *are* a good paramedic," Rory said firmly. "And I'm not going to let you abandon all your training just because you didn't meet your own impossible expectations. You can't keep measuring yourself against your dad, Wys. *Nobody* can do what he does."

"But I should be able to." Wystan rubbed his forehead absently, a brief, habitual gesture that made Rory's heart hurt for his friend. "You said your superintendent knows about shifters. Did you tell him about...me?"

"He knows what you are." Deliberately, Rory put his hand on Wystan's shoulder. The unicorn shifter stiffened, but didn't pull away. "And he knows you aren't...like your dad. That's a *strength,* Wys. Not a weakness. At least you don't get crippling headaches around non-virgins."

"You sound like my parents. *They* think my pathetic animal is a blessing in disguise too." Wystan let out a long sigh. "Well, as long as you're not counting on me actually being able to heal anyone...I'm in."

"Let me see if I've got this straight." The Emperor-in-Waiting, Heir to the Pearl Throne, Crown Prince of the Sea—more commonly known as Joe—leaned back in his seat. He ticked off items on his dark, elegant hands as he spoke. "Glorious untouched forests and sweeping, breathtaking mountains. A close, elite band of brothers, isolated and alone, totally reliant on each other in the wilderness. Honor and glory, protecting both humanity and Mother Nature from devastating elemental forces."

"I don't think I was *quite* that poetic," Rory said, raising an eyebrow. "But that about sums it up."

Joe stared at him as if he'd invited him on a delightful tour of the local sewers. "And you think I would be interested...why?"

"I told you so," Wystan murmured to Rory. "You should have opened with, 'Chicks dig firefighters.'"

"My bro, the *last* thing I need is to become even more attractive to women." Joe waved at himself, encompassing everything from his curling blue-black hair to the slim-cut silk shirt that clung to his lean, hard torso. "All this, and royalty too? If I add 'firefighter' to my excessively long...list of sterling qualities, I'm going to get crushed to death by a hormonal mob."

Rory opened his mouth to argue, but was interrupted by his twin coming up to their corner booth. Ross had a pint of beer in one hand, a shotglass in the other, and an expression of resigned disgust.

"The beer's from the blonde lioness over there," he said, plunking the drinks down in front of Joe. "The whiskey is from her red-headed vixen friend. Apparently whichever one you drink first indicates who gets to take you home tonight."

As one, the three men leaned forward, peering round Ross's stocky form. At the bar, two women whispered, eying their table avidly. There was something remarkably predatory about their expressions, like cats staring at a bird feeder through a window. Rory would not have been surprised if they'd started wiggling their butts in the air.

Joe, for his part, seemed to have no objection to being stalked. Flashing a roguish grin, he gave the two a little wave. The pair waved back, fighting down giggles.

"I hate your life," Ross informed the sea dragon prince.

"Console yourself with the thought of how much your profits go up every time I'm here," Joe replied. "Honestly, I should start charging you a commission."

"Does this happen a lot?" Rory asked Wystan.

The unicorn shifter let out a long-suffering sigh. "You have no idea."

Joe looked thoughtfully at the women at the bar, then contemplated the drinks in front of him. "Hmmm. Decisions, decisions…"

With a flourish, he picked up the shot glass. The red-head clutched her friend's arm so hard, they both nearly fell off their bar stools. Joe saluted her with the glass…and then dropped the whole thing into the beer.

Ross drew in a sharp breath, muscles bunching in outrage. Joe was already lifting the concoction. Never breaking eye-contact with the women, he drained it in long, smooth swallows.

Rory glanced back at the women. They…did not appear to regard the sea dragon's wordless suggestion at all disfavorably.

He shook his head, caught somewhere between amusement and aggravation. "How do you *do* that?"

"With panache." Joe set the empty glass back down on the table. "Thanks for the offer, Rory, but I believe I have just received a better one."

"You." Ross barely seemed able to get words out through his clenched teeth. "Shot bombed. *My beer.*"

"In the pursuit of love, no sacrifice is too great," Joe declaimed. He patted Ross's rigid arm, which proved that he was either extraordinarily brave or remarkably stupid. "Now if you'll excuse me, duty calls."

A shadow fell over the table. They all looked up into the impassive face of John Doe.

Joe sank back into his seat, grimacing. "Or, apparently, duty wants me to stay exactly where I am."

"Forgive the intrusion, but I could not help overhearing." John's indigo gaze switched from Joe to Rory. "You offer my son a place of honor at your side?"

"Well, he'd have to get through a few months of fire academy first, sir, but he should be able to pass that with ease," Rory said. He flung Joe a meaningful look. "If he actually tries."

"I try things," Joe protested. "I am famed for trying things."

"I think the word you're looking for is 'infamous'," Wystan murmured.

"You do indeed try things." John folded his massive arms, light flashing from his bracers. "There was your time with the Seers. Then you decided you had a passion for Smithing, which, if I recall, lasted approximately six months. After that it was the Poets, the Dancers, the Pearl-workers, and a succession of foreign exchange visits with half a dozen different sea-shifter nations."

"Those were educational." Joe let out a wistful sigh, gazing at some fond memory. "In the case of the selkies, *extremely* educational."

John's fingers tapped against his armored forearm, snapping his son out of his reverie. "You have dabbled in practically every art under the sea, and none have kept your attention for more than a year. The Pearl Emperor-"

"-Must be devoted to his people," Joe finished with him, in the weary tones of someone who had heard this lecture a thousand times already. "Strong-willed but subtle, serving with unswerving dedication. But I'm not going to be the Pearl Emperor for a very long time. At least, I sincerely hope I'm not."

"As do we all," John said, a touch dryly. "But you *are* the Emperor-in-Waiting. Enough flitting. It is time to prove yourself."

Joe stared at his father, his walnut skin going a little gray. "Are you actually serious about this? You want me to be a *firefighter*?"

"If you prefer, you may join the novices entering their first year of knightly training." John's blue eyes glinted. "With your little sister."

Smirking, Rory clapped Joe on the shoulder. "Welcome to the squad."

Rory's next target was simultaneously the easiest to find, and the hardest.

Spotting a telltale shock of copper-red hair through the crowd was the easy part. Rory narrowed his eyes, staring at the back of the man's head. He had a one in three chance of getting this right...

As if sensing his scrutiny, the man turned. His mouth curved in an easy, brilliant smile.

Well, that improved the odds to fifty-fifty. "Connor?" Rory guessed.

The pegasus shifter flung up both arms in triumph. "Ten points!" he declaimed to the room in general.

Rory groaned. "Conleth, why the hell can't you three get different haircuts?"

"Ah now, where would be the fun in that?" Even though they'd all grown up together in Brighton, Conleth's voice held a faint lilt of an Irish accent. He'd inherited his father's lanky build and boundless energy too, though his red hair and sparkling green eyes were all Connie. "And now I'm ahead of Connor. It's double points for fooling a griffin shifter."

Rory shook his head, but accepted Conleth's enthusiastic hug of greeting. "I've been away too long. I used to be able to tell you three apart without thinking."

"Well, you only have to be able to spot bloody great forest fires, out there in the arse-end of America." Conleth held him out at arm's-length, grin widening. "No wonder your eyesight is atrophying. You were looking for Connor?"

"Cal, actually." Rory glanced around the pub. "He is here, right?"

"Oh, he'll have found somewhere to lurk and scowl disapprovingly. Hang on, I'll get him for you." Conleth tilted his head, his eyes going vague for a moment.

Rory concentrated, but could only catch the edges of the pegasus shifters' mental conversation, like overhearing voices three rooms away. It generally took close familiarity to be able to talk telepathically to another mythic shifter when out of eyeshot. He *had* been away too long.

"He says he'll join us in a moment," Conleth reported. His mouth quirked. "And he said to tell you that *he's* in uniform, so you can be sure to recognize him."

Sure enough, the tall, red-headed figure that stepped out of the crowd a few minutes later wore charcoal-gray dress slacks and shirt, the insignia of the East Sussex Fire & Rescue Service embroidered on his sleeve. Even without that clue, Rory wouldn't have mistaken him for either of his brothers.

Whereas Conleth slouched at ease, Callum's back was ramrod-straight, like a soldier facing a court-martial. His face was as closed and set as his brother's was open and affable.

Rory had been about to clap him on the shoulder in greeting, but the impulse withered in the face of those cold green eyes. Rather awkwardly, he offered his hand instead. "Hey Cal. Good to see you again."

Callum's chin dipped in a fractional nod. He made no move to shake his hand. "Conleth said you wished to speak with me."

Cal had always been reserved, compared to his brothers...but then, a full three-ring circus was quiet compared to *those* two. Now, he was positively glacial. All of Rory's instincts screamed at him that something wasn't right with his old friend.

"I did. Do. Yes." Concern swamped his pre-planned speech. "Cal, are you okay?"

"Yes."

And apparently that was all Callum had to say on *that* topic. Rory cast a glance at Conleth, who didn't look the slightest bit fazed that his identical brother appeared to have been replaced by a robot sometime in the past eighteen months.

"So what's on your mind, Rory?" Conleth said cheerfully. He draped an arm over Cal's rigid shoulders. "Not going to try to tempt my brother away to the wilderness again, are you?"

"Actually, yes." With an effort, Rory hauled himself back on track. "I'm setting up an all-shifter squad..."

Callum listened impassively as Rory went through his pitch. For all the emotion Cal showed, Rory might as well have been reciting his shopping list. In Hindi.

"I see," was all he said when Rory wound down.

"I don't know, Rory," Conleth said. He was still leaning against his brother, which Cal was tolerating with the silent stoicism of a lamp-post. "Connor's been bugging Cal to switch to smokejumping for months. I don't think you're going to persuade him to join a hotshot crew."

"They're not at all the same thing." Rory couldn't help his lip curling a little. "*We* are disciplined and efficient. *Those* maniacs are all reckless thrill-seekers. Uh, no insult intended to Connor."

"It's an accurate description," Cal said, completely straight-faced. "My brother is right, Rory. I'm not a risk-taker."

Rory blinked at him. "You may be in the wrong profession, then."

"You know what I mean. Wilderness work isn't like urban firefighting. I've heard Connor's stories."

"Connor literally jumps out of airplanes into forest fires. What we do isn't nearly as insane."

Cal's eyebrows rose, ever so slightly. "So you admit that smokejumping is more dangerous?"

"Yes-" Rory started to say—and then the penny dropped at last. "Oh, for the love of—*Connor!*"

"Cal's" face broke into a broad, wicked grin, exactly mirroring Conleth's. In perfect unison, the pair high-fived each other.

"You admitted it!" Connor chortled. He pulled a phone out of his pocket, waggling it tauntingly. "And I *recorded* it."

A rumbling growl reverberated through Rory's chest. His hands fisted, but there was no way he could wrestle the device off Connor without causing an embarrassing scene. "I just said that it was more dangerous. That's not the same as saying you damn idiots are *braver*."

"It's close enough," Connor said, smirking. "I'm sure the rest of my crew will agree."

Rory pinched the bridge of his nose, taking a deep breath. "Do I even want to ask how you got hold of Cal's shirt?"

"That's not my shirt," a third voice snarled from behind him.

Rory turned. Callum—the *real* Callum—stalked up, his curling red hair mussed and his jaw clenched. A couple of grinning firefighters that Rory didn't know trailed him. One of the men was shirtless.

Cal's glare swept over his brothers and fellow firefighters alike. "For the last time, this is *not funny*."

"You're absolutely right," Conleth said solemnly.

"It definitely isn't," Connor agreed.

There was a beat. A muscle ticked in Cal's jaw.

"It's bloody *hilarious,*" his brothers said together, and collapsed into laughter.

Cal's shoulders fell in a long, heartfelt sigh as his colleagues roared with mirth as well. He turned to Rory, ignoring the whole lot of them with icy dignity. "You wanted to talk to me?"

With a twinge of unease, Rory realized that Connor's impersonation of his brother had only been slightly exaggerated. There was a stiffness to Callum's posture that hadn't been there the last time Rory had seen him. *Some* joshing and teasing was inevitable on any fire crew...but there was a cruel edge to the laughter that had his griffin snarling in protective fury. He wanted to wade in with both fists, just like he had years ago: *Leave him alone! Stop picking on him!*

But Cal hadn't appreciated it when he'd been nine. He *really* wouldn't appreciate Rory trying to play the white knight now. Rory drew in a ragged breath, forcing his hands to uncurl.

Wystan appearing at his shoulder was a welcome distraction. The unicorn shifter cast a glance over the scene, not looking the least surprised by either the still-chortling Connor or any of the smirking firefighters. He turned to Cal. "So, are you in?"

Cal's eyes narrowed. "In what?"

"Run while you can, Cal," Joe said from behind Wystan. Even slouching disconsolately, he was still a good six inches taller than the rest of them. "Rory wants to offer you a job."

Cal digested this. "Somewhere that isn't here?"

"A very long way from here," Rory said. "It's-"

"Yes," Cal interrupted.

"But I haven't told you-"

"*Yes,*" Cal repeated, in tones of utter finality.

"All right then." Rory clapped him on the shoulder, which the pegasus shifter bore with stoic resignation. "Three down, one to go."

"One more?" Wystan raised an eyebrow. "But that would only make five. I thought you said there were six on a squad."

"There are." Rory beckoned them all to follow him. "Come on.

There's someone I want you to meet."

~

Wystan looked around the cellar. "You want us to meet...beer barrels?"

"I like this plan." Joe clapped his hands together, beaming. "Never met a beer barrel that wasn't excellent company. Are we here to get staggeringly drunk and bond in manly fashion? Can I build a sweat lodge?"

Cal shot him a sardonic look. "Do you know how to build a sweat lodge?"

"Actually, yes," Joe said cheerfully. "I'm also good at blanket forts. And igloos."

"Why—" Rory started, and then shook his head. "On second thought, I don't want to know." He raised his voice a little. "Here they are. The shifters I told you about."

Nothing happened.

"There's nobody here," Cal said.

"There's a spider," Joe pointed out. His forehead wrinkled. "Do you get spider shifters?"

"I sincerely hope not," Wystan murmured.

"It's just a spider." Cal folded his arms. "I'm a pegasus. Trust me. There's no one here."

"This is Wystan," Rory said to thin air, ignoring the backchat. "The tall one is Joe, and the scowling one is Cal. It may be difficult to believe, but you can trust them. *I* trust them."

"Awww. Thanks, Rory." Joe paused. "Not entirely a ringing character endorsement, of course, given that it's coming from someone who's talking to a barrel of bitter."

Rory rolled his eyes. "Will you all just be quiet for a moment? You're scaring him."

"Scaring *who?*" Wystan asked, a hint of annoyance breaking through his usual polite tones. "Rory, you're being excessively mysterious."

"Be. Quiet." Alpha power echoed under Rory's command, like a rumble of distant thunder.

Joe, who'd been about to say something, shut his mouth with a snap. Wystan's lips thinned. Cal's expression darkened even further.

But they all obeyed. Rory let out his breath, the silence ringing loud in his ears.

"It's all right," he said softly to the air. "They're pack."

The silence drew out for a long moment.

Then the air shimmered.

Joe yelped a expletive in sea dragon language. Wystan recoiled so hard he fell off the stairs. Cal raised an eyebrow.

The enormous, wolf-like creature stared at them all with burning red eyes. Thick, coal-black fur bristled.

Pack? The voice in Rory's mind sounded distinctly dubious.

"Pack," Rory confirmed out loud. "Guys, this is Fenrir. He's a hellhound."

"Rory." Wystan was plastered against the far wall. "I know hell-hounds. My aunts are hellhounds. *That is not a hellhound.*"

"Is it a hellpony?" Joe said, his voice rather higher than normal. "A hellbear, possibly? More importantly, is it hungry?"

"He's a hellhound," Rory repeated firmly. He put his hand on Fenrir's head, which was about the same level as his own shoulder. "Just...a little bigger than average."

"A little?" Cal muttered.

"Well." Joe swallowed, recovering a little of his customary aplomb. He essayed a shaky grin, holding out his hand. "I take it we'll be working together. Fenrir, was it?"

The hellhound cocked his head to one side, eying the sea dragon, then stood up. Joe paled a little as Fenrir padded forward, but held his ground.

"I, ah, was expecting a handshake," Joe said, as Fenrir sniffed at his fingers. "Maybe a fist bump? No?"

"Fen doesn't do handshakes," Rory said. He grimaced. "Or, for that matter, hands."

Joe yelped again as Fenrir transferred his attention to the sea dragon's crotch. "Whoa, bro! At least buy me a drink first."

"What do you mean, he doesn't do hands?" Wystan asked.

"He's...stuck." Rory blew out his breath, as Fenrir went to sniff the unicorn. "He can't shift. Claims he never has."

Wystan tried to shove Fenrir's enormous muzzle away from his groin. He might as well have tried to deflect a bulldozer. "But no hell-hound is born that way. They're always bitten."

Fenrir growled, the sound echoing in the confines of the cellar. **Not a two-leg. No soft-skin inside.** He glanced sidelong at Rory, ears flattening. **No matter what birdcat says.**

"You *are* a shifter," Rory told him. "And don't call me that."

"Call you what?" Joe asked. "Wait, can he talk to you telepathically? But hellhounds aren't mythic shifters."

"I can talk to him because he's decided I'm pack. I found him in the wilderness, or rather, he found me. It's a long story." Rory shrugged. "In any event, he saved my life, and I saved his. So here we are."

Fenrir tried to sniff Cal, and was met by a flat stare. The hellhound paused for a moment, then backed away. He sank to his haunches again, sweeping them all with his burning eyes. One ear flicked.

"Well?" Rory asked him.

Fenrir's lips wrinkled back, exposing finger-long fangs. **Not pack.**

"I know they're not pack *yet.*" Rory scratched the hellhound behind the ear. "But they will be. Trust me."

Cal's frown deepened. "He's on the squad?"

"The hellhound who can't shift is a firefighter?" Joe looked delighted. "Oh, please, *please* tell me he has a little doggy uniform. And a hat. I demand that he has a hat."

Fenrir growled again...but his tail thumped twice against the floor in a reluctant wag.

"He's on the squad," Rory confirmed. "Hellhounds need a pack, or they go...unstable. I think that's why he can't shift. He's been alone too long."

Birdcat promised pack, Fenrir rumbled in his mind. *Proper *pack. Not this.**

"What's he saying?" Wystan asked.

"That we're still missing an essential part of a real pack." Giving Fenrir a last pat, Rory headed for the stairs. "And that's why we need one more person."

~

The sounds of the party drifted up to her room, even through closed doors. As a child, she'd always fallen asleep to the warm, comforting sounds of the pub below. She could remember lying in the dark, listening to that low susurration of half-heard laughter and muffled voices, a fierce hunger burning in her own heart.

She'd been so impatient to grow up. So eager to be allowed into that mysterious adult world, to be part of the conversation rather than straining her ears to catch the occasional word. She'd lain awake night after night, planning, dreaming, mapping out her life. The future had seemed a broad, shining path, leading inevitably to her destiny.

And now, here she was. All her dreams in ashes.

Soft, familiar footsteps echoed down the hall. She barely had time to crumple the uniform shirt in her lap into an anonymous ball of fabric before the door opened.

"Sweetheart," her mother started...and then paused, her gaze flicking down to the shirt briefly.

No hope that she hadn't recognized it, or course. Her own cheeks heated as her mother's eyes softened.

"Oh, my love." Her mother sat down on the bed next to her, putting a hand on hers. "None of this is your fault."

It was a lie. It *was* her fault, all of it. Every clink of glasses, every laugh from the party below cut her like a razor. If it wasn't for her, none of them would be here. They wouldn't have been having to pretend to celebrate...

Her mother's fingers tightened on hers. "It is *not* your fault," she repeated, more firmly. "What happened was a blessing in disguise. An overdue wake-up call."

"But he nearly died." She swallowed, and forced herself to say the truth out loud. "I nearly killed him."

"Which made him take stock of his life, rather than continuing on in familiar channels. Your father is retiring because he *wants* to, sweetheart." Her mother's smile was as warm as summer sunlight. "At last. I've been badgering him for years. You've given *me* a gift, not taken anything away from him. You mustn't throw away your own dreams out of misplaced guilt."

She looked away, down at the shirt in her hands. Her fingertips traced the embroidered crest on the sleeve.

East Sussex Fire and Rescue Service.

She stuffed her former uniform into the bag next to her on the bed. "I was just packing up the last of my old work gear. Can you ask someone to take them back to the station for me?"

Her mother was silent for a long moment.

"You can't hide up here forever, love," her mother said at last, very gently. "You should go yourself."

Just the thought of facing everyone again—the stares, the whispers, the *pity*—made her throat tighten. Every shifter in the fire service was down there. They all knew what she'd done.

What they didn't know was how easily she could do it again.

"I can't." She pushed the bag into her mother's hands. "Please?"

Her mother blew out her breath, but accepted the sack. "Your friends are asking after you. Are you sure you won't come down to the party?"

She shook her head. "I can't."

"I thought you'd say that." Her mother went to the door again, opening it. "Which is why I told them to come up."

Her heart lurched sideways in her chest. Rory stood there, broad and stocky, with that familiar big-brother look of concern in his golden eyes. Others crowded behind him—Wystan, Joe, even Cal. All her old childhood friends.

She only had an instant to gape at them before the biggest dog she'd ever seen knocked them all aside. Before she knew what was happening, a cold wet nose shoved under her hand. The dog whined low in his throat, thick black tail wagging hopefully.

Her mother smiled at her. "I think you should listen to what they have to say."

~

She stared at Rory. "You can't be serious."

"Utterly." His mouth quirked. "Apparently a proper pack needs an alpha female. And you're the most alpha female I know."

"Uh." Joe raised a tentative hand, something clearly preying on his mind. "Rory, if you're the alpha male, does that mean...?"

She spluttered in knee-jerk disgust. To her relief, Rory looked equally appalled.

"Joe, she's like a little sister to me," he said, in scandalized tones. "I'd rather screw *you*."

"Well, obviously." Joe smoothed a hand down the front of his shirt. "Who wouldn't?"

Despite everything, the familiar banter brought a smile to her face. Fenrir, evidently noticing, wagged his tail harder. His nose was still firmly planted under her hand.

A little tentatively, she stroked his pointed, wolf-like ears. The enormous hellhound wriggled like a puppy, tail thumping hard against the ground.

Pack?* The voice in her mind was so faint, she might have been imagining it. *We are pack?

Her smile faded.

"I can't," she said, dropping her hand from the hellhound's head. "Rory, didn't you hear what happened? I can't be a firefighter. Not ever again."

"Yes, you can." A hint of a growl entered his voice. "You were *born* to be a firefighter. You can't throw that away, just because of one... incident. I know you're scared. I've been there myself. But if you run and hide, you'll lose who you *are*. You have to accept the fear, and use it to make yourself stronger."

Those deep, rumbling words seemed to pass straight through her ears and grab hold of her spine, forcing it to stiffen. She found that her shoulders had straightened, without any conscious thought.

She remembered that voice. From when she'd been little, and the three years between them had made him seem like a vast, golden god, delivering commandments from on high: *Of course you can climb that tree. Of course you can pass that exam. You can do anything. I believe in you.*

"You just have to trust yourself," Rory said, in those unshakable, unarguable tones. He leaned forward, his golden eyes intent. "Like we trust you."

She looked round at them all. Joe, utterly serious for once, looking oddly like his father as he gave her a slight, solemn nod. Wystan's kind, intelligent face, quiet understanding in his eyes. Cal, scowling, affecting indifference, but *there.*

They were all there. All her childhood friends. And they still trusted her.

They wouldn't, if they knew the aching, yearning cold inside her. How even now—despite everything—a tiny, traitorous voice still whispered:

Burn.

Rory held out a hand to her. "We need you. So will you join us?"

She crushed that unwanted presence back into the deepest, darkest depths of her mind. She imagined ice freezing around her soul, locking her animal away in an impenetrable glacier.

She took Rory's hand.

"Yes," said Blaise, the Black Phoenix.

The Fire & Rescue Shifters will return in Wildfire Griffin - available Fall 2018

Make sure you don't miss it by signing up for Zoe Chant's New Release mailing list:

http://www.zoechant.com/join-my-mailing-list/

WILDFIRE
GRIFFIN
ZOE CHANT

Printed in Great Britain
by Amazon

36111730R00158